INCUBUS BLUES

A Raven Shakes Novel - Book 1

Rekelle Lexington

Incubus Blues

A Raven Shakes Novel (Book 1)

By Rekelle Lexington

Copyright © 2023

All rights reserved.

This is a work of fiction. Any similarity between the characters and situations within its pages and places or persons, living or dead, is unintentional and coincidental.

Cover design by Daqri Bernardo

For the girls who won't date a guy that plays in a shitty band.

Chapter 1

Willow

Under the Versace gown strangling my hips, four scabbed and scarred claw marks slash across my abdomen. My wide smile aches my cheeks, but I hold the grin as I try not to squint against the rapid-fire camera flashes. Handling the paparazzi registers at the lower end of my skill set, and today, I plan to use them to my advantage.

"Willow, over here!" a voice barks, and I reposition on the red carpet beneath my towering heels. My fingertips dig into the curve of my hip. The wounds itch dully.

"Over here, honey!" shouts a photographer. The pet name makes me snarly, but I can't crack in public.

"Willow!" echoes another.

I'm an ace at quick pivots. It's a good thing, too. If I were a fraction of a second slower three weeks ago, the werewolf would have gutted me.

A smattering of simultaneous shutters is my only warning before an arm encircles my neck. Cool lips press against my cheek as Sloane gifts the paparazzi their money shot. The yells reach fever pitch. Sloane takes it all in stride. She mastered the art of rocking a red carpet long before we became friends.

Waving enthusiastically, she grants them a flash of teeth and ruby lips, winks a lid over one stunning blue-gray eye and poses. The shutters clatter.

She hooks my elbow and with her free hand, gathers the draped silver of her gown, lifting it to show a bit of leg. "Ready?"

Ask, I think, as Sloane tugs me out of the limelight. *Someone, ask.*

"Willow, do you have any comment on the disappearance of Blake Brennan?"

The crowd within earshot draws a collective breath. At my arm, Sloane freezes. As my smile falters, a dozen cameras capture the moment. It'll be the picture decorating the tabloids tomorrow, splashed across social media tonight. I lick my lips as if stalling for time and then loosen my stance, concentrating on softening my expression, making my chocolate brown eyes sympathetic for Blake and his troubles.

Just how you practiced, I tell myself.

"I wish only the best for Blake Brennan," I say, nailing the same inflections I used hours earlier while repeating the sentence in the mirror. Muscle memory gives my lips the slightest downturn. I flick my gaze to the red carpet before raising it to unveil a look of measured intensity. "I sincerely hope he gets in touch with those who love him and are worried for him."

Best wishes for a good outcome from the pragmatic ex-girl-friend.

The claw marks hidden under my dress throb as if to argue.

Blake Brennan will not be getting in touch with anybody. Because Blake Brennan is very, very dead.

"And the allegations of abuse?" someone chimes in. Apparently, once the subject has been broached, it's open season. A vision of blood swims through my mind, both mine and Blake's, spreading over the tiled floor of his Los Angeles villa. I swallow and taste copper.

He raised a hand to me, so I raised a silver dagger.

I wonder how they'd react if I were to say it aloud. 'It was his own fault. He expected me to go down without a fight.' These people have no damn clue what's out there. The average public isn't aware most stars of screens and stages get there with sway and charms and supernatural gifts.

Ignorance is bliss, I remind myself and sigh in a perfect blend of indulgence and hesitation. "Blake had…"

Sloane squeezes my arm in warning. Spitting a curse at myself for using the past tense, I keep going.

"An anger issue. Two months ago, as soon as this became clear to me, I ended the relationship, despite my feelings for him. Violence," I say, "whether it be against someone you love or an enemy, is never an acceptable reaction, and should never be tolerated. Thank you."

It's the best I can do. Sloane's the actress.

At my side, she takes the cue and parades us along the roped off red carpet toward the main building of the theater. When we're out of earshot, she leans.

"Violence is never an acceptable reaction," she singsongs through teeth still clenched in a perfect smile.

"That asshole was a time bomb," I snap, not so careful about my polished veneer now that we're not the focus of the cameras. "I simply disarmed the dangerous thing."

I took Blake Brennan on as a client four months ago. As a newly turned werewolf, he struggled with the change after being bitten in Mongolia where he'd been filming. The lead actress, who played his lover, noticed the signs and got him stateside before reaching out to Sloane for help. Sloane referred me for the job. I'm not the only supernatural handler working the scene. I am, however, the best.

It's been four months since I agreed to help Blake. Two months since I canceled our contract, and we publicly "broke up". Three weeks since he went missing. Tonight, walking the carpet at the premiere of Sloane's movie marks my reintroduction into society since the news of Blake's disappearance broke.

Despite the heat of the late L.A. afternoon, I shiver.

"Hang on. Almost there," Sloane murmurs. She glances at me, brow furrowing.

When she found me on the floor of Blake's kitchen, I'd already been unconscious. There's this memory I have of the windows stretched to the ceiling, the darkness outside swallowing me whole as I fought each breath into my lungs desperate to live long enough for Sloane to make it to me.

I never should have been there, I think.

Blake hadn't been a good person. The wolf only made things worse. But he'd begged me to come over, let him apologize, explain, give me a second chance. He said he needed me, that I was the only person left he could ask for help.

Which was true.

In the month after officially labeling Blake a lost cause, the man burned a hell of a lot of bridges. It had irked me to walk away the first time. I'm a fixer. He's the only client I've ever given up on. I thought maybe, just maybe, I could still eke out a win for both of us and smudge that black mark off an otherwise flawless record.

Two months of the misogynistic asshole and I should have known better, should have expected the set of claws raking away my summer bikini body.

I never killed anyone before that night. Aside from Sloane, as far as supernatural Hollywood knows, I still haven't.

In her gown, with a dainty tiara tucked into her reddish blond curls, Sloane resembles royalty. She leads the way into the bathroom, demands privacy from the attendants, and then leans against the sink. We don't speak as a woman in a stunning dress exits a bathroom stall, washes her hands, and then leaves us alone. Sloane locks the door behind her.

"What made you change your mind?" she asks.

She's offered to heal me every few days since the attack, but I didn't want to forget how easily it had gone bad. I wanted the pain, even at the risk of someone discovering my wounds and putting together what they meant along with his disappearance. Now, the stiffness of the slowly healing scabs is a problem.

And I'm after other benefits.

"Like you said, time to get back on the horse, I suppose." I shrug, one strap of the dress cutting into my shoulder. It fits corset-tight until it flares at my hips. "Help me out of this," I say, turning away from Sloane.

She fiddles with the clasp and the zipper slides down. I gasp in relief, aware of how snug the damn thing is once I'm released from my fabric prison.

"I'm taking on a new client," I say, finally answering her question.

She blinks in surprise before concern wrinkles her brow. "Tell me it's not another wolf."

"God, no." My tone comes out more exasperated than I planned as I struggle my arms out of the dress. I'm pretty sure I won't be signing any werewolf clients for the foreseeable future. "He's an incubus."

Sloane hits me with a level look. "Wow," she says. "When I said, 'get back on the horse', we had vastly different ideas of what you'd be riding."

I snort a laugh. "He's a client."

She doesn't entertain my protest. "It's not the healing you want from my blood, after all."

"Added bonus?" I offer. Because vampires are immune to incubi, with her blood in my veins, theoretically, I will be too. Fabric crumples to my hips. The cool breeze of the air conditioning chills my chest and stomach, bare save for an adhesive bra. "You're the only one I trust to do this."

The play leaves Sloane's expression. She pets my dark curls before lifting my jaw with two fingers. "You need to be working," she says, her eyes on mine. "Not dwelling on shit that couldn't be avoided."

"I need to be working," I concede. Killing Blake almost cost me everything. Still might. "To be working, I have to be able to move."

"Arms up," she says, and I stretch. She smacks twice at the sensitive skin below my armpits. "Higher."

My right arm shoots straight, but my left side slumps as I favor it. "I can't."

She grabs either side of my rib cage. Her fingers settle into the depressions between my bones, tightening for purchase. "You are always welcome to come to me for extra protection. This is not a weak move. It's using every advantage to keep yourself alive."

It took me an eternity to talk myself into this single dose. The whole idea squicks me out. "Do it quick," I say and wince in anticipation of what's coming.

"One...two—"

She yanks.

My flesh rips apart as the scars and scabs separate. Red and black stars explode in my vision. My knees give out and I catch myself on the edge of the counter. Burning lances through me.

"Hurry," I slur through the pain, but Sloane's already raised a wrist to her ruby lips. From behind them peeks a pair of deceptively tiny and utterly lethal fangs.

"I am hurrying," she says before biting hard on her own wrist. The trickle of blood slides down her arm and she shifts her hand over my gaping wounds. Maroon courses over her fingers in four rivulets, one for each of the furrows Blake's claws left behind. I hear dripping. The vampire blood tingles, numbing as it goes to work on the slashes. In minutes, it'll be as if the wounds never existed.

"Don't forget you need oxygen," she reminds me. "Can't have you passing out on me."

I manage a shaky inhale.

While keeping a wary eye on me, Sloane washes away the trail of blood on her arm, checking the satiny silver of her dress for wayward droplets. The self-inflicted gashes torn at her wrist are already sealed shut. Soon, the skin will be flawless again. She wets a towel from the missing attendant's abandoned basket with warm water. I work the dampened cloth over my ribs and stomach as she leans in close to assess.

"Damn, I'm good," she whispers, and I hear the smile in it.

Grateful, I fan myself to dry the last moisture before Sloane helps me into my dress.

She gives me a once over as she zips. "Remember," she says, "that shit has side effects."

I nod, as if it's old hat. My entire body tingles with a strange current.

"Hopefully nothing crazy," she goes on while I adjust the dress. "Extra energy. Little more joie de vivre. It could take a few days to work through your system."

"Life of the party. Got it." I give my hands a quick wash in the sink.

"What's the job?" Sloane asks as she passes me a towel. "When does it start?"

Besides being my best friend, the girl is a vault when it comes to supernatural details and client lists. It also helps to know a vampire has my whereabouts in case shit goes south and I need a rescue. I don't have to worry about her stumbling into something she can't handle.

"Tomorrow," I tell her. "Bit of bad press over some pictures, I guess? Needs a sobriety coach. I don't want him glamouring my ass."

Her brow wrinkles. "They're rare, his kind. I don't know much about them."

I shrug, but it's more to work out any lingering tightness. "So, by the end of this job, I'll be the leading expert."

In the mirror, her reflection grins. "With all your extra energy, this means we're going out tonight, right?"

Sloane started the tradition with my second client. When I announce a new gig, she insists on a night out, wild times to purge my system before I knuckle down and focus on my client's needs. We usually end up doing shots in a small-town bar that's hours outside of L.A., wearing T-shirts and jeans, wigged and without makeup, anonymous. Part of me wonders if those nights are more for her than myself, though I'll never call her out on it. Then again, she'll find any excuse to blow off a Hollywood premier, especially for a movie she stars in. Expectations always make her cagey.

"First round is on me?" she adds.

The way her face lights up makes the next part of my news a bummer. "Can't," I say. "I'm meeting him in Austin."

Sloane looks excited anyway. "Austin is a blast. Sixth Street. The music is fantastic!" she gushes.

I wilt against the counter. Aside from the healing, any extra go-go juice in my blood hasn't kicked in yet. Going out is the last thing on my mind. "Not tonight."

"Look," she says. "You know how couples get all lovey-dovey about staring up at the same stars when they're miles apart?"

I raise an eyebrow. Though the internet comment sections constantly offer "proof" otherwise, she and I have never been more than friends.

"Same principle," she says. "We might not be in the same bar, but baby, we can drink the same whiskey."

I shake my head with a smile, push off the counter and tentatively bend to the left, then the right, mimicking a stabbing motion. The moves are hesitant, stilted in the dress, but more than I could achieve ten minutes ago.

"Listen, I appreciate our tradition, but it won't be the same without you," I say. "Besides, my flight leaves in an hour and I'm not scheduled to land until eleven. Once I get there, I'll need to—"

"Plenty of time."

"Prepare properly," I go on. "Brush up on incubi. Look up The Raven Shakes."

"Wait, what?" She grabs my arm to force my attention to her.

"Ouch," I blurt.

"Willow, you need to tell me right now," she says. "Is your client the singer?"

"You know The Raven Shakes?" In my phone call with the manager, he'd described the group as an up-and-coming bluesy rock band. I hadn't expected Sloane to recognize the name. "Are they any good?" I ask.

"Fucking amazing, but that's not the point!" she blurts.

Someone pounds on the door. Sloane's influence has apparently dried up. A simple turn bolt stands between us and the power of inconvenienced women in fancy dress.

"One minute!" Sloane calls.

"Then what *is* the point?" I ask as I cross my arms over my chest. The motion still feels strange, having so much range. I don't bother denying the lead singer is my client. Soon, images of the two of us will decorate magazines and social media feeds. Step one, positive press manipulation.

"Have I ever steered you wrong?" Sloane asks, her voice serious.

I bark out a laugh. "Sure," I say. "Lots of times."

She gives my shoulder a sympathetic squeeze. "Willow. Please. Bang the shit out of a hot guy to tide you over. Because trust me, incubus or not, you're going to want to bed your client."

"Highly unlikely," I say, rolling my eyes. My skill set is honed and specialized. Enter a supposed and very public relationship with the client. Use said relationship to nix any bad press while providing the guidance needed. Each job is different.

This job, I'll get the rockstar on the wagon and keep him there.

"He's gorgeous, Wil," Sloane says. "Those eyes! That voice! I—"

"Not happening," I laugh.

The show put on for the public will be nothing more than that. A show. I've never invited a client into my pants. I never will. As soon as I've satisfied his record label, who hired me, we'll have a tearful mutual breakup that'll leave him the hot new catch and myself a media darling and celebutante. Female clients get an adorable bff treatment that finishes in a more open-ended way.

Turning to the mirror, I check my mascara. The tears I blinked away have smeared the corners of my eyes with black. I fix it with a fingertip.

Only then do I meet Sloane's nervous gaze in the mirror. Luckily for her, vampires not having reflections is bunk. A carefully applied layer of sunscreen and a pair of designer sunglasses take care of another myth. The bloodlust, and the need to feed? Those are unfortunately real.

"I promise I'll be careful. It's a straightforward job," I say. I don't dare tell her the incubus isn't the only one with supernatural abilities in the group. "I can handle myself."

Sloane's mouth opens, closes, opens again. Her expression sharpens. "Last time you told me that, I found you nearly gutted."

I wince. "That's an important nearly," I offer.

She studies me as if sizing me up. Finally, she clutches my upper arms and runs her hands down until her fingers find mine. "You're my best friend, Wil. But we both know I'm the reason you're able to use this lifestyle to survive."

I draw a breath to protest.

"It's true," she says before I can. "It started with me. You get your clients by word of mouth." She hesitates. "Which means it's my fault you took on Blake."

My heart breaks a little. "Sloane—"

She'd been my first unofficial client. She hired me as her personal assistant, but between my interview and start date, a vampire turned her, and my job description radically changed. Suddenly, I found myself working as the handler of a starlet with extreme bloodlust. It was a lot to adjust to. But I did my job. When another of Sloane's friends needed help, I helped. My talents kept me in elite Hollywood circles, on all the Who's Who lists. But after what went down with Blake?

I think I need a break from Hollywood.

Sloane frowns. "I can't heal the damage he did up here, Willow." She taps a finger against my temple. Her tone drops low. "Are you *sure* you're ready? You can take more time."

She grimaces as I attempt a smile.

"It's a simple job," I promise. "Sober up the singer, polish him like the shiny diamond he is and set him free." I brush my hands together. "Easy peasy."

"How's your PTSD?"

She's not pulling punches.

"Christ, I had a few nightmares!" I say as if she's being absurd. The truth is, aside from a slight case of coma, I haven't slept through the night since what happened at Blake's. Werewolves are territorial, and asshole or not, Blake *belonged* to them. If anyone finds out I took him from them, I'm dead.

Blowing out of town with a band on tour will keep me on the move. Rumors of a new boyfriend on the heels of my reemergence will have the press salivating. The only thing gossip rags love more than a tragedy is a girl getting back on her feet *after* a tragedy. It's everything I could have asked for in a job.

Still, fear adds the slightest tremble to my voice. "Blake had friends, Sloane. He was part of a pack. They know he didn't wander off on sabbatical." I sigh, uncertain how much to divulge about what's been going on. "It's smart to put space between myself and L.A. right now."

With a roll of her eyes, Sloane gives my hands a reassuring squeeze before she drops them. "Honey, half the vampires in Hollywood consider you friend, not food. That means you're off limits. The wolves will respect that."

"No," I admit. "They won't." I debate whether or not to say anything and then blurt out what I've been hiding. "I found paw prints."

"When?" she demands. "Where?"

"Last night." I clutch at the nape of my neck and close my eyes. "On my front porch. They came up the walk. Right to my door." I force myself to take in her worried expression. My voice lowers to a whisper, as if I'm afraid even in this empty room I'll somehow be overheard, that my secret will get out. "They know what I did."

"They don't," Sloane says. Her gray eyes flick silver. "Blake is missing. We have no idea what happened to him. Say it."

I shudder. "Blake is missing."

She nods once in encouragement to urge me on.

"We have no idea what happened to him." The words curdle on my tongue. My mouth tastes sour. "But—"

"But nothing."

She never said what she did with Blake's body or how she cleaned up the scene alone. Technically, I'm not positive she *was* alone.

"Now you see why it's best I take this job? Get out of here for a while?" The door rattles again. I use the opportunity of Sloane's distraction to head toward it. "Go celebrate your movie," I tell her. "I'll text you later."

Before I click the lock, I spin and raise my hand to my side. "Thanks," I say.

She nods and I know she's gotten my meaning. That night, lying on the tiles at Blake's, the blood spread a frightening warmth underneath me until it puddled against my cheek. Helpless and hurting, I watched Blake's chest rise and fall and rise and fall and stop. Adrenaline fading, I snagged my phone, unlocked it, and tapped a name.

I remember darkness beyond the windows. I remember the lights of L.A. winking out as black rolled inside like a foul tide, my vision fading. I remember scrawling words in red onto the chilly white tile, his blood or mine, it hadn't mattered anymore, my fingertip bent and squeaking against the floor.

Don't turn me.

That close to death, the risk of Sloane yanking me over into undead territory as a last resort was too great. And despite the blood loss, despite the gaping fissures at my waist and the serious problem of the dead werewolf beside me and the shallow pulls of air wheezing through my lips, I'd woken up a few days later in agony, but I'd woken up human.

Am I walking into another nightmare? I wonder. Blake wanted my life.

I have a feeling I know what the incubus will be after.

15

Chapter 2

Roanoke

I am fucking lit.

My whole body hums, aches, needs. I want more. The memory of standing on that stage with my arms outstretched is on a feedback loop through my brain. It's been hours and I can't shake it. We were the *opening* band. No one should have given a shit about The Raven Shakes, and yet the crowd knew my songs.

Every word of them.

My ears still ring with the thundering sound of six thousand fans chanting my name.

"You guys!" I manage leaning against the side of the shithole Winnebago that serves as our tour bus.

"Right?" Damien says, like he can't quite believe our lives, and I shake my head in bewildered agreement. Every show gets more insane. Every night ramps up closer to the sort of next level shit that means headlining tours. That means we could make it. Big.

Our grumpy asshole of a bass player, Carter, is the only one not grinning. The rest of us—me and December and Damien—are laughs and hollers and arms looped over shoulders, linking and unlinking.

The adrenaline rush I'm still riding keeps the fire pumping inside me. My lungs add oxygen with each whoop I unleash until I'm all backdrafts and unstable air. Heat roots at the base of my skull, but it's got nothing to do with liquor. Feeling this good should be illegal.

It almost makes me forget my hunger.

I push off the Winnebago and start us on the stumbling celebration across the hotel parking lot. At my shoulder, December, the drummer, is wearing this crazed look, her sea-green eyes blazing with the few celebratory shots the four of us downed backstage while Timber Boom took the spotlight and did their thing. Behind December and me, Carter and Damien bring up the rear.

I have to hold on to this, I think. *These people...this band is what's keeping anything left of myself together.*

Goosebumps flare across my skin. I flush and break into a sudden cold sweat.

No, I think. *No, no, no, not now. Not this moment. This one's mine.* I fist the hand hidden at my side and ride out the wave of nausea.

Oblivious, December gives me a playful slug. "Fucking nailed it," she says. "I told you adding a violin solo to Once and Future would change everything!"

Plastering on a grin, I run my unclenched hand through my

curls. They hang to my chin in loose brown waves, just short enough that they've slipped from the leather tie I used to hold them back when I'm on stage. I unwrap the few strands still stuck in the knot and a black feather spirals down onto the asphalt. I stoop to snag it. The world tips uneasily.

A surprised "ope" escapes me before I straighten too quickly. I overcompensate into a stumble and cock my elbows out for balance as either Carter or Damien grabs my shirt to yank me out of the tumble.

"Gravity, Roanoke," Carter snaps. "Gravity."

"Yup!" I say cheerfully. "Slipped my mind and caught my feet!"

December giggles and I scrunch my nose at her. I hook a thumb over my shoulder with a shrug. "Loose rocks."

She shoots me an incredulous look. "Liar, liar, pants on fire."

Her voice is light and airy, but she's careful to keep the words from slipping into actual song.

I rub at the five o'clock shadow on my left cheek before I realize I've probably sweated off the three black dots I wear there on stage. December's are gone, too.

Behind me, Carter scoffs at some joke Damien told, and I laugh though I missed the punchline.

"Hey," Damien says. The guitar player's voice strains to sound casual. "Let's go out. All of us. Together. Celebrate. We can find Roanoke a friend for the night."

From the corner of my eye, I see December wince. The fevered thrill of the concert sputters out of me like a sparkler against fingertips.

"Damn," I say, trying to laugh off his comment and failing miserably. "Do I look that bad?"

The other three members of the band have the good sense to suddenly be very interested in anything other than me. A tall chain-link fence at the rear of the parking lot sits just beyond where our Winnie is parked. After driving from the venue, our new handler left us to our own devices and went to check us into the hotel. The dude's only been with us a couple of weeks. He's *supposed* to be a label sponsored babysitter, but we're constantly slipping away, me in particular. He doesn't exactly make it hard.

"You look a little..." December hesitates and tucks a blonde lock behind her ear. "Worn out," she says finally.

"I'm always wrecked after a show." It's a lie. Inside me is a void, hungry and gaping, so strong my fingers stiffen. *You're being dramatic*, I chide myself. *Your fingers are stiff because you just played the best set of your life.*

Sure, I've had the shakes since I woke up this morning, the sheets on my bunk soaked through with sweat. I planned on riding it out, though, to go eight days without feeding. I've made it that long before. But once Damien's mentioned it, all I can think about is satiating the demon. I purse my lips and blow.

"Roanoke," December starts cautiously, and I tip my palm in her direction to cut off the speech. She doesn't realize she's already won the battle.

"I'm fine," I say.

Not remembering what city we're in, I glance around the hotel parking lot as if it'll offer a clue. Dallas? No, Austin. I've been here before. Partied with Damaged Atlas, the other opening band.... Where? I search my addled brain for the memory.

Sixth street. That's where the crowds will be. I'll find a bar. Grab a drink and do what I need to get this parasite inside me placid again. I won't think of the dead girl.

Those sightless eyes.

A shiver runs through me. She died while I was onstage. Three weeks ago, while I gripped the microphone and sang about love and loss, her pulse stopped in the small cave of a room the band used before the show.

She was still warm when a pair of employees stumbled on her and called their boss, who called the cops. By the time we got offstage, the backstage area was a circus.

I'd gripped shoulders and pushed forward through the gathered bouncers and bartenders. Around me, the crowd whispered that she must have overdosed. That there were no needles. That it could have been pills. I saw her then, crumpled against the cinderblock wall, head tilted as if to take in all the attention, eyes open with vague surprise, not even clouded.

I read in the paper that her name was Everly. The toxicology came back clean, the autopsy inconclusive. No one, including me, had a clue how she got there. Because a venue employee ushered us onto the stage, there'd been a witness that we left the room empty.

It had nothing to do with me. It's become a mantra. *It had nothing to do with me.* The words lose their syllables, bump together and round off until they mean nothing at all. Dissonance. *It had nothing to do with me.*

So why had she looked vaguely familiar?

I do my best to cast off the memory of the dead girl and focus on the issue at hand. Beside me, December keeps her eyes on the broken asphalt. She walks with her arms crossed over her chest. "You don't always have to go out alone when you—"

"It's not really a spectator sport," I say before I can help myself.

"Forget it," Damien mumbles. "I thought maybe we could all go together and—"

December's voice hits as hard as she'd slammed her snare earlier. "Trust me, none of us want to watch you screw a few years off the end of some girl's life." The words ring in my ears. "We want to make sure you're—"

"Not fucking some groupie that winds up dead?" I grind out at the same time December says, "Safe."

She purses her coral pink mouth into a patronizing snarl. "Ass," she says under her breath before her scowl softens into confusion. "Is that why you didn't go out yesterday?"

"No," I say. "I wasn't in the mood yet."

"You have to feed that demon, Roanoke."

I swallow hard. "The dead girls. They're getting closer. Each one." It's the part that freaks me out most. "Christ, if Carter hadn't moved rooms," I start and then cut off when I see him fall back a few steps, his discomfort obvious.

Six days ago, a commotion in the hotel's hallway drew both Carter and Damien from their rooms, though December slept through it. He and Damien watched from an anonymous distance as a random old man started chest compressions on the body leaned against the door of Carter's vacated room like a macabre gift. Earlier, Carter had gone down to the front desk and changed to a different one because his air conditioner gave off a high-pitched whine. I'd been in the Winnebago, oblivious until it was all over, the police departed, the scene cleared.

That'd been the third body. It made us connect dots with the others. Before her, there'd been a corpse found in the same parking lot where the Winnebago was parked. We didn't know until later when Gregory started paying attention.

"Someone's fucking with us," December says. "Gregory already called for backup. We're going to find out who's doing it and get it stopped, okay?"

I grunt in a non-answer. I'm starting to wonder if it's not the band someone's fucking with. I'm starting to wonder if it's me.

I spent the last couple of days obsessed with the profile pictures of those three dead girls on my phone. One of them, I swear I remember in flashes of a tossed back head, red lips open in a moan of pleasure. I can't tell if it's my imagination going dark and terrible. The blur of drunk sex and guilt. But if I'd been with her, it'd been cities before, states even.

You're losing it, I tell myself. My guts feel like they're curdling, the blood sluggish in my veins despite the rush from being on stage earlier. I'm not an idiot. I wasn't going to make it until day eight.

"It's just...we have Houston tomorrow," I say quietly. I shift my hands into the pockets of my tattered jeans where it's easier to hide the tremble. "If I'm sick..."

Sick, I think. When there's nothing but need. When I get dangerous. Such a nice term for the shudder in my bones, the way my eyes darken to a muddied rust color as the thing inside me takes over. If I ever let it, the demon will trample everything good left in me.

I've never killed anyone. Never took from someone who wasn't willing. Never even came close. I have to feed the demon while I still have control. I know what it means for the girl I hook up with tonight.

I'm going to do it, anyway.

"I gotta go," I mumble, afraid if I stay any longer, I'll come clean on my hunch; that whatever's happening is tied to me somehow. "Alone," I add, in case any of them get ideas.

Carter reaches to clap me on the shoulder.

"You being on your own, Ro," he says, and then pauses. A clump of his shockingly ice blond hair droops in front of his eye before he whisks it back, showing off the ink on his tattooed arm. "We're worried about you. I mean, I get it. What you do...it's...it's not really a..." He hesitates. "A group activity."

"It is if you're doing it right," Damien says quietly, like he can't help it. No one laughs and I kind of feel sorry for the dude.

I glance over and one of the multitude of tattoos on Carter's collarbone fades and flares underneath the unbuttoned collar of his shirt. The scripted writing reads NECK DEEP. I try not to take it as a sign.

Carter has it easy. As a shapeshifter, he doesn't depend on others to sustain him. All he has to do is remember what tattoos he's been too lazy to ink yet or concentrate that his irises don't flicker between brown and blue like a bug zapper. When Carter makes a mistake, it's passed off as contacts or creativity.

What's cocooned inside me nibbles away at lifespans. Then again, someone else always has it worse. My eyes snap to December. She's focused on me as if debating whether she wants to let me out of her sight.

If tradition holds, another corpse will show up after the concert in Houston tomorrow. Maybe New Orleans if we're lucky. Until then, my theory dangles over my head like a fucking guillotine.

Over December's shoulder, through the glass doors of the hotel, I spot Gregory, our new corporate spy, waiting for us in the lobby. He waves.

"Tell him sorry," I say. Gregory had wanted to talk to me, no doubt about whoever he called to help solve our problem. I can't face that conversation. What if what's happening *is* somehow my fault? Just in case, tonight's going to be different. I didn't pick out a groupie from the show. I'm striking out on my own. I'll find some anonymous girl, one with no ties to me, to the band.

When I turn to take off, December's fierce grip on my arm stops me.

"Keep your shit together, Ro. Do what you have to do and get back here, okay? Keep it low-key tonight?" Her tone has the slightest plea in it.

Rather than argue, I nod.

Her expression darkens. I drop my gaze to the place where her fingers squeeze tight, and she loosens her hold on me.

"I'll be good," I say. I press a thumb to her nose. "I promise."

She tousles my hair as if we're siblings with a rivalry before she takes a step backward, then another, watching me with haunted eyes. "I hate it when you lie," she says.

A blast of air conditioning swirls the briefest of chills around me as the automatic doors open to let her in. Carter follows, and then Damien.

I bolt. My stride lengthens as I increase my pace. The last thing I need is a guilt trip from Gregory.

You're not a prisoner, I remind myself. And then, *You haven't done anything wrong.* Maybe December's right. Maybe the guilt is all in my head. Doesn't make much of a difference, though. It's still there. Drowning me. Invading the empty spaces.

The demon scuttles and shifts. I curl my arm across my stomach.

I need a drink to get through the next couple of hours. *Just to take the edge off*, I promise myself, but December's voice echoes through my mind.

I hate it when you lie.

Seven days, four hours, fifty-six minutes.

The demon wriggles, sensing my surrender. Claws curl into my ribcage from the inside.

Eight days would have put me minutes from taking the stage tomorrow night. I wouldn't have been able to perform. Not tomorrow, when I would have been so much worse.

"Fuck," I mumble as I head off across the still hot blacktop.

I was always going to lose this one.

CHAPTER 3

WILLOW

O utside the hotel, I inhale the strange scent of Austin into my lungs. It rained earlier and the patchy way the moisture is drying on the sidewalk makes me think of the wolf's paw prints again. The streets are wet with shine.

Despite the humidity, windows are open at every cafe, tavern, and bar that I traipse past, advertising the music playing within, the food. My stomach growls. I haven't eaten since breakfast. I'd been in hair and makeup all morning and afternoon and then, after my public appearance, it'd been straight to the jet.

After we took off, I googled for updates on the Blake fiasco and my dramatic speech. The articles covered the same ground—Blake Brennan, star of films such as The Dragonfly War and In the Time of Velvet Saints, hasn't been seen since June 13th, no foul play suspected, a search of his house revealed nothing. Linked romantically to Willow Taverson until a video leaked in April showing Brennan allegedly roughly handling Taverson following an argument the two had. Shortly after, Taverson ended the relationship. This is her first public appearance since her former boyfriend went missing.

And then my face.

I don't look like that. Not in real life. I redid my makeup at the hotel. Now, I'm wearing the barest beige eyeshadow, my eyeliner brown and smoky and utterly unlike the trademark slice of black wing I usually wear. I taste the cherry cola flavored lip balm that turned my mouth wet and red.

At the premiere, in all the pictures, there's a glint in my eyes that makes me look like I'm in over my head. Awkward and hesitant doesn't equate with someone who has the skills to take out a werewolf. I never asked what, if anything, Blake told his pack about our arrangement.

Half a country away, I'm fighting the urge to glance over my shoulder. I finally make it to the sign in front of The Wooden Barrel and whip out my cellphone. Blonde hair frames my face. I'm wearing a wig cut into a cute bob, my own brown curls secured underneath. The outfit I hastily changed into when I arrived at the hotel is designed to throw off anyone who might think they recognize me. Surely Willow Taverson wouldn't show up in a dive bar dressed in a lacy white tank top and distressed jeans. The blonde wig seals the deal. Not to mention, every single gossip site put me in L.A. at Sloane's premiere tonight. I'm officially off the radar.

A shot and a song, I promise myself. Popping off a quick selfie, I send it to Sloane and then add a follow-up message.

Jack Daniels, my star-crossed partner in crime.

Without waiting for a reply, I tug open the wooden door.

Sound assaults me. Over whoops of enthusiasm that drown

out the bar's small talk, an old school blues band plays. The stage they're on takes up the rear third of the room. It's bowed dangerously under the weight of a drum set and a standup bass, along with an ancient Black man crooning into a crackling microphone that looks like it was made the year he was born. Paint peels from a leak in the ceiling, a yellow-brown stain seeping down one wall and almost hidden in the dim light. I've somehow found the perfect dive bar. My grin widens.

I barely register that I note the angle of the door behind me and the exits at the rear of the bar, both lit by glowing signs. I wonder absently if I snap the metal microphone stand in two if the pieces will make a decent stake.

Stop it, I demand mentally, in a harsher tone than I would ever let anyone take with me. *Relax. Now. Not everyone is out to get you.*

The haunting, bluesy baritone fights against my nerves as I glide through the crowd and up to the counter. I roll my shoulders and the joints click and crack as the tension draws them up again. Eyes flash to me from dark corners. Big men, sizing me up.

I'm acting like prey, I realize, and so they're treating me like prey. Goosebumps race over my exposed skin. I'm not used to this new me. This After Blake me. I'm suddenly lightheaded, my breathing swift and shallow. It's the vampire blood. Every emotion is dialed up to eleven.

In the back of my mind, Sloane's voice cracks like a whip.

PTSD.

Closing my eyes for a beat, I ground myself with a slow inhale and then open them again. I'm the predator. I'm the one hunting. Nothing can hurt me.

The bartender, a sprig of a girl with a gray towel over her shoulder, gestures to me with a raised eyebrow. Her head tilts to ask if I'm okay. I wave off her concern and step up to the bar.

"Get cha?" she yells, the first half of the question swallowed by the lonely warble of a slide guitar.

"A shot! Jack!" I call, leaning forward on crossed arms to be heard. The bartender nods and tips a bottle with practiced precision. She slides the tumbler down the bar and into my outstretched hand. When I catch it, a smile bursts onto my lips.

A barstool opens and I drop onto it, the polished wood stained and sticky with spilled liquor. I don't care. A couple minutes to enjoy the music and I'll order something greasy to go, eat it at the hotel while I pour over the information the record company sent on The Raven Shakes. Tomorrow night after they play, I'm officially in charge of the band and Gregory will assist me in whatever capacity I deem most helpful.

My evening of debauchery might be short and sweet, but at least I'm not breaking my promise to Sloane, aside from 'banging a hot guy'. It's honestly good for me to be out, though. The show I put on at Sloane's premiere was one thing, but I need to deal with this random paranoia.

Maybe I *should* find a stranger to toss some trust into tonight...like a test.

I tell myself it's in the interest of therapy that I'm casting my gaze over the crowd. No one seems younger than sixty, though I can't quite see the tables in the back corner. I check my cellphone for the time. Twelve thirty-seven. If I stay until one, I can work until two, get a good night's sleep, and arrive completely prepared for my meeting with the band at eleven.

A good night's sleep. What a joke.

My phone vibrates in my hand.

To us, and to the stranger quenching your fires, Sloane's text reads.

I laugh, loud and bold, before self-consciousness overcomes me. I'm not here to be the center of any scene.

Sadly, the crowd is geriatric, I text her and then tuck the phone into my pocket. I tip back the shot, barely wincing as the whiskey coats my throat.

"You know," says a voice. "Drinking alone is a sign of alcoholism."

Goosebumps raise across the nape of my neck. The timbre of the words rattles through me.

Now that *sounds like the kind of trouble I'm trying to get into*, I think.

Amusement plays at my lips as I resist spinning to face the owner of the sexy voice. "Who says I'm drinking alone?"

When I adjust to give him a smidgen of a profile shot to pique his interest, I catch a flash of movement in my peripheral vision. The liquor hasn't dulled my reflexes enough to keep me from flinching. To cover the move, I relent and swivel my seat to face him. My eyes settle on the stranger, a single empty barstool between us.

Shit. It's the first thought that bursts into my brain. He sweeps tousled honey-brown curls from his forehead as my gaze wanders over his form. He's built, but not gym-ripped, and tan. The threadbare jeans he wears are battered into ragged holes at the knees.

Despite the heat, a red patterned flannel is locked in a knot around his waist. His white t-shirt gleams, sending an ethereal glow haloing him against the darkness of the bar. He should come across as rumpled and tossed aside, only to land in a place like this. Instead, the rough edge of the surroundings takes him from unkempt to alluring.

He holds two fingers to the bartender before flicking them at my empty whiskey glass.

"Saving me from a life of alcoholism?" I ask. The line's tired, but he's gorgeous enough that I'm willing to give him the benefit of the doubt.

"You?" His mouth crooks in a half smile. "Not at all. It's me I'm worried about," he says.

A laugh bubbles from me. I cock my head and gift him with a nod of admiration. "Nice twist."

I can't quite pin down the color of his eyes in the dim bar, somewhere between cerulean blue and a jade tone depending on how they soak up the light. Half of his brownish waves hang free, the other half tied back. His jaw is sharp, cheekbones a little less chiseled than the "cut-glass" actor look. There's no part of him that equates with slumming it. He's gorgeous. And those eyes. They flicker from blue to green as he tilts toward me.

"You're staring," he says. I catch the slow temptation of his tongue sliding across his lips. Heat crawls up my neck as I rip my gaze away.

"I'm deciding whether or not I want to save you from that life of alcoholism," I say, my tone unapologetic. A moment slides by, time for me to appear to be thinking it over, a move that would make Sloane damn proud.

Finally, I lift my shot glass. He mirrors the motion, clinks his against mine, and we both tip back the liquor. His eyes fall to the throb at my throat as I swallow.

"Are you a fan of Walker Roads?" he asks to break our shared silence, jutting his chin in the band's direction.

On stage, the old man is wailing into a harmonica. His foot stomps rhythmically on the warped wood.

I shake my head. With my fingers cupped around his ear, I shout, "I promised a friend I'd come for a drink!"

When I lean away, his brows are knitted. He searches the crowd.

Grasping his meaning, I smile. "She's not here," I say, placing the tiniest amount of extra emphasis on the pronoun. "Long story."

"Got a name?" he prods when I don't fill in the details.

Usually, I lie. I tuck a lock of hair behind my ear, habit, but the blonde strands of the wig are too short and swing free. I'm not sure why my real name is on the tip of my tongue. I hesitate and the instant I do, it's obvious.

"I'm only here for the night," I settle on.

"Me too." His gaze snags on my features and I think he recognizes me despite the wig and outfit. That he knows my face even if he can't place it. He does the awkward lean again to speak to me. "That Gretsch guitar he's playing has gotta be a hundred years old, easy!" he says, and for a second I'm lost before I realize his attention wandered to the singer. "Guy's a legend!"

We part, and I watch him watching Walker Roads. There's almost a disbelief in my guy's expression as his lips move along to the gravelly lyrics. His mouth purses on a word and I imagine that mouth on me, his warm breath on my collarbone as he kisses his way across my shoulder.

I bite my lip and release it with a pop, considering. I can't kiss him here. If a single picture surfaces of me making out with some rough and tumble guy in a random Austin bar? Taken days before I'm going to be declaring my love for the lead singer of The Raven Shakes? And on the same day as my chin-quivering speech about Blake? Shit will hit the fan.

It's the hotel or nothing.

Mine, I think, and just like that, I'm back to being a predator instead of prey, feeling loose and reckless in a strange city without a care in the world. God, I needed this to remember myself. The music's got my muscles relaxing for the first time in weeks. The gorgeous guy in front of me will take me the rest of the way.

Tonight, I'll be able to sleep.

It's a pipe dream and I know it, but if I'm facing another sleepless night, I'll spend it tangled around and underneath the guy sitting next to me. I tilt my head a little to appear shy. "You doing anything? I'm about to take off..."

There's a clunk as two full shot glasses are set on the bar behind us. He nods his thanks before turning to me.

"He's playing James Don't Lie," the guy says. His eyes are glued to the stage. "Next one will be Devil Take You Cold, which is always his last. You hang out, dance with me to that final song." Only then does his gaze flick from the old man to me. He raises an eyebrow as if in challenge. "And I promise the reward will be more than worth it."

I deflate a bit. So, apparently, the blatant invitation into my pants won't shake him free of his bar stool. "Next time," I say as I stand.

His hand catches my wrist. "Why? You got somewhere else to be?"

There's a playfulness to his tone as his thumb absently strokes my skin. "You're so eager to get me into bed you'd pass up the opportunity to hear the best delta bluesman alive? This is once in a lifetime. Can't believe I wandered in here and caught this." He shrugs. "Now granted, you might be a goddess between the sheets, but honestly, if you don't see blues this good as foreplay, we're doomed."

I wonder how many women before me walked at the line, why it intrigues me so much more than it should. He's not afraid of me shutting him down. And damned if I can't help wanting to live up to his strange standards, which is a well-known trick of pickup artists even if this guy doesn't seem sleazy enough to be one.

"Music isn't foreplay," I counter to test my theory and then I hesitate. I have files to go over. He probably isn't worth it after all. All smooth talk and a lousy fuck. "I should go. I start a new job tomorrow and—"

He moves onto the barstool separating us and slides closer until he's perched behind me.

"And that," he says, "is tomorrow." His fingers skate across my shoulder blade and then down my arm in a series of feather-soft touches. "Give me the chance to prove you wrong about the foreplay."

Chapter 4

Roanoke

When it comes to feeding the demon, I'm usually going through the motions, the steps rote. But I'm actually enjoying this little chase. She's indisputably gorgeous, snarky ...we'd probably have fun hanging out if we got to know each other.

Of course, that's not going to happen.

This banter—hell, even small talk—feels gratuitous. I'm used to being groped in dark corners by girls after bragging rights, unconcerned if I'm barely conscious, as long as they can technically claim they fucked me. Instead of a goodbye kiss, I'm left with a camera flash as they snap proof for their friends. My feelings don't factor into the exchange. Only getting the demon fed matters.

"Two songs," I say as I drift my calloused fingertips over the softness of her shoulder. "What's an extra ten minutes?" A thrill runs through me. I should have already sealed this deal. It's risky, staying. But I'm enjoying the moment, the conversation, her company. How our barstools align her between my thighs.

"Ten minutes?" she asks.

Draping my arms over her shoulders, I hold her closer, fold her against me. My other hand finds hers.

I trace the edge of her ear with my tongue and then flick it against the lobe. The tiniest moan breaks from her, almost involuntarily. I tighten my arm around her waist. It's been a damn long time since I've been this turned on by a kiss. I unwind my fingers from her, eager to touch, play, explore as much as I can get away with in the crowded bar. My fingers graze her side.

She recoils and freezes.

"Are you okay?" I ask, dropping the sultry tone to my voice. If she's not into this, I won't push. "If you want me to stop..."

"It's not you," she insists, but she doesn't sound right. She's gone from flirty to a frayed nerve. As if to prove herself, she settles against me again, presses herself tight to my body. "Keep going."

Instead, I stroke her arm with my thumb, my attention on the stage to let her recover from whatever startled her. Walker Roads eases into his next song.

The arm I've draped over her shoulder rests across her chest. The heartbeat underneath is frantic, her chest rising and falling in shallow gasps. She's smiling, but inside, she's pure chaos. I'm guessing it's the start of a panic attack. Some memory tied to the reason she flinched from me.

She's clutching my hand tighter. If I don't stop this, she's gonna spiral until it's full blown and I won't be able to help. I don't bother with anything supernatural. Instead, I use an old trick I learned when I used to freak out before shows. Back when I was fully human.

With our fisted fingers, I start a steady tap at half-speed to the rhythm of the music, distracting her from her own heartbeat. She doesn't notice it, nor when I time my inhales and exhales to hers so that when I slow mine by degrees, hers follow. As hers go normal again, she relaxes into my embrace. We spend a few minutes in silence.

"He's good," she admits, and I grin, though she can't see it. Between finding her and stumbling into this place, my night is on an upswing I don't understand. It feels like a trick.

Until it backfires, I'm enjoying it, I think, as I adjust her in my arms. My lips find her neck. I don't kiss her, though, only drift my mouth torturously close until I lift to her ear.

"Imagine the things he's seen," I say, my voice husky from singing earlier, the whiskey. Goosebumps rise on her arms, and I run my grip over them, enjoying her reaction to me. "Imagine the pain needed to write lyrics that incendiary."

The music throbs through me, my every atom aching for the wavering slide down the guitar's neck. "He's brilliant," I whisper, and though she shouldn't be able to hear me, she turns ever so slightly.

"You're a musician," she says over her shoulder.

The words hit like a drop of soap in oil. "What makes you say that?" I ask.

Her chocolate eyes weigh on me. Is she toying with me? Does she know who I am? "It was a question," she says.

I grunt, not sure if I believe her. Her pout of confusion eases my tension.

"Listen. Tonight, I'm just a guy in a bar," I say. "Enjoying things as they come." It's a careful middle ground. I glance up and her eyes meet mine again. "Who are you tonight?"

Her expression flashes to alarm for a split second before it shifts to uncertainty and then morphs into amusement with an eyebrow arch. When she speaks, her voice is even. "Whoever you want me to be," she says.

I sniff a laugh and shrug. "Fair enough," I say before I snatch one of the shot glasses the bartender brought us earlier.

"To lonely souls," I say in a way that makes it unclear if I'm toasting lonely souls in general or specifically the two of us.

"And keeping them that way," she adds. We're obviously after the same thing here.

"Noted," I say before I gulp down my shot. She mirrors me. We both swallow hard, wince before we slam the shot glasses upside down on the bar. The remnants of the amber liquid slip to the rim and soak into the old wood.

It hits me that the jukebox is playing. I whip around. On the stage, the band is packing up, the ancient Walker Roads already gone. "Damn it," I manage.

"So," she says, giving me a once over. "What was the music foreplay to?"

I wave the bartender over. "Whatever we both drank, on me," I say, whipping out cash. Without the advance we got from the record company, I wouldn't be able to pull this move, but I peel off a generous amount of twenties and shoot the bartender a conspiratorial grin. "And we'll take the bottle."

"Want an unopened one?" she purrs and a trickle of guilt slides into me. "You can just take it. Take them both."

It's the incubus sway. I try so hard to keep it locked down. I snag the opened bottle, thrust the twenties at her, and grab the hand of the woman I'm leaving with, much to the bartender's dismay.

"Ready?" I ask. At least *she* seems to still have her head about her. Mine, for the record, is a mess. *I'm too sober for this*, I think.

We make it out the door and half a block down before I raise my touch from her waist to tease the lace strap of her tank top. Need sends an ache first through my chest, then straight to my cock as I swell against my jeans. I can't wait for wherever we're heading.

"Hey," I say.

When she turns, I've already leaned forward. Her mouth meets mine, an inferno to match the surrounding night. She throws her arms over my shoulders, grips the back of my neck, her fingernails scratching lightly.

With a guttural groan, I stumble us backward over the sidewalk, toward the face of a shop. Her feet tangle, but I throw a hand up and use it to pivot at the last second, saving her bare shoulders from the rough brick. The bottle clinks as I take the brunt of the force myself. I slide my fingers up her ribs, ride the ridges until I'm unveiling the bottom edge of a pink bra. I tip my mouth to hers again, kiss her, slow and searching.

She starts to return the kiss, but snaps her lips free of mine, her nervous glance darting to either side, like she's afraid we'll get caught or embarrassed. The other night revelers and pedestrians stream around us, some smiling as they avert their eyes.

"Not here," she says as she cuddles into me.

My fingertips trespass under the cup of her bra, to the tight bud of a nipple. "A *little* here?" I murmur against her neck.

"Um..." She wavers and then shifts until she's blocked from view by me. She's hiding from someone.

Husband? I wonder. She's not wearing a ring. *Boyfriend?*

I'm not about to screw up anyone's life. Before I can ask, though, she's kissing me again, her hands wandering first to my chest, then south, curved against my hips at the waist of my jeans. She tugs my belt loops to yank me against her. I'm hard and I know she can feel me against her thigh from her smile as her head tilts. My mouth crests her jaw, my teeth nipping her neck.

"Jesus," she murmurs. "Okay, wait. Yeah, we need to go somewhere."

The humidity already has our skin damp, the added heat of the warm Texas night strangely erotic. I lick the erogenous spot behind her ear, trap the lobe between my lips and suck.

A single and very naughty word breaks from her, and I smile.

The tease about her being a bad girl with a dirty mouth is right there, but I don't take it. I'm too distracted. Her tongue edges against mine, the kiss going deep and passionate and all I can think about are the other places I want to taste her.

"Are we going to my place or yours?" I ask, praying she'll offer a location with an actual bedroom. As we adjust against each other, her head taps softly against the brick, the blonde strands snagging. Normally, I have a thing for brunettes. It's another attempt at breaking free of any habits. No brunettes. No sex with anyone from the show. No hooking up with anyone who knows who I am. Which is why the Winnebago is out, even as a last resort.

An image of Carter's bunk, laden with dirty laundry, swims through my mind. It'd be interesting trying to explain December's schoolgirl skirts and random lacy underthings hanging off her bunk hooks. Only Damien's bunk is tidy, save for his collage of 'hot girl' pictures taped on the wall, mostly celebrities.

"Tell me where to take you," I mutter in the space between our mouths. She moans, but I can't tell if it's an answer. Reluctantly, I draw away to let her speak.

"I have a hotel room," she says and then we're kissing again. Finally, she breaks away to tell me the name of the place. "Do you know it?"

I shake my head. It's not one of the nationwide budget chains. If it was, I'd have stayed there. "Taxi?"

She nods and I peck her on the lips once more and raise my arm toward the curb. A minute later, we've spilled into a cab. We sit like behaving adults for three seconds before we're making out again. Her teeth graze against the pulse point in my neck. The sensation sharpens into a soft bite.

My throat goes thick as her hand finds my thigh. She crawls it upward, almost as if in an accidental motion. My eyes flash to the rearview, but the driver is intent on the road. "You like that?" she whispers.

I give her a quick nod before she uses my shoulder to lift herself onto my lap in one smooth motion and swings a leg around to straddle me. As she settles, she adds the slightest twist to her hips. A noise steals from me, low and guttural, before I swallow it away. At the bar, we were talking, flirting, interacting, but more and more, this is feeling like she's after a transaction.

Taking the involuntary reaction from me as a cue, she slides herself against the outline of my cock where it's trapped inside my jeans. *Okay*, I think. *Maybe I don't need the connection after all.*

Gripping the nape of her neck, I guide her to my lips. "I can't wait to get those pants off you," I confess as the cab crawls to a stop.

I grab the bottle off the seat beside us. She swings open the door and clambers off me. Once she's out, I dig into my pocket to pay for our ride.

"No change," I call over my shoulder to the driver. My eyes never leave hers. She considers me before she reaches to cup my face and tips it toward the glow of the streetlights.

"Blue after all," she says.

"Was it a mystery?" I ask before something else occurs to me. "Oh!"

I straighten, my posture formal and hold out my hand.

She gives me a nervous laugh. "What?"

I raise an eyebrow and wait her out. We were connecting at the bar. I want that back. At least a little.

She shrugs and hooks her fingers in mine. I raise them to give her a twirl. When she rotates into my arms, her smile is radiant. I rock us to an imaginary beat, the whiskey bottle clasped behind her. The air thickens with possibility. The moment feels prophetic, like the blip between before and after. Like the start of something.

I know better, but that doesn't mean I can't pretend.

"What are you doing?" she asks, amused.

"Enjoying this," I admit. "We never got to dance to that last song."

The city hums a melody. I dip her low, enjoy the strange rush when she trusts me to hold her. It's only then that I peek over her shoulder and take in the hotel. "Wait, you're staying *here*?"

For a night at this place, you have to have fuck-you-money. Thank God I didn't take her to the Winnebago, in the parking lot of that shitty roadside hotel, an exact copy of the last shitty roadside hotel we stayed at on this tour.

She shrugs like this level of opulence is normal. "Did you want to come up for a few minutes?"

She's not shy about what she's after with me. Still, it bothers me she seems determined to get it as quickly as possible.

Finally, I hold a finger up in frustration. The other three and my thumb grip the neck of the bottle of Jack. "One rule," I say. "Before we do this..."

Her tenuous smile falters and I nestle in for a kiss before it disappears totally. "What's your rule?" she asks.

"Make sure you get your money's worth," I murmur. "Don't rush tonight." We're still swaying to our imaginary beat. "You let me fuck you good and proper. Agreed?"

She kisses me once, a tease.

"Quite confident in your abilities?" she snarks but when I don't bite, she hesitates. "Wait, get my *money's* worth?" The heat of a blush I don't understand rushes to her cheeks. "You're not an escort, are you?"

My laugh bursts out before I can stop it, genuine for the first time in too long. A second later, she joins. I hook my arm over her shoulders and kiss the crown of her head. "It's an expression," I say as she starts us into the hotel. "I mean...are you willing to pay, though? Cuz..."

She smirks and smacks me, but I wonder if it was the right joke to make considering this place. Whoever she is, she's loaded. As we pass the front desk, I pore over a picture opposite, my face turned from the clerk. It hits me she's doing the same thing. Interesting.

What are you hiding? I wonder, not for the first time tonight.

We keep our hands off each other in the elevator, waiting while the door slides shut. My shoulders press against the mirrored wall, arms crossed as I watch her take a keycard from her pocket.

"What floor?" I ask, finger poised to hit the button.

"Oh, um...here," she says. She nudges me aside and pushes the card into a slot next to a letter P. It lights up.

Okay...so it's restricted, and she's got access. It occurs to me what the P stands for.

"Penthouse?" I mouth.

If she hears me, she doesn't react, her expression hidden in the wobble of the polished chrome. The elevator dings to a stop. The door opens.

CHAPTER 5

WILLOW

"**R**eady?" I ask without looking back.

He trails me, his footsteps a gentle crush into the plush plum carpet. Outside my room, a plaque illuminated by a half circle of glow reads Suite A.

Should I have warned him? I wonder. The guy probably thinks he's hit the jackpot, being so blatantly picked up in a bar, and now this. But when we cross the threshold, he doesn't so much as glance at the impressive collection of rooms, save to gather where the bedroom is, take me by the hand, and lead me there.

He searches the wall and clicks the switch. Warm light floods the enormous, gilded bed.

"Not bad," he says, like he expected the decor. Crossing the room, he bounces his ass once on the mattress as I fold myself over and unzip my boots, first one, then the other, before nudging out of them.

"Here," he says distractedly and hands me the nearly full

bottle of liquor.

I snatch it and unscrew the cap. Raising it to my mouth, I take a decent-sized swallow to calm my nerves.

"You want any?" I ask, my voice rough with the liquor. He shakes his head, and I set the open bottle on the nightstand.

He considers me before he draws his hand from his pocket. "This going to bother you?"

Cupped in his palm is a small baggie of white powder. From my years attending afterparties and intimate gatherings of Hollywood-types, I'm familiar with a treasure trove of illicit substances, even if I avoid most. And while I may be a ruthless sobriety coach for my clients, I'm off duty.

"You do you," I murmur as I cross my arms in front of my chest, snagging the bottom hem of my tank top and raising it over my head. It drops to the floor with a soft hiss of lace and fabric. I climb onto the bed, the silky sheets rustling beneath me.

For a split second, the files I should be reading about the band flit through my mind. The folder is open on the desk in the other room. The guy turns, follows my gaze, but can't discern what caught my attention.

I hook a finger on the bottom of his shirt and draw him closer as I raise up onto my knees. I've got his attention. A mischievous smile creeps onto my lips. He mirrors it.

"Hi," he says, his voice low and breathy.

"Hi," I echo.

Laying on the mattress, I tug him until he's straddling me. Only now does he crack open the baggie. He spills a thin line of white powder on the skin between my breasts. I still as he rocks forward. His loud sniff breaks the silence. Holding his thumb against his nostril, he reaches over my shoulder to the nightstand, grabs the neck of the bottle and brings it to his lips.

I watch, fascinated by his abrupt descent into insobriety. "Damn, Boy. You are not fucking around," I say at the third and final swallow. An amber droplet slides free.

There's a clink as the bottle finds its way onto the nightstand. I sit up and flick my tongue across the rogue drop of liquor slipping to his chin, catch it and follow the trail to his mouth.

He tucks a lock of the short blonde hair of my wig behind my ear. "Tell me you want this," his lips whisper against mine.

I raise an eyebrow. "I basically propositioned you in that bar."

His blue eyes meet mine. He's searching for something in them, though what, I can't guess, his need so blatant a shiver runs through my body.

Okay, so not backing out, I think. *Just making one hundred percent sure I'm into this.* It's slightly endearing. I pat his cheek. "You're cute, but if you don't fuck me soon, we're gonna have a problem. Clear enough for you?"

Relief spills across his expression. His forehead taps against mine and then his arms encircle me as he unhooks my strapless bra. It tumbles off. He runs his hands over the tops of my shoulders, down my sides, and finally raises a palm to cup my breast, thumbing the curve. He leans. His teeth skim my nipple, then find flesh. As the bite softens, his tongue returns to the still pebbling bud.

"What happened to slow?" I say.

He chuckles against my ribs. "You like to be kept on your toes," he says at the same time he trails a line of sweet kisses down my side, my waist, across my hip bone. His baritone voice eases through me. "I'm going to do that for you. Though, those toes may be curled," he adds.

His fingers tease into the waistline of my jeans, undo them and drag the material down, catching my panties, tugging them free as well. *Okay*, I think. *We're getting to it.*

As I raise my foot to kick the clothes to the floor, he catches my calf. "Now we go slow," he says.

He slides his thumbs up the arch of my foot, the motion repetitive. He wasn't kidding about keeping me on my toes. The last thing I expected was a foot massage, but as I settle against the sheets, it was obvious he knew what I needed. I've been wound so tight for so long; my body doesn't know what to do if it's not in fight or flight. "God, that feels good," I whisper.

His strong fingers knead my calf muscles, move higher. My legs part for him as he traces the outsides of my thighs. Seizing me by the hips, he tugs me toward him. His mouth presses against my mound, once, twice, each touch torturous.

Don't rush him, I think. *He wanted to take his time. Let him.* The anticipation has me throbbing. A half-pant escapes me. I wriggle, needy and aching. "Please," I whisper, already breaking my own rules.

He slides two fingers through the wet heat of my folds, parting them, but it's not until his tongue edges my clit that I keen. I grip the sheets, slowly twisting them around my wrists as if to keep in my cries as he licks, sucks, savors.

One of his fingers steals inside me. He adds another and still I thrust my hips forward, craving more. He matches my rhythm. Even as he fingers me, his tongue sweeps and strokes in the exact way I need, as if he's known my body for years.

My jaw clenches as I bite down on a moan, helpless and squirming against his hand. Heat flushes my chest. My eyes roll back, unblinking as I concentrate on how his fingers coax me closer to release. Moisture gathers at the corners of my eyes, my mouth opened wide in a silent oval of gratification. Like he promised, my toes curl.

A ball of heat starts between my legs at the same time my fingers go tingly. *I can't be this close*, I think. *Not yet.* My thighs clench and for once in my life, I really, really want things to go slow. Glacial. I want him eating me out all night. "Stop," I gasp.

"Stop?"

I feel the start of a smile against my skin.

"I haven't even started," he says.

The words give my body a chance to relax, the orgasm I'd been on the cusp of fading. Raising onto one trembling arm, I stare at him in wild wonder. "Who *are* you?" I ask.

"Does it matter?" he shoots back. The defensiveness in his tone makes me instantly sorry. He rises from between my legs, crawling up my body until one of his hands drifts across my hairline as if in apology for his harshness.

I sigh and lean into his palm. "I didn't mean anything by it, I—"

It's only then that I remember the wig, realize how I've been grinding against the pillows. I freeze.

He offers me a wry grin as he tugs on a blond lock. The pins catch. The wig is off kilter, showing my real hair underneath. Which means he's not apologizing.

He's calling me out.

People wear wigs all the time, for tons of reasons. But the redness crawling up my neck makes it clear I'm hiding something. The final pin dislodges. The wig slips free. He dangles it between us.

"I can explain."

"Don't," he says.

This time when his fingers slide through my hair, it's my own brown curls he brushes away. A shiver of vulnerability rolls through me, but he kisses it away.

"I told you at the bar," he says. "I'm enjoying things as they come. You're obviously doing the same." There's no judgement in his mesmerizing cobalt eyes. "Still in?"

Instead of answering, I pop the button on his tattered jeans.

"Take your shirt off," I command as I slide his zipper down and tempt his pants over his hips.

He stands, unties the flannel, and drops it. Strips off his t-shirt and tosses it aside, too. The way he obeys sends a thrill of pleasure through me. I admire his sculpted abs, the intoxicating dip where his hip meets his leg, all the places on him I want to explore. He's got the body of a marble Adonis. A muted sound of appreciation steals past my lips.

He laughs, embarrassed, until I slip off the bed, sink to my knees. My fingers find the hem of the only clothing he still wears. As I lick my lips to wet them, I open my eyes wide, doe-like, and raise them to meet his gaze. His smile freezes. A shudder runs through him as I tug his boxers down. His cock springs free, erect against the carved plane of his belly.

"You don't have to—" he starts.

I wrap my fingers around the thick shaft. It swells against my palm and his sentence cuts short. "Shh," I say. "I know I don't. I want to."

Pressing my lips against the tip, I push forward, allowing it to penetrate the seal of my mouth. My tongue rolls, undulating against the velvety soft skin before I take him into the warmth of my mouth, sudden and deep.

He groans, fingers reflexively sweeping through my curls as he cups the back of my head. I flick my eyes up only to see him close his, lost in pleasure. I work my lips up to the crown again, alternating between pressure and suction. Broken gasps catch in his throat. I take each one as a compliment.

My fingers, slick from the moisture of my mouth, sweep his shaft as my lips retreat, then return. With each minute that passes, he's more jittery, his touch moving from my head to my shoulders and back before he laces his fingers over the nape of his own neck. He groans low and desperate, his abs tightening.

"I think," he starts and then cuts off when I flash my tongue across the tip to catch the salty bead leaking from him, enjoying myself as he fights against unraveling. "We need to...I..."

I lick the cleft that runs up the underside of his shaft and he gives up on talking, his inhale choking off at the touch.

"This wasn't supposed to be about me," he says finally.

I raise an eyebrow as he pops himself free of my mouth.

"Can't it be about both of us?"

Crawling over the bed, I grope the nightstand until the condom crinkles. Before I catch the wrapper in my teeth, he climbs on top of me, his fingers winding up my arm to my wrist.

He pins me with a chiding look as he takes it from me. "Not yet."

Frustrated, I bite my lip. "But—"

He cuffs my wrist with his hand and kisses me deep to quiet my protest. "Not," he says. "Yet."

Electricity crackles across my skin at his words. With every demand I make of him, whether or not he grants it, the confidence Blake's werewolf claws stole from me flares to life.

I break free of his hold and thumb his stubbled jaw. "What do you want instead?" I ask.

His forehead knocks gently against mine. "I want to taste you again."

My nipples tighten at the thought. I nod. He reaches for my hand and straightens two of my fingers. "What are you doing?" I ask.

"Keeping you on your toes," he whispers, before guiding my hand between my legs. He steers my palm, directing my fingertips into the throbbing heat of my opening. "Tell me what you like."

He starts a slow rhythm. His fingers urge mine deeper, my second knuckle disappearing, the third bumping against the webbing at my palm. "That," I barely manage. "I like that."

With every pump of his hand against mine, my thumb strokes my clit. I swallow hard, arch, spread my legs farther. My inhales quicken, sharp and shallow.

As if to torture me, he draws my hand north. He smiles at my groan.

Eyes half-lidded with pleasure, he sucks my fingers into his mouth before he moves his body between my thighs and runs his cock through my sodden slit. "You feel what you're doing to me?" he asks as his mouth meets mine.

I'm past the point of politeness. "Fuck me," I murmur as I grope his shoulders, the nape of his neck, desperate to get him closer. "Now. Please."

"Do you want me?" he asks against my collarbone.

"If you ask me that again," I start before I glance up.

He's motionless between my legs, swaying, his eyes glassy, unfocused. The pupils are blown wide. He looks entirely too fucked up to be doing this.

"Hey," I say. "Are you okay?"

His attention snaps to me as if startled I cared enough to ask. He blinks twice. I'm fairly certain the sheen of sweat that's broken out across his forehead has nothing to do with the workout we're in the midst of.

I scan the bottle, doing the math. He had a few generous swallows...the shots at the bar.

The coke.

As if sensing my trepidation, he ducks to catch my thighs with his arms, lifting my legs to balance on his shoulders. "I will be," he says.

He plunges forward. I'm ready and wet, but I still cry out, pleasure drilling through me on a flicker of pain. Our passion pauses as he caresses my neck, its nape, my bare shoulder. His honey-brown curls slipped from his tie and now hang loose to frame his face. He murmurs something, and I realize he's apologizing.

Cocking my head, I offer a tiny chuckle. "That's sweet and all, but you didn't hurt me," I promise him. "Not in any way I didn't like."

His brow pinches. "I—"

I surge my hips forward to meet him. His answering moan raises goosebumps across my flesh. I drop a flurry of appreciative kisses against the sweaty skin of his shoulder as he settles inside me again. Each thrust from him encourages a roll of my hips that ends in a gasp from both of us.

"Jesus, how do you feel so good?" he rumbles against my ear. He slides halfway out of me and teases his way home, one of his hands splayed against the headboard, the other beside my shoulder.

A keening sound breaks through the room that almost embarrasses me silent until I hear the carnal groaning echoed to me from his lips.

"More," he murmurs. "It's got to be more."

I don't answer. I raise one of my legs high and drop the other, tilting my hips to bury his cock to the hilt. "Like that?" I ask as he thrusts.

A strangled cry of pleasure erupts from me. He grins at my reaction. The next scream I stifle into my shoulder before he grips the side of my jaw, twisting my head to face him. His eyes lock on mine. "I want to hear you."

He pumps harder. My nails dig into his biceps in reflex. Another animalistic growl breaks from my throat. I throw my hands back, desperate and searching until my fingers wrap around the bottom edge of the headboard. I strain, gripping tight, coiling underneath him. "That's so good," I blurt. "Don't stop."

His hand finds my shoulder, uses it for leverage as he ruts into me, harder.

"There!" I scream it, the word a high-pitched plea.

That perfect cock strokes my inner walls twice more before every muscle in my body contracts. My pussy clenches around him. I writhe, arching under him as the orgasm buckles me. His mouth meets mine. He swallows the moan as it breaks from me, amping up his rhythm until stars prickle across my vision.

His abs tighten and I know he's not far behind me. He scoops his arms under mine, wrapping me tight, his fingers gripped at the nape of my neck as he stares into my eyes. It's too intimate, runs a flush over my cheeks. Inside me, his thickness swells, contracts, and then pulses out the last of his pleasure.

For a long moment, there's nothing but the sound of our desperate breaths. Finally, with a grunt of a satisfied sigh, he collapses on top of me.

I raise my arms in a languid stretch. "Damn," I say, my voice quaking as hard as my legs. "I'd say that qualifies as a good and proper fucking."

When he speaks, his lips are smooshed against my skin, slurring the words. "Told you I'd curl your toes," he says, grinning at the laugh that bursts from me.

"Yeah," I admit. "Definitely some toe curling going on."

He slips himself out of me, drops a kiss on the tip of my nose and rolls to sit on the edge of the bed, his feet on the floor. After a sigh, he scoops his shirt from where it landed earlier. Now that his washboard abs are hidden from view, I wish I'd taken more time to appreciate them.

When he reaches for his jeans, I raise an eyebrow. "You know, no one's kickin' you out of bed yet."

"Oh," he says with what seems to be faux awkwardness. "I mean...usually after..."

"You take off before the sweat dries?" I snap at the same time he says, "They want me gone. Rush, rush, rush."

I flash back to the bar, how I'd cajoled him into heading out. Catching onto the joke at my expense, I balk dramatically. "What kind of bitches have you been screwing?"

I huff as if in disbelief and a smile creeps onto his beautiful mouth. I want that mouth on mine again, want those fingers touching me, want him even with my skin still flushed. I draw my knees to my chest and pat the mattress beside me.

"You...want me to stay?" he asks. The hesitation in his voice calls to my heart.

"I do," I confess. "For a little while."

He crawls into the bed beside me. His lips make gentle presses, once against my temple, then tender against my shoulder. He pulls back and gazes at me.

After almost a full minute, heat flushes my cheeks. "What?" I ask.

He runs his hand through the air alongside my face, fingertips skittering millimeters from my skin. And again, he surprises me. "The way the light hits your cheekbones," he says and trails off as if mesmerized. "It's such a symphony of shadows and light."

I expected some typical post-sex compliment. How I'm so beautiful, something vague about my eyes, a fake phone number programmed with a fake name. Thrown off, I lower my head to my knee, watching him.

A sudden certainty overwhelms me. I don't want the night to end. Not yet. "Tell me something about you," I say quietly. "Anything true."

His paleness from earlier is gone, his cheeks carrying a ruddy glow. He doesn't have that drunken faraway look anymore. I'm so lost in those damn blue eyes that I almost miss how his hand fists on the mattress in frustration between us. "I...no," he says.

So, everything is off limits. "Some little detail. Anything," I push. "It's not like I want your name."

"I wish I could," he starts and swallows. His brow furrows. "Something true?"

I nod.

His lips part and close again as he talks himself out of whatever he'd been about to say and then presses forward, anyway. "Truth," he says slowly before the rest spills from him. "I wish I *could* see you again."

And just like that, the spell is broken.

I shear my gaze from his, uncomfortable.

"I don't think so," I say. "I'm kind of..." I hesitate. Tomorrow I'll be meeting my new client. If all goes as planned, soon there'll be pictures of us together dotting the tabloids, splattered across the internet. I wonder if this guy will stumble upon them. If he'll regret this night. If he'll remember me at all. Part of me wants him to. Part of me knows how dangerous that could be. "I'm kind of involved," I say.

He tilts his head, incredulous. "You've got a boyfriend."

My mouth opens, but I don't have an answer. The words all seemed damning.

Not really. Not yet. Sort of.

"No," I say, settling on the truth. I figure I owe him that much, though I'm not sure why. He's a stranger. Nothing to me. A quick, anonymous fuck. "It's a job," I say. "A new job."

"So, you're living here? In Austin?" He seems eager for any morsel I'll gift him. It makes me cagey and uncertain. What if this guy latches on, figures out my name, makes problems for me with this job? Why couldn't I have said yes? Yes, I have a boyfriend. It's an open relationship, but this is a one-shot deal. Don't worry your pretty little head, Random Fling.

"No, I don't live here." *Stop talking*, a desperate voice in my head demands. *Every word you give him is too much.*

"This is ridiculous," I exclaim and fight out a laugh so cringingly fake I let it fade away mid-attempt. Frustrated, I shake my head. "I feel like you're breaking the rules!"

"What rules? You opened this up to questions, didn't you?" he asks playfully, settling those mesmerizing eyes on me again and it's all I can do not to lean forward, kiss him. A moment later I do. For a split second, his mouth stays taut before he opens to me, his tongue massaging mine. All I can think of is how good it felt between my legs. I shiver. Without the heat we've been generating, the air conditioner has the room freezing.

If we only have tonight, I think, *I might as well enjoy it.* Get my money's worth, he'd said. I lean against the mess of pillows propped against the headboard, tug the sheets aside and crawl under them. I hold an arm out in invitation.

I'm almost convinced he's going to walk away anyway, but he snuggles closer, and I lay his head against my chest.

"What are you—"

"Shh," I whisper. My fingers run through his hair, the leather tie lost somewhere between the sheets. I trace a fingertip across his forehead until the lines smooth, then his temple, brush his cheek, his chin, and raise my hand to repeat the pattern. Gradually, the tension fades from his expression. His eyes slip shut.

I study him. Memorize those honeyed curls, the smooth silk of them sifting through my fingertips. His lips, swollen and red from our frantic kissing. The curve of his jaw, my scent on his skin. In the morning, I'll have to convince myself he wasn't a dream.

I'm almost sure he's drifted off to sleep when he murmurs, "That feels so good," in a drowsy voice. It brings a small smile to my lips. Exhaustion drags at my eyelids. It must have been the day of travel. The booze. The perfect fucking to cap the day.

I swear I only blink.

I hear a jingle—the change in his pockets as he slips into his pants.

"Sorry," I say, stretching. "I...did I fall asleep?" It's impossible, though. I don't do anything more than doze these days.

He shoots me a smile in the dim room. The only light comes

from the exit sign in the other room of the suite. It shines in from the open bedroom door. Before, the lamp on the nightstand was burning. Did he turn it off?

"You crashed out. It's okay," he whispers. "It always happens."

He's not wrong. Sleep pulls at me. It takes everything in me to fend it off. My body tingles, warm and floating.

"You drank too much," he says. "You'll feel it in the morning."

An argument bubbles up that I'm too tired to voice. I barely had any of the whiskey, none of the coke. We left the bar hours ago. Anything I drank would have worn off by now. But I can't deny the dizziness stealing over me. One desperate word escapes.

"Stay."

"I can't," he says instantly. I'm dimly aware of the sound of his footsteps crossing the room, taking him from me. In the main room of the suite, I hear the lock click, the door opening.

Not yet, my brain screams. *A few more minutes.*

"Wait," I blurt and clear the sleep from my throat. I get one arm under me to sit up. "Tell me about Walker Roads."

"What?"

"The blues singer. From the bar," I murmur as my head sinks into the pillows again. "Tell me why you love listening to him play. Why is he your favorite?"

There's silence. And then a tentative step. Another. "You...you really want to know?" he asks. He crosses the room and climbs back into bed. "You're sure?"

Nodding, I smile as he draws me closer, stroking my hair as I curl against him.

"Tell me why you love his music," I say, drowsy against the warmth of him.

He starts to speak, the words a deep purr in my ear. He tells me about the lyrics and the sadness and the stories behind the songs we heard played earlier tonight. He tells me about dissecting the rhythms and using them to learn how to make his own.

So, he is a musician, I think, but by this point, I know not to ask. I'm half dreaming, imagining him on the tiny, raised plywood square of a stage, a crowd of ten, maybe a couple more if the bar got busy. I bet he'd be happy, I think.

Peace steals over me until, impossibly, I sleep.

Chapter 6

Roanoke

Stroking my fingers through the dark curls of the beautiful girl asleep against my shoulder, I'm well aware of exactly what kind of monster I am. I envy her, at least now, before the pain hits her.

I don't remember the last time I stuck around after sex, the last time a girl invited me to stay, asked me things that seemed important. Tried to get to know me. I hold her, stretching things out as long as I dare.

Usually, the process of getting the demon fed starts when a groupie sticks her hand down my pants and begs me into a dark corner backstage. The vibe changes after, the lust sprouting a growing discomfort that makes them shy away, close off. I've always wondered if it's some sort of primal reaction to the demon, or if part of them, at least subconsciously, knows what I did.

I run my fingers gently over the girl's cheek and her brow pinches, then relaxes.

She's only dreaming, I promise myself as if it's not my touch that repulses her. She inhales, sudden and deep and sighs before settling against me again, her arm tightening where she's slung it across my ribs. I close my eyes, pray for sleep.

My brain spins daydream scenarios—she's important to me, this girl. She isn't anonymous, didn't pick me up in a bar. She's my girlfriend, cuddled up next to me. Maybe it's our anniversary. I've done something special for her, ended the night with her in my arms.

My fingertips brush her naked shoulder as the dangerous daydream plays out. I'll never have these things. Never grow close to someone without whittling them into nothing.

Like Cassandra did to me. The name roams into my mind and I slam shut the train of thought before it takes me.

This girl in my arms, she'd been careful, in the same ways I'm careful. From the wig and how she watched to make sure no one looked at us too closely outside the hotel, I thought she might be somebody important, or escaping a bad situation. Though looking around this enormous hotel suite, if she's running away, she's doing it in style.

I wish I could see you again.

I hated myself for saying it. I want someone to hold on to for myself. A body underneath me whose curves I know.

I want it to be her.

Thoughts like these mean it's time to go. There are repercussions for being with me.

I slip my arm from underneath her, settling her head on the pillows. Slowly, so as not to wake her, I crawl from the bed. One of my boots is abandoned by the dresser, the other near the bedside table. I debate liberating the bottle of whiskey and instead, I unscrew the cap, take far too long a drink, and return it to its spot. When she wakes up sick and disoriented, she'll think it was the liquor instead of being drained by an incubus.

In this whole mess, I have one consolation. I never have to admit to them what I've done.

I wish I could see you again. Even if it's true, who am I kidding?

I want to wake her, kiss her again, and feel her take all of me into her mouth. The spiral and suck as she hollowed her cheeks. In my pants, my cock twitches, more than willing to go again despite the demon's need being fulfilled. I lick my lips, taste her there.

I'm so used to bare minimum exchanges. Giving, as if good sex will somehow make up for what I've done. But Jesus, with her...

You didn't hurt me, she said when I stumbled and lost myself and told her I was sorry. As I rocked into her and the demon did its work, I tried to focus on the warmth of her, the small sounds she made in the back of her throat, her body she curled into me, but instead I'd been caught on how the colors took hold.

The deep red tentacle of energy surged from me as soon as I entered her. At the base of her spine, her lifeforce wriggled, its brightness concentrated like a pearl inside an oyster. Brighter than any other I've seen. Just before the demon's own red spread to it, it blazed as if ready to fight. But the tentacle wrapped tight, nibbling at its edges, suckling on weeks, months, never satiated.

And then she'd asked me if I was okay. Noticed I wasn't. I'd been thinking about the reason I went to that bar, the bodies.

The chance she'll become one.

A shiver of dread worms through me. I hope for both of our sakes, my last image of her will be this; her asleep, one bare shoulder peeking from the sheet I tucked around her. I'll only scare her if I try to warn her. What would I say anyway? *Yeah, you're great and fucking you rivals being on stage, but the parasite inside me ate the end of your life which, if it's any consolation, might not be that long considering there's a serial killer stalking my band.*

Instead, I chug another swallow from the bottle and set it on the nightstand. Holding a hand out, I fist it. The tremors are gone. There'll be no trouble when I play tomorrow.

Snagging the pen and pad of hotel stationery off the dresser, I glance at the girl asleep in the bed.

I wish I could see you again.

I don't think so, she answered. It's better this way. Safer for both of us.

I make a pit stop in the bathroom. Standing in front of the sink, I tap the pen against my lips twice before I scribble a quick note and then run the water on low to wash my hands, scared the noise will wake her.

I ease the door open and slip through the crack into the light of the hall, shutting it behind me. I hit the stairs, because they're closer than the elevator, faster if she's woken, if she comes after me.

I don't trust myself to resist if she calls me to her again.

I spill out of the stairwell and into the lobby. As I cross it, I shove my hands into my pockets, trying to look nonchalant, like this isn't a pre-dawn version of a walk of shame. The clerk working the desk glances up to give me a knowing smile. It freezes on her face, her mouth dropping open. I round the corner of the overstuffed couch. Almost in the clear.

"You're...oh my God, you're..." she sputters.

"Nope!" Spinning to face her, I hold my hands out as I walk backward, giving my head a sad shake. "I just look like him," I say.

"You...really do," she says, one finger tucked between the pages of a book. I wonder how bored she must get, sitting here alone from dusk until dawn.

"Get it all the time. Hope they don't get any more famous!" I add. It's not being the lead singer of The Raven Shakes that has me getting recognized. It's the shot of me a month ago on TMZ shitfaced.

She gives me an uncertain look, as if not quite buying my story, but willing to play along. It doesn't matter. I'm already at the door, hear it sliding open behind me. I whip around to walk out into the hot darkness.

Seen.

The word skitters over my brain in a terrified mantra. I got spotted. Recognized. I made things worse because I denied who I was.

Christ, what the fuck is wrong with me?

No one knows what you are. You had drinks with a woman you met in a bar and a night of mutual fun. That's it.

Except it's not. I'm trying to break any patterns, but I can't be one hundred percent sure her body's not gonna show up in a future city we're playing, days from now, a week, maybe more. And that clerk is going to remember seeing me. Seeing me *with* her.

The press assumed the dead fan in the greenroom was just that, an overzealous concert goer who, in her excitement, snuck into our prep space and took too many party favors. She's the only one that's been connected to us publicly so far.

Someone's fucking with us, December says in my head. But what if there's no us, no boogeyman torturing the four members of the Raven Shakes with a trail of unexplainable, dead fangirls?

I suck a lungful of humid air.

Get your shit together, Roanoke. Now that my god damned brain has started though, it's not going to stop. The thought crosses my mind to walk toward Sixth Street. The bars will be open another hour. The last of the whiskey I drank in the hotel room is settling in, my buzz growing. What I should do is head to the bus, take a couple of pills and forget everything for a while.

Instead, I walk, aimless.

Decorative cherry trees line the fence of a yard, their pink petals dusting the sidewalk. The blossoms float around me and I think of the damn girl again, picture us dancing under them like we did outside her hotel, her head thrown back in that laugh as I dip her low. Despite the heat, a shiver racks through me.

Two blocks down, long after the flowered trees have ended, I can't shake loose the image. I swear I can smell her. Only then do I realize it's coming from my own skin. She's on me like a bruise.

I dig into my pocket for the pen and square pad of stationery I stole and scribble a few words to catch the mood. The song will be a good one. She'll never know it's about her.

Around me, despite the hour, the city's still wide awake. Car horns blare, music leaching into the streets, guitars, voices struggling to be heard. The noise crowds out the images in my head. I sigh. Another drink, two, and I'll be able to sleep. What the demon took from her crackles at the roof of my mouth, a brush of vanilla that inexplicably sharpens to mint. I tongue at my teeth.

A memory invades me. Until tonight, it'd been a month, more, since I thought of Cassandra, though she left me almost three years ago. The first time I saw her, I'd been playing a gig on a stage much like the one I listened to Walker Roads on, long before The Raven Shakes.

She'd been a beauty, though I couldn't quite say why. Her hair had been a dishwater blonde, her features forgettable, eyes a washed out blue. I'd been mid-lyric when I spotted her. My gaze had tried to skip her and stuck instead.

I'd stumbled over the lyrics, and the band had stuttered to a stop, the drummer giving the cymbals an angry smash that only made it worse. Cassandra had ducked her mouth into her hand to hide her smile, tilting her head to the side and looking abashed. I remember how her hair spilled over her arm, caught the stage lights in a cold glow, though they shouldn't have reached her. She'd taken her hand away to mouth "Oops," as if my reaction to her had been expected.

I hadn't finished the set. She'd stood as I stumbled toward her, desperate to touch her, to please her, to give her anything she wanted, and she'd held out her hand and led me into the darkness. She never seemed ashamed to change someone's will, to force them to love her, to get them to give up their life without a second thought.

It's the reason I fight so hard against using those powers now that they're mine.

My head snaps to the side as if I can shake loose the memory, rid myself of it. The street sways.

Not enough, I think. I follow the music. I enter the bar.

I drink until I think of nothing.

Chapter 7

Willow

I shoot upright in bed, instantly awake.

"Oh fuck," I blurt, not because I followed through with the silly tradition Sloane and I started. Not because I had a couple of drinks and banged a hot guy. But because in the instant I come awake, I remember that when I was caught up in the incredible sex with him, I totally forgot to set my alarm. "Shit-shitshitshit," I chant, forcing my wobbling legs underneath me.

"You gotta go," I call over my shoulder.

I'm fumbling toward my suitcase when I actually look around. The dude from last night ghosted me, which is just as well. Better even.

I roll to grab my discarded jeans from where they're crumpled in a pile on the floor. Digging in the pocket, I search for my phone. Nothing.

Oh my God, did he steal it? I think before I zero in on it sitting on the nightstand. Next to it is the mostly empty bottle we brought from the bar. *Did* he *drink all that?*

I sure didn't. Then I notice the condom beside the bottle. It's still in its wrapper. My brain stutter stops.

I don't remember either of us stopping, hesitating, thinking about anything but our own pleasure. I catalogue the shots I took—two at the bar—add another to account for my swallow straight from the bottle once we got here. Three shots would never qualify as wasted enough to risk unprotected sex with some rando. I'd never be that irresponsible.

You're falling apart, a voice in my head whispers. *Every day it's a little worse. You're cracking, Willow.*

I don't have time for this. Last night I felt powerful, in control, confident. I want that back. I claw across the bed, desperate, and whip the alarm clock around to face my fate.

10:40.

I can still salvage this. It means no shower and a quick touch up of yesterday's makeup, but I can get things on track. I stumble to the bathroom and click on the light.

On the counter is a torn piece of hotel stationery.

For your head, he had scribbled. On the paper are two aspirins and a glass half full of water. I contemplate them. How much of a lightweight did this dude think I was? And where did the aspirins come from? Did he carry around a pocketful?

Well, add dubious critical thinking to the fact that I passed out almost instantly after the act... I remember the stroke of him inside me, lighting every nerve ending on fire at once.

Because there'd been nothing between us.

I grab the bottle and tip it, examining the amber contents. I'm more than familiar with the pounding crush of a whiskey hangover. What I'm feeling isn't it.

A mystery for another time, I tell myself, fighting to focus my thoughts. I'm due to meet the band at eleven in the lobby of their hotel. Yesterday, I had my driver cruise past on the ride to my own. It's only a five-minute walk.

Running a brush through my curls, I fashion my hair into a messy bun, hoping for an effortlessly thrown together look instead of the sexed-out vibe I seem to be channeling.

Rock bands are casual, right? I tell myself. The haphazard makeup will help me fit in. Groaning, I glance at my reflection in the mirror. I rub the pad of my ring finger over the delicate skin under my eyes to clear away bits of last night's eyeliner and flakes of mascara. My eyeshadow is barely there, but it'll have to do. I smack my cheeks and then give them a pinch for good measure. My face only looks pale and sickly against the red splotches.

"So stupid," I whisper to myself as I struggle into a pair of boutique blue jeans from my suitcase.

It's my first day on this assignment. They'll be judging me. Both the band and the other handler I'll be working with. I'm going in cold, with no idea what they have and haven't heard about me.

You already fucked it up. Cut your losses and go home.

I can't head back to L.A., though. Those wolves are onto me. They know something.

Bad choices, my brain spits. Bad choices like not using protection. Bad choices like the one that left me choking on my blood while Blake's eyes went vacant.

I whisk a layer of mascara over my lashes. *It's only an incubus*

73

this time, I remind myself. *Not a werewolf or a vampire or a wraith. Just a guy with a penchant for overdoing the partying in public...and a creepy sex demon making a home some place inside him.*

I can't lose another high-profile client.

Roanoke, I remind myself. *His name is Roanoke.*

Notecards. I move them from my carry-on bag to my purse. They outline the generic plan for mine and Roanoke's relationship that I drafted on the plane, the headlines my connections will influence, and the ones we'll have to push for ourselves. I wanted to wake up early, go over everything to make sure I'll maximize the positive exposure for him as our cute little Hollywood coupledom chugs along, but there isn't time. My half-scribbled thoughts will have to do.

My fingers fumble over the shirt I wore yesterday, brushing past it to snag the bra I cast aside last night. I clasp it around my chest, miraculously finding each of the three eyelets on the first try. I catch a whiff of sweat and citrus. A memory flashes—my forehead pressed against his, our breaths mingling as I clutched onto his shoulders.

"Fuck." I stumble to my knees and unzip the second of my two oversized suitcases. I draw out a tailored chocolate brown button down shirt with cap sleeves.

New day. New boyfriend. At least on paper. My sultry one-night stand will have to tide me over as far as sex goes. Somehow, I'm pretty sure it won't be a problem.

I strip the plastic off the toothbrush lying beside the unused bottles of shampoo and conditioner and scrub my teeth and tongue. Gargling with the water in the cup the guy left me, I spit into the sink and watch the bubbles spiral away down the drain. Finally, I swipe a pink lip stain across my mouth.

Done and done, I think.

I grab my purse, the two folders of files I intended to look over last night, and a room key, then take the elevator, impatiently waiting through the floors. Heels clicking, I race down the sidewalk, conscious of the sweat already pooling between my shoulder blades, no doubt slipping to stain my shirt. My underarms will be worse. I can't remember if I reapplied deodorant.

Quick meeting, I promise myself. *Just touching base.* Bands aren't super into being productive before noon. I'll introduce myself to the tour manager so we can do our formal expectations, to the band if they're around, and most importantly, to the enigmatic, if slightly messy, lead singer. We'll all smile and shake hands and I'll be on my merry way until the band plays tonight. Once the singer and I are publicly official, I'll be on duty twenty-four seven.

Outside the glass door of the hotel where the band stayed last night, I stop. Anyone looking out will see me here, frozen. I force my feet to move forward, my hand coming up to catch the revolving door. Even though I'm almost late, the walk passed too quickly.

What if Sloane was right?

What if I'm not ready for this, after all?

Directly in front of me and across the lobby is the front desk. To my left, through a set of doors open in welcome, I spot a dining room. The smell of sausage and eggs wafts over me as I follow the clank of plates and silverware into the breakfast area. Despite my lack of hangover, my stomach rolls.

Most of the round tables are empty, the buffet already cleaned up though the restaurant still seems to be serving. But not all the tables are empty.

Sloane described The Raven Shakes as up and coming. The lead singer is at least recognizable enough that he got caught in some compromising pictures. I'd been so tied up with Blake, and then healing, that I missed the trending story. Then there's me. It makes a public hotel dining room a weird place to choose to hold what's supposed to be a clandestine meeting.

One point against their tour manager.

Fortunately, anyone who sees the meeting today will chalk it up to my secret relationship with the singer. Hell, maybe someone will leak the story early and save me the trouble. Lord knows I could use a break.

I loop the edge of the booths along the wall until I spot a table in the corner, out of earshot of the other patrons. At it are four people. All of them are wearing varying expressions of fury. A gorgeous blonde, the only female among them, rises from her chair, stabbing a finger at a shabbily dressed guy across from her whose back is to me. As I get closer, I pick up on words and phrases.

"Doesn't know...think he'd ever go for this!" she growls. Her braided pigtails swing forward, the black checkered ribbons tying the ends dragging dangerously close to the plate of fruit and eggs in front of her. "...under false pretenses...dead fucking bodies, Gregory!"

So, the guy cowering is Gregory, who I'm supposed to be working with.

Great, I think. Then I process the words. Well, mostly the three important ones. Dead fucking bodies.

Gregory called it a straightforward job, sober up the incubus and keep him that way. Recalling our conversation, though, he definitely quizzed me on my other areas of expertise with a little too much interest. Specifically, what I was and wasn't qualified to handle when it came to supernaturals. I assumed it was because the rest of the members of the band weren't strictly human as well.

Dead bodies, plural, don't exactly go hand in hand with a straightforward job.

Her tirade over, the furious blonde slams herself into her chair again and stabs a piece of cantaloupe between her cherry red lips.

"Thanks for the vote of confidence, December," Gregory says, and I instantly don't like him. He sounds whiny and petulant.

The muscular guy beside December has one foot raised to balance on the seat of his chair as if he's folding in on himself. Tattoos cover most of the skin I can see. He runs a hand through the ratty white-blond tufts that stick out several inches from his head before his mouth snicks into a sinister curve. "You blew the one thing we needed you to get right," he says to Gregory as he picks up his fork. "Un-fucking believable."

"Hey, I hooked this band up. You all should be grateful!" Gregory gripes.

December rolls her eyes at the pushback. "Hooked us up how?"

The self-satisfied tone in Gregory's voice sets my teeth on edge. "Wait until you see who I got to help."

He's halfway through the sentence when I'm noticed. It's the third band member who spots me, a guy with a shaved head. He's jangling one knee under the table, dragging his fingers through the condensation on the side of his juice glass, absently glancing around the room while December and the tattooed guy hash things out with Gregory. When his wandering gaze stops on me, I offer him a small smile. He goes stock still, the change in his limbs from frenetic to frozen so jarring that December turns toward him, then toward me.

Her eyes blow wide in recognition. So at least two of them know who I am.

The guy who noticed me first crosses his arms on the tabletop and leans into the hollow they make until I can't make out anything more than the crown of his shaved head. He's almost...hiding?

That can't be Roanoke, I think. He's definitely not the type Sloane had me picturing, attractive in a cute neighbor kind of way, not enigmatic lead singer material.

The tattooed guy is oblivious as he loads the tines of his fork with pancakes from December's plate and then drags them through her syrup. She doesn't react, completely caught up in me as I approach the table.

"What?" Gregory finally asks her before he whips around as I come up behind his chair. He brightens. "Willow!"

His greeting booms in the small dining area and I give a subtle shake of my head. The last thing we need is attention. He stands, grabs a chair from another table and, to my horror, noisily drags it over before he points me to it. I sit as quickly as I can, anxious that one of the few patrons left in the dining room will recognize me.

Now that I'm getting a look at Gregory, I like him even less, though I'm not sure why. He's dressed in a pair of black slacks and a white button-down shirt with his sleeves rolled up around tanned forearms. He appears to have at least a decade on me and the band, in his mid-thirties. The sun damage on his face is starting to show.

I wait for an introduction, an icebreaker, anything. Gregory's grin looks pinned onto his mouth.

"Which one of you is Roanoke?" I try, my tone overly chipper.

Sleeper sits up in surprise. December snorts and gives her head a sharp shake, like she can't believe the faux pas I've pulled. The muscled tattooed guy only chews. The ink near his neck seems to wriggle and I blink to clear my vision. My head throbs dully. Finally, he untangles his crossed leg and drops his foot to the floor, swallowing the mouthful he's chewing.

"Here's the deal," he says, sounding bored as he leans in close enough that we won't be overheard. He flops a hand onto the table in a chopping motion and finally, finally, meets my eyes. "Gregory fucked you over on some of the finer details of why you were hired. Luckily, we're all in the same boat because he also left out the fact that our lead singer's fake sobriety coach is tabloid fodder, which is exactly the sort of attention we *don't* want."

"*Fake* sobriety coach?" I manage.

He yawns without bothering to cover his mouth. "I hope to God you didn't sign a contract," he says.

"Damn it, Carter," Gregory mumbles. He has no control over this band. If this is the precedent he set, this job is going to be harder than I thought.

"What false pretenses am I under?" I ask. "Who's dead?" Color flares in Gregory's cheeks as he realizes I overheard part of his and December's argument. "You said I was needed immediately. That your singer was having blackouts."

"Really, Gregory?" December spits, her voice brimming with betrayal. "That's what you led with?" Her eyes catch the lights, so green they're nearly glowing.

The siren, I realize.

A glare passes between them. There is no love lost between these two.

Gregory tents his fingers on the table, his words deliberate. "I had thought, December, that perhaps getting Ro healthy would clear some other situations affecting this band as of late, no?"

I glance between the four of them. "Is Roanoke not on board with this?" I ask.

A chorus of chuffs and bitter giggles cut me off.

"With dragging you here to play his fake girlfriend and solve all our problems, or with him getting clean?" Carter asks. "Because Roanoke doesn't know about either, so I'm guessing no, he's not on board."

Anger rolls through me and, hot on its heels, fear.

I need this job. I need to be on the move, surrounded by others, and as far from those damn wolves as I can get.

I'll gladly deal with dead bodies as long as I don't end up one of them.

Clenching my jaw, I give myself a moment to consider my words. "Where is he?" I ask. "Roanoke. What room?"

The two guys glance at each other, mouths pressed tight in twin lines. At least they're loyal.

My attention shifts to Gregory. I'm appalled when he shrugs. "You don't know where your client is? Aren't you supposed to be handling this band?" I demand, and in my peripheral vision, I see the other members straighten.

I'm in, I think.

He gives me a smarmy once over and suddenly I don't care about overstepping. He's the one who called me, but I'm technically on the record label's dime. I'm more than comfortable cutting Gregory out.

December's the one they seem to have chosen as the voice of the group, so she's my point person. I direct my attention to her. "You said I don't know why I'm really here. Tell me."

I wait.

"At least tell me if Roanoke is somewhere safe or if I need to start putting out fires?" I insist.

I think she might hold her ground, and then, blessedly, she cracks. "Ro sleeps on the Winnebago. He took off last night to feed, so chances are he's still sleeping off whatever he got up to," she adds, biting at the last of the red nail polish on her thumb.

I might have a fighting chance at this. "You've talked to him this morning?" I ask.

"Well, no. He usually gets moving around one." She hesitates. "Roanoke runs on his own timeline."

Pushing myself away from the table, I stand. "Not anymore, he doesn't."

The four of them stare at me.

"Like Carter said, I'm going to be playing fake girlfriend while I'm fixing all your problems, which, if we execute this correctly, means the potential for a lot of media attention on your band." My dramatic pause catches their attention. "I have no issue with my job description changing slightly. I'm not, however, risking my reputation for an out-of-control junkie."

The siren's eyes tighten into slits. "Ro's not a junkie," she says quietly. "You don't know him."

"Neither does anyone who bought the copy of Scold with his picture in it," I hurl back. I hadn't seen the article, but I'd heard about it from Gregory on the initial call. "Do you have any idea how many shares it got?"

None of them will look at me. I only received a description of the snapshot—the singer latched onto some female fan, both of them half-conscious and pawing at each other on a bench, another of him taking a drag off a bottle, a smaller inset of a blurred baggie that could have contained anything but implied scandal. That had been the initial incident. The second headline hit TMZ a few days later before it went wide in minutes. Since then, he'd been on a tear.

"Has he fucked up a show yet?" I ask, my voice innocent

enough that it sounds like I'm genuinely interested. "How long after that first slip up on stage do you think it'll be until he costs the rest of you everything?"

None of them move, save for December, her fingers tapping lightly against the table. "He's under a lot of stress," she says. "We all are. He's just not dealing with it well."

"Your band hasn't hit the mainstream yet and he's imploding."

The third guy, the one with the shaved head, whose name I don't know, rubs his hand over his buzz cut before he groans low. "She's right," he says. "Ro's gotta be reined in."

The siren stops her tapping, one fingertip going white as she presses it against the tabletop. She scoffs. "And somehow you feel Willow Taverson's the best choice to do that, Damien?" she says, as if I'm not here at all, sounding vaguely baffled by his agreement.

"So far? Hell yeah." He turns to me. When he speaks, Damien's voice has the slightest shake to it. "But our problems are a lot bigger than you know."

The hope in his expression has me softening. "I'm a fixer," I tell him. "That's why I was hired." I glance between the three band members. "Trust me when I say whatever's going on, I've handled worse."

Carter scoffs. "Not a chance."

To my left, Gregory scoots back his chair. "Why don't you take fifteen minutes to wake up Roanoke and we'll do this all together, okay?"

"No," I say, the word curt. Gregory flinches even before I turn my caustic smile on him. I'm working out the dynamics of this band and he's gumming up the works. Not to mention they all clearly hate him. "Your services are no longer needed."

Damien chokes a surprised laugh and then covers it with a cough. Carter gives him a mocking smack across the back of the head as he juts his chin at me to acknowledge his approval. Only December doesn't react.

I have a feeling she's been keeping this band above water. She doesn't trust that I'm here to help her shoulder the weight. Not yet. But I'm going to win her over.

For now, though, my best bet is giving her a little power, the impression of control. "Why don't you go convince your singer he needs to be on board with the original reason I came, okay? Put in a good word for me. We'll head out to your Winnebago in fifteen minutes."

Before she can answer, Gregory gives his abandoned coffee cup a shove. It clatters across the table. Carter grabs it as it starts a dangerous tip that sends pale brown liquid sloshing over the rim.

"Good riddance," Gregory growls and then turns his attention to me. "And good fucking luck. You're going to need it with the four of them."

We watch him go, flouncing angrily across the dining room until he disappears into the lobby. A moment later, we hear the unmistakable sound of a disturbance as he screams at someone, then silence.

"What a prick," I whisper.

The barest trace of a grin teases December's red lips and then fades. She turns and scrutinizes me. I don't break eye contact. *Come on*, I think. *All I need is a chance.*

December looks first to Carter, then to Damien. Apparently, whatever she sees gives her the approval she needs. She clambers to her feet, arms crossed over her chest.

"Give me fifteen," she tells me. "I'll get Ro on board."

CHAPTER 8

ROANOKE

I become dimly aware of pressure on my shoulder, someone shaking me hard. I nudge the sensation away and tumble into the darkness again. A hummed note follows me down, down, insistent. I sink deeper, fleeing into unconsciousness, searching for the girl from the blues bar.

Her form appears, a shadow projected onto cobwebs, thread-thin and impossible. She holds out a hand.

Yes, I think, reaching for her. Our fingers almost touch. *I want to stay with you.*

The humming swells. I groan, distracted, as the song grows deafening. The notes morph into barbed hooks. They curve, catch me. *No. Please.*

The lines snap taut. My heart slams against my ribcage. I struggle, but it's no use. I suck a lungful of air as the song drags me awake. Trembling, I press my palms over my ears, open my eyes to the familiar interior of the Winnebago.

"Stop, December," I say, my throat hoarse. I'm uncertain

how I'm able to respond to her at all. Normally, when she sirens out, I'm as malleable as any other creature trapped in her snare.

Her singing cuts off.

I wait a beat and then lower my hands. "Jesus," I say.

"Last night a rough one?" she asks. Luckily, her spoken words don't have the same effect.

"Yeah," I croak, not bothering to sugarcoat. I press the heel of one palm against my eye. "Why'd you wake me up?"

She sits cross-legged on the stiff carpet of the tour bus, next to the bottom bunk I finally crashed out on just before dawn. Instead of answering me, she reaches toward my face and rubs at the skin under my nose. Pain shoots through my sinuses and I wince. "Who'd you fight?" she asks.

I have a mental snapshot of sinking against a brick wall, one hand cupped to catch the blood plopping from my nose. A flash of a leather jacket. Big guys.

"I don't know," I admit. What the hell did I get into last night after I left that fancy-ass hotel room? I remember walking. I remember trees. Music. Everything else is a fucking blur.

The memory of a female voice whispers through my mind, but I can't decipher more than the cadence.

"You're covered in blood," December says, bringing my attention back to her. "You smell like a back-alley, and it took a full minute of a siren's song to get you conscious. Do you know how far gone you need to be to resist me like that?"

I shoot her my most charming grin. "Maybe I'm getting better at ignoring you."

December doesn't bite. "Your breathing was wrong," she

says and the last of my buzz from the night before winks out. "Shallow and choppy. Takes a lot more than liquor to get you that way."

The little baggy pops into my brain. I finished the contents on a park bench. I swivel myself into a sitting position and drop my feet to the floor. "Hey," I say lightly. When she doesn't look up, I tuck a finger under her chin and tilt her head until our eyes meet. "I'm fine."

Her face twists, and I wait for the lecture I know I deserve.

It's not like I haven't been worse, which is exactly why they all wanted to supervise me last night and exactly why I hadn't wanted them to come.

"Last night was..." *I wish I could see you again.* "Last night was..." I'm not sure what to fill in. The best night I've had in a long time? The worst?

How can I explain what it's like? How I need something to dull the guilt of what I help the demon steal? Last night though, I laid in bed, and told that girl about my favorite blues player and I know it's stupid, the actual connection I felt. I know it isn't real. Doesn't matter. Couldn't last.

Didn't.

I gulp down the sick feeling that threatens to overwhelm me, taste spent liquor at the back of my throat. If she ends up dead, I'll never forgive myself.

December inspects the wounds on me that she can see, her expression pinched. This is the part of the conversation where I'm supposed to promise not to touch a drop of liquor ever again, but I can't endure the nights anymore without hard swallows, a couple of uppers to get me moving after a show, a set of downers to stop the self-destruction.

I have no memory of how I made it to the Winnebago.

I paw at the crusted blood under my nose. "I should probably get my shit together, huh?" I say in the most casual tone I can muster.

She sighs hard. "Honestly, Ro? This is getting a little fucking old."

Her anger flips a switch on my own. "Jesus!" I snap. "I have one bad night and you're riding my ass?"

"One?" she yells. The nail polish is missing from her thumb. It's a nervous tick of hers, to peel it and judging from the flake of red shine caught in her lipstick, her morning hasn't gone so great. I wonder how much of that has to do with me.

I reach for her to start an apology, walk this thing down, but she yanks away. "December," I try gently.

She glances at me, emotions warring in her pale green eyes. "Maybe we should cancel the rest of the tour," she says.

The words hit me like a gut punch. "What? No! That's not happening."

We've worked too hard. A thousand memories flash through me, sweating out the last ounces of my energy as I drive a crowd into a frenzy, December behind me on drums, Carter and Damien on either side. A unit. A conduit for the energy running over the crowd and spilling onto the stage. And still a voice at the back of my skull berates me. *People are dying because of you and all you can think about is your stupid little band?*

A sharp throb starts over my left eye. "We're not canceling.

I'm not that—"

"Stop talking!" she cuts in, her face going red as her voice raises. "Listen to me for five fucking seconds!"

The silence spirals out while she struggles to calm herself and I realize how much I've worried her, how stressed she is.

"Okay," I say, the words barely audible.

She swallows hard and forces herself to go on. "Gregory got the label to hire someone to help with our problem." 'Our problem', she says, not my problem, so I know she's talking about the bodies. Six dead, one still missing. To her, we've got nothing to do with it. We're victims, too.

Me, I'm not so sure.

"As per usual," she goes on, "he fucked things up."

I perk, glad for a bit of blame shifting. "Oh?"

"Who he hired? She's qualified. She's vetted. But he didn't tell her why she's really here."

"Wait," I say, confused. "What does she think she's here for if not..."

December hesitates. "A sobriety coach. For you."

My new goodwill falters. "What?"

She tilts her head to take me in. "Ro, it's Willow Taverson."

December drops the name like a bombshell. Clearly, it's supposed to garner a reaction, except it means nothing to me.

She balks at my blank look. "Willow fucking Taverson!" she says. "She's straight up Hollywood."

"What like an actress?" I ask.

"No!" December moans, as if me not knowing this chick's name physically pains her. "Oh my God, she's like, friends with the upper echelon of them, though! She's a socialite."

For December's sake, I'm trying to understand, but with every word, I'm more confused. "One of those people that's famous for being famous?"

"Yes!" she says, and I recoil at the thought. "Glam. Gorgeous. Christ, she could probably tweet once about The Raven Shakes and we'd chart." December shakes her head as the shocked look on her face grows. "She can get us press. Get us noticed. Ro, you two pretending to hook up could—"

"Hook up?" I repeat, too stunned to react.

"She's going to pretend to be your girlfriend. She can stay close, find out what's happening, if someone is targeting the band, framing us or..." December starts over, her tone newly cautious. "She'll only help us if you agree to sober up. She's worried a relationship with you will fuck up her reputation."

"You can't be serious." This is all too much. "A random Hollywood hang around is going to Sherlock us back to normal?"

December grins at me. "She fired Gregory."

I jolt in surprise. "Really?"

"Came in, took control, fired his ass. Didn't take her two minutes." December isn't easily impressed and yet, clearly this actress not actress has done it. "We need help. You know that. And this could be a really good thing for the band. Come on, Ro. She asked me to get you on board with this."

I consider it. When I speak, the words are heavy with embarrassment. "Feeding this demon with a clear head is a lot to ask."

December bites her lip. "You've got a solid week before you need to worry about that again, right?" she says.

I nod.

"Then it shouldn't be a big deal for you to hold off on partying until you're due." Her tone hardens into a challenge. "I mean since it's not a problem and all. Since you're *fine*."

My brain spins as it cycles through a thousand excuses, stories, lies, all of them too flimsy to get me out of this. It looks like my best bet might be helping this actress do her thing as fast as possible. Then everyone will go back to worrying about their own lives again and stop making such a big deal about mine.

December leans in, waiting.

I'm not getting out of this. "Okay," I say, giving in. "Whatever you want me to do."

She rocks away to grab my chin, tips my head to the side at a strange angle. "You've got blood in your ears."

As I wipe at it, she digs her phone from the pocket of her jeans and checks the time.

"Was there an expiration on your little one-woman intervention or something?" I ask, trying to lighten the mood.

Her look sharpens. "Better get your ass in gear. You've got less than five minutes to get ready. She's in the hotel dining room."

I balk. "You couldn't have mentioned that at the beginning?"

A smirk lifts the corner of her mouth. "Don't skip the shower," December says. "You've got a hell of a first impression to make."

$$\bullet \; \bullet \; \bullet \; \bullet \; \bullet \; \bullet \; \bullet \; \bullet \; \bullet \; \bullet$$

T he RV's shower is dark and claustrophobic, shoved in beside a toilet and an airplane-style plastic sink molded to the wall. I grab the shampoo I brought in, lather it over my hair and body in the trickle of lukewarm water. Dried blood sluices from my face. The bubbles turn maroon.

I check for wounds and find a heinous bruise on my abdomen, a couple of tiny scratches on my neck. The fight must not have been much. I just bleed easy.

A girlfriend, I think. Of course, it's only going to be for the cameras. And if this goes on longer than a week, December, and Carter, and Damien, they'll know I have to feed the demon, help distract my jailor. No one will expect me to do that part sober.

I shut the water off and stand there, trying to calm my suddenly racing heart. This is nothing. I can do this. I'm going to be charming, use my powers for once, woo her into trusting me. It's going to be fine.

I'd been so distracted with hurrying, not keeping anyone waiting longer than necessary, that I forgot a towel.

Sliding open the accordion door, I head for my bunk to find clean clothes, dripping onto the stained, crushed carpet. We bought the bus second-hand, maybe third. The band's getting known, but there's no money to blow. Not yet. Staying in hotels, one perk that signing with the label gained us, feels extravagant, even if they're cheap airport accommodations.

Beyond the bunks is a table. Of course, it's only while I'm standing naked with one hand groping through my T-shirts that I realize it isn't empty. I can barely see past the half wall of storage after Carter's bunk, Damien's space above it, to catch movement. I don't see the flash of color that would give away Carter's tattooed arm, and I'm guessing December didn't hang around once her duty was done. Which means they sent our guitarist to fetch me.

"Sorry, Damien," I yell in his general direction, adding a brightness to my tone I'm not close to feeling. "I'm hurrying. Lobby, right? Can you go ahead? Tell this chick I'm on my way?"

I find a towel, ignore the scent of mildew, and rub it violently across my wet hair before wrapping it around my waist. Traveling together means no privacy. The rest of the band likewise gave up on it long ago. I've seen December's tits more times than I care to admit as she dressed or undressed or fooled around with some poor sap after a show. None of us react to each other anymore.

"The chick is ready when you are," comes a female voice.

Surprised, I step forward.

The table is full, three spots of the booth occupied by my bandmates. And beside Damien in the fourth, mouth dropping in shocked confusion the second she sights me is—

It's her. *Her.*

I said I wanted to see her again, but she made it clear that wasn't going to happen. Did she change her mind? How did she hunt me down? How did she get the band to bring her onto the Winnie?

"You," I say. Between one breath and the next, I recover enough to not make a fool of myself. "Are not who I was expecting. Hi."

I hold out my hand. I have to touch her to make sure she's real. Her fingers wind across my palm and at the last moment, I twist hers and place a chaste kiss on her knuckles.

You fucking idiot, I think as soon as I do it. The move is so cringy even I want to squirm. To her credit, she doesn't react, lowering her arm as she sweeps me with a calculating look. Her fingers smelled like sex and soap.

"Don't get caught up in those baby blues," December tells her. "We're all hopeless against them. Even me." She's teasing. As a siren, her powers far outweigh mine. My sway is useless against her. Still, she knows it's better not to make eye contact with an incubus turning on his charm, though I rarely use mine.

Carter holds his fingers in L shapes as if framing for a camera. He pans first over the girl, then me. "Not sure I buy the chemistry," he says.

Should have seen us last night, I think.

I focus on her. "What are you—"

"An incubus with a drug problem." She lobs the words like the weapons they are.

I freeze. She knows what I am.

Did she know last night? my panicked brain spits. No. It's impossible. No one would fuck an incubus knowing the cost.

She stands and then scoots aside, gesturing to the spot she vacated next to Damien. Confused, I drop into it.

I cast a helpless look across the table at December, then Carter, and finally settle on Damien beside me. Carter might think it's funny to bring last night's fling back to haunt me for laughs, but December? Damien? His sense of humor never veers to cruelty. And this is absolutely fucked up.

"We tried to tell you to tone things down," Damien says, spreading his arms. "You didn't listen. It's time for backup."

My gaze flies to the girl standing at the head of the table, hovering beside me. She's acting like we never met, distant, almost professional. Like this is a job.

"Oh shit," I whisper.

She didn't con her way in here to come find me. *This* is the fixer, the famous not-actress who's supposed to work the press, uncover a murderer. My new girlfriend. December said her name. I can't remember it.

"I changed my mind," I say suddenly, my voice monotone. "I don't want to do this." Not anymore. Not with her.

As I glance around the table. One by one, the other members of The Raven Shakes drop their eyes.

December shrugs weakly. "You've been blacking out, Ro. Losing time. With what's going on, that's...that's really bad."

My words are out before I can stop them. "Makes me sound guilty when you put it like that."

I wait. No one jumps to my defense. No one will even look at me. "Wait, you don't think I'm the one who—"

A hand grips my shoulder, cold on my bare skin where it's still warm from the shower.

"Relax," the girl from last night says. Her tone has a calculating edge to it, like she expects me to go from hurt to homicidal any second, like she wants me to know she'll drop me if I do. "No one said that."

I might not know her name, but I know the high-pitched

moan she made as she came last night. It echoes through my mind with a bit too much familiarity.

She waits a long second before she lets me go, pulling some sort of dominance play. "Look, I don't want us getting off on the wrong..." Her attention skims my naked chest before the slightest pink tinges the base of her neck. "Foot."

As if to distract from her embarrassment, she taps a manila folder sitting on the table in front of me, where she'd been parked when I came out of the shower.

"Carter and Damien looped me in on what your dysfunctional..." She pauses and looks around the Winnebago. "Wait. Please tell me I didn't inherit the job of driving this thing? One of you knows how to operate it, yes?"

Carter runs a hand through his haphazard hair. "Gregory only came on board a couple of weeks ago. Do you think we walked before that?" he snarks.

Even though he's clearly trying to get under her skin, she gives him a beatific smile. "Well, Carter, run your feet half as fast as you run your mouth and I bet you beat us to the next show."

For a split second, he blanks out and I wonder how long it's been since someone other than the three of us shut down Carter Cole. He gives her a once over as he assesses her. December's no longer the only one this girl has gotten onboard.

"Anyways," she says before her attention flicks to the group as a whole. "Gregory's gone. Everything goes through me. Understood?" There's a pause as she stares at each of us until we nod our agreement.

I clear my throat. "Okay, but you know you're not really here as a sobriety coach, right?"

December deflates. Damien drops his head subtly into his palm, and judging by the vicious look from Carter, I'm on my own.

The actress sighs. It's not me she lashes into, though. It's Carter.

"Tell him what you told me." When he doesn't answer, she presses. "In the hotel. Tell him."

I have a feeling Carter's using his shapeshifting abilities to hide the flush of embarrassment from his cheeks. Still, he squirms. He runs a thumb over the edge of his sharp jaw twice before he fists his hand and drops it to the table. He turns to me. "I told her I'm fucking worried about you," he grinds out.

The admission catches me off guard.

"Every time you go out alone," Carter adds, his finger drilling against the tabletop until the nail goes red, then white. "I wonder if whatever creature is munching on our fans will eat that demon out of you instead. Leave the leftovers for us to bury."

I scoff. "Carter, that's not—"

"Same," Damien whispers.

I swivel between the two of them in shock.

December frowns. Her red lipstick darkens the corner of her mouth like a wound. "I know as long as the demon is inside you it'll keep you from dying," she says. "But Christ, Ro, it's not an excuse to destroy yourself every damn night."

Her words from earlier echo through my mind. *Your breathing was wrong.*

My heart begins to pound. I scared her. That's all this is.

"Honestly, I'm fine," I say automatically. Only minutes ago, I swore the same thing to her alone, a broken record. But for the second time in as many weeks, I woke up bloody with a blank spot in my memory. "It's not me you all should be worried about," I remind them. "I'm not the issue here."

All eyes rotate to the fixer to see how she'll handle my push-back. For a long moment, she contemplates me. "I need to be alone with Roanoke," she says finally. "Now."

Despite the gravity of the situation, I see the start of a joke forming in Damien's mouth before a mere warning look from December sucks the life out of it.

Carter snickers anyway, the first to slide out of the booth and head toward the door of the bus. "Good luck," he tosses over his shoulder.

I'm not sure if it's meant for me or her.

As I stand to let December out, she squeezes my arm. I'm not sure if it's in comfort or pity. Maybe it's a reminder to toe the line. The siren slides past and follows Damien to the front of the Winnebago. The door wheezes closed.

I heave a sigh and turn. "This is—"

Pressure clamps around my throat as I'm shoved against the bathroom doorway. I stumble, crash into the paneling. Her grip tightens on my windpipe. I drop the towel in surprise and grab her wrists.

"You're a fucking incubus?" she spits like I infected her with an STD, stabbed her with a dirty needle.

"I'm sorry! Please!" I pry at her fingers. "My throat! I have to sing tonight."

She releases me. I sink to the floor, coughing.

"You tell me right now. The truth," she demands. "Did you search me out in that bar? Did you know who I was the whole time?"

I hit her with an incredulous sneer. "Really? Come on."

She paces above me. After a full minute, she offers me a hand. Once I'm up, she scoops my towel from the floor. "Here," she says.

As I wrap it around me, her eyes catch on the bruises decorating my waist. "What happened?" she asks.

I shrug. "Picked a fight and lost."

Twin lines of confusion burrow between her brows. "When?"

"After I bailed on you," I tell her before my words twist with sarcasm. "The night was young. Can I get dressed?"

Without waiting for permission, I grab a pair of boxers from my bunk's drawer and ditch the towel as I step into them.

I make my voice cool as I yank on my final clean pair of jeans. "Look, I didn't want to run into you again or I would have left a number." I hate the smarmy tone I'm using, but I have to get her out of here. As far from me as possible. Safe. "Any authority you planned on lording over me is null and void after what we did. Your idea," I remind her. "Not mine."

"Are you trying to shame me?" She laughs. "I had a couple shots, a good time, and slept great. You chowed down on my golden years, ghosted me, and then threw yourself a pity party rowdy enough to scare the shit out of your friends."

I've been playing at the anger, but the last of my patience

evaporates for real. "Spare me the high and mighty act," I snarl. "I was doing coke off your tits twelve hours ago."

A memory surges, her helpless sounds while I tongued her clit. I drag my attention off her and concentrate on finding myself a shirt, tugging it on and past my waist to hide the bulge at my crotch.

"Willow," she says suddenly.

Annoyed, I glance at her. "What?"

"You'll need to know eventually, right?" Her brown eyes search mine. "My name. It's Willow."

Flecks of gold ring the centers of her irises. I hadn't expected to add any new details about her. "Well, go home, Willow," I say. "The label will send someone else. This isn't fair to you. Not after what I did."

I don't mean to be so damned honest.

She watches me as I finish getting dressed, then tucks her fingers into the back pockets of her jeans. "An incubus," she says quietly, as if chiding herself. "Christ, I should have known once you dropped that music as foreplay bullshit."

"Hey," I say, copying her slightly friendlier tone. "No part of that was bullshit. Walker Roads is a legend."

"He was pretty good." She grins and then toes the ancient carpet. "Swear you just stumbled in there?"

"Hand to God," I say.

She bites her lip. "Once we left the bar…" Hollow sickness rolls through me as I realize what she's about to ask. "What I did with you, it wasn't because…"

She knows about my powers, the sway I *can* call upon, but

101

she doesn't know me. She doesn't know I would never, ever do that. I lean against the bunk. "You're asking if I forced you to have sex with me?"

"I'm not *asking* anything," she says and my stomach sinks until she goes on. "I wasn't drunk. You never pressured me. You got my consent countless times. You didn't bespell me. I want you to know what I did was my choice."

In my relief, the tiniest of laughs breaks from me.

She gives me a quizzical look.

"Of all the bars in Austin," I quip. She might claim I didn't bespell her, but I can't say the same. "We really fucked ourselves, didn't we?"

Ever so slowly, her edges lose that calculated distance and in her smile is the version of her I met last night. "How long have you been an incubus?" she asks.

My good mood falters. "Three years."

I'd been twenty-two, joining local bands that collapsed inward like stars after a few gigs in the small venues near my hometown. That's where Cassandra found me.

I fight the urge to apologize to Willow. What I ripped from her can't be given back. And then a thought breaks in. "Why aren't you sick?"

Her brow wrinkles. She's clearly not following.

I've never had to have this conversation, never faced anyone in the morning. "With what the demon takes, you should have a wicked hangover." It took Cassandra a month to explain to me the headaches I couldn't shake, the nausea, the horrible vertigo. "It fed off you, Willow. I *know* it happened because of how *I* feel. But you're not sick."

She stays silent.

"You seem pretty sure I didn't influence you," I add, increasingly suspicious. "Is it because I can't?"

Willow smirks. "Are you wondering about my health or are you concerned I'm immune to your tricks?"

I think of how quickly she subdued me with that choking hold. Now this.

"So, you really are qualified to do more than babysit drunk rockstars?" I ask.

"I'm qualified to do more than babysit." From her expression, I expect another laugh. Instead, her voice is thick with gravity. She sinks into the booth. "I need this job, Roanoke."

Something inside me twitches at the sound of my name on her lips. I sit opposite her.

"Do you want my help?" she asks.

I don't answer.

When she speaks again, her tone is hard. "Did you kill those girls?"

It takes everything in me not to lash out. Laying my hands on the tabletop, I press my thumb against a fingernail, letting the motion soothe me even as my nail bites into the cuticle. "If you truly thought I did, you wouldn't be here."

She nods once. "But you know more than you're letting on, don't you?"

Heat crawls up my neck. There's a stickiness to the cuticle I'm grinding my nail against. "I've been watching for missing persons cases. I check their social media posts, see if they watched us play."

"Carter told me three girls have shown up dead?"

I lick my lips, not sure how much to tell, if I trust her. "Six," I correct. "Six that I know of. I think it started two months ago."

"And you think it's going to happen again?"

Like a portent, I glance down and see blood on the hangnail I snagged. "Willow, I—" When I don't go on, she gives me a nod of encouragement. "I don't know how to stop this," I whisper.

"That's my job." She reaches across the table and separates my hands. For a long moment, she seems to contemplate the growing droplet of red.

If she's able to resist me, she's supernatural, which means she has a fighting chance to stop whatever's happening. If she's lying though...

Then I need to keep her close, I think. She already gave me the perfect excuse. "Can you help me?" I blurt. "Stop drinking, maybe? Get clean?"

Her eyebrow raises at my sudden change in attitude. "A huge part of this job is going to involve me putting my public reputation on the line. If you slip up, even once, it affects my ability to land future work."

"I understand," I promise.

"Anything you need to be weaned off?" she asks. "Pills?"

I shake my head.

"Good. And the coke?"

I shrug. "Not an everyday thing."

"Drinking?"

"Is," I admit. The word feels like ripping off a Band-Aid.

"We'll ease you off the alcohol."

I set my jaw. I'm in this. I need her to know it, so she'll trust me. "No. I'll go cold turkey."

"That's too dangerous. Your body could shut down."

"It won't," I answer and then add, "I'm no good to the demon without a pulse."

I let a few seconds pass and give her a once over. The eyeliner below her left eye has slunk low. I fight the urge to reach out a thumb and wipe away the mark. "This relationship thing," I start carefully and then find I'm not sure how to continue the sentence.

"Gets me close." She tucks a lock of brown hair that slipped loose from her bun behind her ear. "To you. To the rest of the band. I can change what the public thinks of you."

"I don't care about that," I say.

"Fringe benefit. You'll need it. Especially if the press catches on that your shows have a body count." She lets the words hang in the air. "I think it would be better for us if we kept what happened last night private. Agreed?"

"Yeah-no," I say as casually as I can. "That makes sense." I rub my palms across my knees. "The rest?"

"Rules—" Her tone stays neutral and detached. "Caffeine's fine. Anything else, you don't touch."

I know better than to take time to consider it. "Got it," I say. "I'm on lockdown and we're madly in love."

"For the *cameras*," she reiterates. Willow's serious expression wilts and with it, my tension. "I mean, don't get me wrong. You're a fantastic lay. But let's forget it ever happened, okay?"

"Fantastic, huh?"

A hint of pink blazes on her cheeks as our eyes meet.

On the table, my fist moves on its own accord, only a few millimeters closer to where her hand rests.

Without breaking eye contact, Willow slides her hands into her lap. "A fantastic lay," she says again as she stands. "But not worth dying over. Not even a couple of years at a time."

I watch her go, sauntering down the aisle. Not once does she look back.

She's right. I'm not worth dying over. Which means I've got to do everything I can to keep Willow alive.

Chapter 9

Willow

T he phone drones against my ear. "Pick up," I whisper as I pace my hotel room. "Pick up, pick up, pick up."

When the call connects, I hear Sloane groan at the other end of the line. "Early," she says, stretching the word out.

"Wake up, Peanut," I say, raking a frustrated hand through my curls. I need a shower. I need to wash the scent of Roanoke off my skin. Have the sheets changed. Turn back time.

To Sloane's credit, she instantly sounds more alert. "Hang on."

I hear mumbling in the background, a rustling noise.

"No, it's fine...stay..." she says to someone else.

I picture her tiptoeing through her white bedroom, into the hall, down through the entryway of the mansion she bought after her third film to hit number one at the box office. I ache to be in the spacious kitchen, drinking the expensive coffee she keeps on hand, far from this damned incubus and the hot mess I've caused.

"Whiskey," she says to me as she lets out a yawn. "I'm fine with how much of it I drink, but then *they* drink and spiked blood goes straight to my head!" A tiny giggle escapes her. "Dinner ran a little late."

Despite everything, I smile. Sloane might be a vampire, but she doesn't take life. Instead, she keeps a discreet harem of "roommates" to feed from. Occasionally, the intimacy of bloodletting leads to other such intimacies.

"Is something wrong? You sound upset. Did you meet the incubus?" she prods now that she's relocated to somewhere private where she can speak freely.

"Yes?" I say.

"And?" she presses.

How the hell am I supposed to explain what happened between our texts last night and this phone call?

"Was I right to send you out into the night seeking a piece of ass before you met him?" she says with a laugh.

I hold my breath, wincing my eyes shut. *Out with it*, I tell myself.

"I fucked him," I blurt.

I hear Sloane choke. "It's not even noon! How did you manage to—?"

"God," I say, raising a hand to rub my temple. A headache throbs there, off and on, as if trying to break through the bit of protection the vampire blood affords me. Apparently, Roanoke really did me a solid by leaving the aspirins on my bathroom counter. I wander over, shove the tablets in my mouth as I fill a tumbler with bottled water, and then slug them down.

"We were at the same bar," I tell her after I swallow. "Last night. He did this whole music as foreplay thing and..." I trail off. "Are you there?"

"He's an incubus, Wil." Sloane sounds utterly heartbroken. "He fed off you."

"Yup." The confirmation comes out quiet. Once I got over my shock in the Winnebago, I played off the time stolen from me as inconsequential. Roanoke's demon took a few years. A pittance when Blake almost stole them all.

I knew about the werewolf's claws, knew the danger always there beneath the surface.

Roanoke I never saw coming.

"He asked me why I wasn't sick this morning," I say. "That you?"

"Well," Sloane says slowly, as if considering it. "An incubus, or a succubus, is basically a vampire. We both feed on life force. But blood can be replenished. What they take is permanent." She hesitates. "Still, they're weaker than us. They can't control us. Which is probably why you're not reacting as he expected."

"How long? Before he can influence me again?"

She lets out a noise of uncertainty. "Couple days?" she says, venturing a guess. "Less? It's not an exact science and they're pretty rare creatures."

"Ask around," I say. "Discreetly."

For a moment, there's only confused silence. "But, why?" Sloane asks. "You're coming home, aren't you? You can't possibly still want to help him?"

"I..." My gaze strays to the bed. A dreamlike memory surfaces of last night. His fingers running through my curls. How easily I drifted off as he held me. Him today, minutes ago, heartbroken and defensive, yet desperate enough to accept my help.

I picture his face when I asked him if he killed those girls. *If you truly thought I did, you wouldn't still be here*, he said.

"Sloane, he's a mess."

"Let someone else clean it up," she says.

"He needs help." I clutch the phone to my ear. "Do you not remember what that was like?" I ask. I hate myself a little, even as I say the words. "When I found you with Michae—"

"Don't," Sloane warns. Bringing up her worst memory hardly counts as fair play.

Years ago, I'd knocked on the door of my first LA job, nervous and ecstatic that Sloane Marquette had actually hired me as her personal assistant. A total dream job. When she didn't answer the door, I went in, following a trail of darkening droplets. I found Sloane sobbing, curled around the body in her bed, the white sheets stained and torn in her bloodlust. By then, Michael had already been cold, his eyes clouded. Anyone else would have turned tail and run. I still can't explain why I didn't.

"You were a mess, too, Sloane." I give her time to argue and then go on when she stays silent. "I am very good at my job."

That, at least, is something she can't deny. By all rights, when I found her with the body of her boyfriend, I should've gone full horror movie final girl and shoved a makeshift stake through her. Or panicked and ran up a flight of stairs. One of the two. Instead, the handler in me kicked in, and I did what I was hired to do.

I solved her problem.

Which is exactly what I'm here to do for Roanoke and his band.

"Sit down for this next part," I tell her and then, before I can talk myself out of it, I spill all the details I know about what's going on. Six bodies, maybe seven, according to Roanoke. And not much else to go on.

"Any chance I can get you to do some research?" I ask. "I have names. I need anything useful." I'll interrogate the band on the almost three-hour drive to Houston where they're playing tonight. Between my efforts and Sloane's, I should have a decent base to unravel this mess.

On the other end of the line, Sloane sighs hard. "I know you want to help him. You want to save all the lost little things that go bump in the night. And if they can be saved, you're the girl for the job. But don't forget Blake," she says. "Don't forget, sometimes the humanity is already dead. All that's left is a predator."

Even though the claw marks are healed, even though they're gone, I raise my hand to the spot. I still feel the pinch of phantom pain sometimes when I move. There's a reason I clung so long to the reminder. "I know," I whisper.

"Figure out which one the incubus is."

Chapter 10

Roanoke

The Winnebago hits a bump.

"Carter, slow the fuck down!" December yells from where she's seated across from me at the table. He whoops from the driver's seat and she groans, her head balanced in her hands. She looks about as sick as I feel. Damien's beside her, on the outside.

The Winnebago is cruising along somewhere between Austin and Houston. Me, though? I'm in Hell. Sharing my booth seat is Willow and with every sway Carter's driving causes, she slides the length of my thigh. And with each touch of her, the ache in my balls worsens.

Last night in that bar, she'd been beautiful. Today, her hair up in a complicated twist and her makeup perfect, she's breathtaking. After a quick Google, I know the circles she rolls in. Stars like Maggie Briggs and Octavia Penn and Sloane Marquette and Dez Tennay and Kincade O'Rourke. Those names, even I've heard.

No one is going to believe Willow Taverson would date some random singer like me. No one.

My brain wanders to the name attached to hers in every recent article I read. Blake Brennan, her ex, the douchebag who laid hands on her and got deservedly dumped four months ago. Apparently, he's missing, has been for weeks.

Good, I think. I saw the picture of them on the sand dunes, the closeup of him gripping her upper arms, her head snapped back with the force of his shake. Remembering it curls violence in my gut.

I cross my arms over the table and lower my forehead to them. I'm pretty certain the tension roping through my shoulders is the only thing holding me together.

Though my eyes are closed, I hear the flutter of paper as Damien passes the printouts to December. "Sorry," he says. "None of them look familiar except..."

He trails off. Except the girl found dead backstage at our show.

During our private conversation not three hours ago at this same table, I gave Willow everything I discovered. The names, links to their social media with their walls choked in memorials, pleas from their parents for information, leads, anything.

"Wait," he says, and my insides clench. "Why are there ten pictures here if there were only three bodies found?"

Ten? I think. I showed her six names. The pause grows too heavy to ignore. Dread floods me. Willow's going to out me.

Why didn't I tell them what I found before, when it didn't make me look so damned guilty? I lift my head and swallow, taste bile. December's watching me, waiting, like she knows I've been hiding something, that tinge of vindication already tweaking the corner of her mouth. "I—"

Under the table, Willow squeezes my thigh. "Because those are other women who mysteriously disappeared after attending one of your shows," she says, interrupting my confession. "Eight of them have shown up dead. Two are missing. I expect to find more."

"More?" December says.

"Yes," Willow says without hesitation, and I turn to look at her for the first time since she sat beside me.

December taps her fingers on the tabletop. "Jesus, this is so much worse than we thought," she whispers. "How did we not notice this?"

"Why would you?" Willow points out. "And yes, it's bad. But it gives me a lot to go on. I'll find out who's doing this and why."

To my shock, December relaxes. She believes in Willow. She believes this is all going to work out. God, how I wish I could, too.

Willow turns toward me and her hand wraps around my wrist. It's strange to have her touching me, here, where others can see. My pulse speeds up as she fingers the leather tie I wear, dragging a nail against the silver beads knotted on it.

"Do you always wear this bracelet?" she asks.

"Yeah...yes," I say.

She poses my wrist at a strange angle. "Stay like that."

Reaching down, she snags her hotel coffee from the cup holder and sets it on the table a good eight inches from my hand before she snatches up her phone. "Don't..." she says as she lines up her shot. "Move."

"What are you doing?" Damien asks as he watches Willow snap a photo of her cup, then another, another, another.

"I am," she says slowly as she types on her phone. "Laying groundwork."

After furiously tapping at the screen, she turns it toward me as if to bring me in on her plot. She ran the picture through a filter that gives it a warm tone and then posted it to her social media. *Sometimes it only takes one thing to brighten your day*, the caption reads. My wrist, complete with my bracelet, is barely visible in the shot's corner.

Willow tilts the phone to December, then Damien.

December's face screws up with uncertainty. "I don't get it," she says.

Instead of answering her, Willow hits a button, scrolls, and then holds the phone to her ear. "Piper Finnigan!" she squeals a second later. "How's my absolute favorite person in the whole world?"

At the unfamiliar name, December, Damien, and I exchange confused shrugs.

"Well, of course they promoted you. You always have the best stories." During the pause that follows, her grin only spreads. "We definitely do, but I'm not in L.A. I'm calling you with a scoop." She pauses. "I'm seeing someone."

Willow winces at the screamed swear of surprise and then returns the phone to her ear. Another pause passes before she laughs, the sound throaty. I remember her laugh from last night.

This one, though? It's fake.

I shouldn't know that. That I do makes me want to bolt from this table, from this bus. A few hours ago, she'd been pretty livid for someone who said her lifespan didn't matter. What if she's after revenge for what I did? What I can't stop wanting to do again?

Beside me, Willow lowers her voice to a whisper. "We started talking right before Blake disappeared. It was my call to keep things quiet, but after yesterday..." Her pause is calculated. "It's not fair to him, Piper. He's so worried about us getting caught, this looking bad on me...his reputation looking bad on me..."

Heat burns my neck. I cuff a palm over the skin as if to hide it when December and Damien rotate to catch my reaction.

"Tonight, we're going public," Willow says into the phone.

Is she...she's outing us now? "Wait," I blurt. "What?"

Willow grabs my arm and shoots me a look that steals my protest. "But you'll break the story first," she says to Piper. "I'd love a little intrigue. Make it cute. Can you do that for me?"

The grip Willow has on me shifts. Her thumb strokes absently while she goes on with her phone call. Inside me, something settles at the same time another bit knots. The Winnebago fades, December and Damien and Carter, all of them, gone.

"Yup, the one I just posted. See that bit of bracelet in the corner?" she asks as she glances at me. Her thumb stops. There's only her touch on my skin, her heat against my heat, her brown eyes locked on mine. "You'll want to look up the lead singer of a band called The Raven Shakes. Be gentle with us, Piper."

Willow ends the call.

December bumps her shoulder against Damien's before she slides out of the booth and heads toward the bunks. He follows, shooting me a wink before he goes. I ignore it. "She's good," I hear December whisper to him.

Willow's still gripping my arm. "Are you okay with this?" she asks, her words only for me.

I give a single nod. "Of course."

She studies me for a long moment. "This won't work if we lie to each other," she says.

Her mouth moves around each word, driving me mad. I swear to Christ I could drown in her eyes and never be sorry. She doesn't want us to lie to each other, but what would she do if I were honest? If I told her how desperately I want to kiss her?

"What happens next?" I ask on a breath.

"Tonight, at your show," she starts. "I'll stay in the crowd, draw attention to myself. After, I'll come backstage, and we'll do an official sighting of us together. Some coy hand holding. Maybe a stolen kiss if I can make sure it gets on someone's camera without being obvious about it." Her tone makes the words mechanical. "Think you can handle that?"

I don't answer.

"Roanoke?" She leans until her forehead presses gently against mine. "This is your call. If you don't want to—"

"Do you believe me?" I ask. My fingers raise to her cheek, the touch too intimate, but we're only playing pretend, so what does it matter? "Do you believe I didn't kill anyone?"

Willow's tongue flicks to wet her lips. "Not yet."

It hurts to hear, but it's the answer I wanted. Black spots

117

haunt my memories. Swaths of time where I might have done terrible things. "Okay," I say as I lean from her. "Then I'm in."

CHAPTER II

WILLOW

Outside the venue, fans line the sidewalk. Most wear black feathers in their hair, tied to their wrists with string, drawn crudely onto cheap white T-shirts.

In the Town Car that drove me here, I nervously pick at a tattered thread on my jeans. I've rehabbed actors and actresses. Never a musician. This isn't my scene. I didn't even do the damage to my denim; they came pre-stressed from a boutique.

But Roanoke clearly needs help. I know in my gut, if he were human, he'd already be dead. He spends his nights isolated, desperate to dull the reality of what the demon requires of him. Removing it kills the host, so I can't do anything about that.

Sighing, I watch the line slowly march into the building, excited fans chattering, taking last drags from cigarettes. I wipe my palms on my knees.

Once the driver communicates with venue security, he opens the door and offers me a hand. The few stragglers who haven't flooded into the venue to fight for the front row turn to see who's causing the fuss. Several gape. A handful raise hesitant phones, filming me. I pretend not to notice while the driver walks me down an alley to a rusted side entrance. He raps twice, his knuckles echoing dully against the metal.

The bouncer who opens it gives me a cursory glance, a walkie clutched in his fingers. He lifts a tree trunk of an arm to allow me to slip under and indoors.

"Thank you," I call over my shoulder to the driver.

Once my eyes adjust, I make out a hallway spray painted with a mural of assaulting colors. "Where do I go?" I ask.

His hand drops to the small of my back, steering me forward. "I assume you want front row?"

That was the plan. I hesitate, unsettled and unsure why. "Can you take me to Roanoke? He sings for The Raven Shakes."

He chuffs a laugh. "You wanna meet Ro?" he asks with a raised brow. "Yeah, I can do that."

I'm led through a maze of halls. We pass a musician with green hair, a guitar across his knees with a broken string. Nigel Lee, I realize. He sings for Timber Boom, the headliner.

The bouncer points. "Take your time. I'll be over here when you're done."

I nod, distracted. A thick red drapery curtains off the crowd, but the backstage area is far from empty.

Before I lay eyes on him, Roanoke's smooth baritone lures me forward. I observe him from my vantage point behind a large speaker.

From one lock of his honeyed curls dangles a black feather, mirroring what I saw on the fans outside. Three black dots decorate his left cheekbone. His flannel patterned button-up is shorn at the sleeves to show the muscles cording his upper arms. His guitar hangs from a shoulder strap.

In his hands is a coffee mug. Amidst the frenetic energy of milling people and roadies moving equipment, he takes a careful sip.

I frown. I need to know what's in that cup.

Before I can move forward, a woman taps Roanoke from behind. He turns, startled from his peace, and sets his mug on a speaker to give her his full attention. She hugs him, a shy smile playing at her pink mouth, her fingers sliding up his neck into his curls.

A flare of possessiveness ignites in me. We're supposed to lay the seeds of a believable relationship tonight. How do we do that with this woman groping him in public?

I surge from my hiding spot. My overly forced grin must look nervous, which is fitting because suddenly I'm scared shitless that I'm not going to pull this off. The woman sees me first. Her annoyed glance over his shoulder at my approach shifts to confusion as she places me.

"Surprise!" I call.

I raise my arms as Roanoke rounds toward my voice. In his shock, he catches me. I press my mouth against his.

I intend to give him a quick peck, but Roanoke breaks from his surprise to clutch the nape of my neck, stalling my retreat. The delicate prod of his tongue asks permission even as he deepens the kiss. My tiny moan is all he needs, my body eager for his touch.

It's for the cameras, I promise myself as I let go of my reservations, throw myself into our so-called reunion.

Finally, Roanoke leans away.

I press the back of my hand against my mouth as if I can't believe what I've just done, as if I couldn't help myself.

When I glance up at Roanoke, he's wearing a stunned expression. One of his hands squeezes my arm like he's testing to make sure I'm real.

Good, I think. *It'll sell the scene.*

We've got an audience. Several people stare. Others pretend not to. At least one holds a camera at his hip, slyly recording our encounter.

"What are you doing?" Roanoke blurts.

Around us, idle chit-chat falls to a hush.

I shrug, trying to look apologetic and adorable at the same time. "I missed you! I didn't want to wait for the show in New Orleans, so I flew out early."

Come on, I beg him silently. *Don't blow this.*

Roanoke snaps from his trance and I oof against his shoulder as he yanks me into a hug.

"What the actual hell?" he hisses into my ear.

I stiffen. *Is he angry?*

"You said a public PDA after we played, not making out while I'm trying to prepare my voice."

I kiss his jaw and then skim my lips to his ear. "December's the siren," I snarl. "So don't tell me it was your voice that had that girl flocking to fuck you."

His fingers find my spine, slide upward to hold me to him. "I don't know her," he says defensively.

"It doesn't *matter*. I told you this morning. *Everything* you do reflects on me."

His grip on me softens as he retreats a step, his expression crestfallen. It's my turn to be caught off guard when he kisses me gently. "Don't be upset with me," he says against my lips, voice low, for only me to hear. "I'm sorry. I wasn't ready."

I lick my thumb and fix the smearing black dots on his cheek. It's an intimate move, implies we're comfortable with each other.

His forehead touches mine. "You smell like cherry trees under moonlight," he murmurs. "I couldn't shake it last night after I left the hotel."

For a moment, half, those blue eyes do their damnedest to slay me where I stand.

His fingers curl gently to stroke my arm. "It's intoxicating," he says.

I blink before dragging my gaze from his. *Incubus.* The thought throbs through me. "You're supposed to be staying away from intoxicants," I say.

You panty dropping asshole, I don't say.

"You're going to watch me play, right?" he asks.

I nod and tuck into the space between his neck and shoulder. "I'll be in the crowd."

It's a risk but gets me in front of as many eyes as possible, amps up that social proof we need.

"Okay," he says, tipping my chin for a last kiss. "I'll sell this, Willow. I promise."

From the corner of my eye, I spot December sauntering in our direction. I use the excuse to put some space between me and him.

I pry myself out of Roanoke's arms and dive into hers.

"It worked!" I yell, beaming. "We surprised him!"

"Yay? Oh!" December says as she catches on. She gives my shoulder an awkward pat. "I was actually looking for you."

Something presses into my hand. I pull away and open my palm to find a package of violet earplugs.

"I sing during the second and fifth song. It won't hurt you to hear me," she says, not meeting my eyes. "You probably won't remember. But I wanted to give you a choice."

Her gaze flashes to Roanoke, follows him as he picks up the mug again and swings his guitar around to his front.

"I'm giving you a choice," she says. "But he won't be able to. When he's on stage, that sway gets stronger than he'll admit, even to himself. The more you're around him, the less it'll affect you, but still..."

She gives me a once over and I can't help but think I'm being weighed, measured. That I'm falling short. The blood Sloane used to heal me *has* made me immune to Roanoke, at least for a few days, but I'm keeping that little secret. Will it protect me from December as well?

"Thanks," I say and tuck the package into my pocket.

"Those are specially made to block all sound," she says. "Just so they don't catch you off guard."

I nod and turn to find Roanoke has wandered off, sipping from the mug. Her face is unreadable as we watch him cross the stage and move into the shadows.

"One more thing," she says as she sections half her hair and begins braiding the pigtail. Her tone goes caustic. "If you hurt him, in any way? I will *end* you."

I almost laugh until I realize she's serious. "What?"

She drops the finished braid and starts on the other side. "What happened to your ex, Willow?"

I blink.

"Blake Brennan," she presses. "Roanoke might keep himself in a bubble, but I don't."

I try in vain to keep the uncertainty from my voice. "We broke up," I say. "Before. Two months ago."

"Yeah, I saw the clip of your speech yesterday. Touching. Were you actually dating, or was he a job?"

I don't say anything.

"He's dead, isn't he?" she asks me.

I shake my head, but it's obvious I'm saying no to the question rather than answering it. "Blake was *bad*," I confess, my voice haunted with all the things I'm not saying. I flick my gaze in Roanoke's direction before returning it to her. "Not like him."

A muscle twitches in her cheek, the only crack in what seems a flawless poker face.

"Am I wrong?" I ask.

She hesitates. "Ro would never intentionally hurt anyone."

"Intentionally?" I repeat, not missing the careful word, the slight inflection she put on it.

December ties off her braid with a thin strip of leather before she sighs. "It's true that he's been having blackouts," she says.

"Well, he has a serious drinking problem."

Her nod of agreement is thoughtful. "And when he spirals, he goes hard. But he's never been like this."

"December, if he's responsible for those deaths, I need to know."

Her brow furrows. "Him? Never. The blackouts, though, I think they're a Band-Aid."

"They don't seem to be fixing anything," I say, but December shakes her head.

"You don't understand," she says. "They're covering up something."

Guilt over the years he steals? Or secrets about the deaths? It's on the tip of my tongue to ask, but it feels like the wrong direction.

December hesitates. "He's wrecked, and he won't talk to me. I thought it was the bodies, but we've only known about them for a month. This is different."

A roadie walks behind December and squeezes her shoulder. "Fifteen minutes."

"I should go," she tells me, a little too relieved. As she pirouettes, I clamp onto her arm.

"Wait! Covering up what?" I demand.

"I don't know. But you better figure it out quick." She takes a small step back, then another. "Because whatever that Band-Aid is hiding?" she says. "It's festering."

Ten minutes later, I hover at the edge of the crowd, but I can't get December's words to stop echoing through my mind.

He drinks. He blacks out. There's nothing unusual about that. And yet...

Something's festering. Surely the record company wouldn't have hired me if he's dangerous. This ending badly would be a PR nightmare. I remember the two aspirins he left me at the hotel. *For your head*, he'd written.

The piped in music dies. When the house lights follow, I startle in the sudden dark, barely have time to react before the curtain rises to reveal an empty stage, save for a microphone stand and December's drum set.

The crowd surges forward on a wall of cheers. I'm caught in the rush, stumbling with it until I'm four rows from the gate separating the fans from the band, slightly to the right of center stage. Screams ring in my ears. I hold my ground as people elbow and jostle for position. Cell phones glow with an eerie light, recording.

December takes the stage first, sporting the twin braids she wove backstage. On her cheek are the same three black dots Roanoke wore. She skips to the front and curtsies, holding out the edges of the pleated schoolgirl skirt she's wearing. Scrawled on her white tank top is the crude feather drawing so many fans have inked onto their own clothes. I don't know whether The Raven Shakes simply haven't had time to figure out merchandizing or some marketing genius made their gimmick easy to replicate.

Once December takes her place behind the drum kit, Carter follows. He strips off his shirt, balls it up and hurls it into the crowd far beyond where I'm fighting for my tiny piece of ground, his ice blond hair spiked and glowing under the stage lights. Tattoos sleeve his arms, his chest, strangle up toward his chin in a way that makes me claustrophobic. It's weird because I sat across from Carter in the motorhome when we'd awkwardly awaited Roanoke. I remember noting his neck tattoos in the hotel, but not on the Winnebago.

He's shapeshifting them, I realize. *They're not real.*

Aside from the shirt throwing, he doesn't play to the crowd. He saunters to the left side of the stage and holds out a hand. A roadie passes him a gleaming blue bass guitar.

I'm still watching Carter when a flurry of activity draws my attention. Damien waves wildly, bouncing on his toes. With a grin, he laps the edge of the stage to gather fist bumps and high fives before he settles into place almost in front of me with his guitar.

December lifts her arms. The single beat she slams down hits my chest in a shock wave. Damien's guitar squeals feedback.

From off stage, a wicked laugh breaks into a microphone. Every pair of hands in the venue but mine shoots into the air like they've all received a signal I missed. Angled toward the stage, their fingers wiggle frantically. I glance around behind me. The entire place is movement and anticipation and smiles.

I am out of my element, overwhelmed and confused.

"Hands up!" the girl beside me yells, laughing as she knocks her shoulder into mine in encouragement. "Is this your first Raven Shakes show?"

I offer a tentative smile.

Roanoke's voice oozes from the speakers, low and sultry. "Do you..." he rumbles. "Have the shivers?"

And God, if goosebumps don't prickle my skin, race up the nape of my neck.

The screams swell to an ear-splitting volume.

The dark leather of one of Roanoke's tattered boots peeks from the curtained edge of the stage, then his hand, holding the microphone out as if to encourage the crowd to a frenzy. He curls the mic toward his hidden mouth. "Anybody out there feel some tremors starting?"

I wouldn't have thought it possible for the crowd to grow any louder, but they do, screaming, eager to please him. The girl beside me releases a piercing whoop of utter ecstasy.

"Are you ready?" Roanoke starts as he strides onto the stage, rushing to the microphone stand, tipping it over as he curls into himself. "For The Raven Shakes!"

The whole band launches into the first song. December's hands fly, ravaging the drums. Carter leans, plucking the blue bass slung low across his hips. Damien absolutely wails out chords. My eyes skip madly between the three of them. I don't know which one of them to watch.

Then Roanoke sings.

The crowd hushes instantly, caught in his spell. A smooth dream-like fog spills over the edge of the stage, flowing into and around us. Some part of me understands it's only a smoke machine, but it's otherworldly.

The lyrics break from his lips. My chest aches with his mourning calls for a touch taken away too soon. Behind me, the crowd knows every word of the song, mirroring his pain to him as he prowls the stage.

God, I want him. It's a need so stark and unrelenting that I shudder. I want his laugh, his smile, that soft kiss as he whispered his apology to me backstage. I want to fall asleep in his arms again and this time, wake up in them. Surely, this reaction isn't normal, some part—some tiny, rational part—of me thinks. And then I remember Sloane's blood, the protection it should afford me.

Maybe it's already wearing off.

At my side, the girl who asked me if it was my first show slings an arm around my shoulder and sways us like we're old friends as the song ends. She tightens her grip and presses her mouth to my ear. "I told you they're fantastic!"

Damien strips his guitar off and hands it to someone behind the curtain, trading it for another.

On stage, Roanoke paces. "How's it going out there, Houston?" he asks.

The place explodes.

My head cocks as I watch him. His chest rises and falls, his blue eyes sparkling. He raises two fingers and kisses them before blowing across his hand and sending the kisses out to the crowd. A grin slices his face as he raises the microphone again. "You guys are everything, you know that, right?"

"He looks so different," I murmur, unaware I've spoken aloud until the girl beside me yells, "What?"

I give my head a distracted shake. Happy. Roanoke looks truly happy.

He grabs his guitar from the stand and then peers out, shading his eyes from the light. "So, I'm gonna break some hearts, but I need to do this."

A ripple of uncertainty rolls through the crowd and Roanoke laughs as if chickening out of whatever he's going to say.

What's he doing? Confusion keeps my attention rooted to the stage. Is the banter a normal part of the show?

Carter wanders over and gives Roanoke a fist bump.

"Alright, hell with it," Roanoke says suddenly into the mic. "Um, there's a girl out there with you guys somewhere, and this is her first time seeing me play."

A tingle of nerves creeps into my stomach.

He rolls his eyes skyward, a shy smile plastered on his lips. His voice falls to a confessional whisper. "I really like her," he says. "So, I'm kind of nervous tonight. If you guys could sing along extra loud for this next one, it'd really help."

The crowd bursts into an encouraging cheer.

"Anyway," he says and strums a few chords on his guitar before quickly adding, "This one's for Willow."

Damien fiddles with his guitar as Roanoke flushes a bright pink.

You clever, clever bastard, I think. For the first time, I wonder if I've underestimated him. Vastly.

The girl beside me spins, shock on her face. "Oh my God. You're...that's you!" she says in a joy-filled voice. "Holy shit, how did I not know Willow Taverson and my favorite singer were an item?"

"We...it wasn't..." Heat warms my cheeks. Why am I so damn flustered?

"You bitch!" The words ring with congratulations instead of the bite of jealousy I expect.

Luckily, Roanoke spares me when he sings. This song isn't like the first with its heavy drums and guitars. His voice bounces along, the chorus a sort of call and answer the crowd happily takes up. "If I am a lover lost, you are my ocean, crossed, a changing of fate and a bit of blank slate." Then it turns darker, slowing into a melancholy lullaby. "An Irish goodbye to tonight's guilt trip," he hums. "Any port in a storm couldn't save this ship."

I know an Irish goodbye is another term for ghosting, what he did to me at the hotel, but the girl beside me is singing along, so the song isn't new.

Recycled love songs, I think, but the lyrics catch in my head as I watch first Damien and then Roanoke slip oversized headphones over their ears. In the song, the lover lost is clearly Roanoke. An ocean crossed...December? A changing fate could refer to Carter and damned if Damien isn't a blank slate, no matter how many times I've read through my notes from Gregory.

Another voice cuts in, a dueling vocal slicing over Roanoke's and drowning it out.

The siren's.

I sing during the second and fifth song, December told me backstage.

I dig frantically for the earplugs and then notice what's happening around me. The entire venue goes absolutely still, silent save for December's singing. The crowd, the bouncers, they all face forward. Only my head swivels. It's fucking eerie. Things only get worse when I connect eyes with a blond woman a couple of rows back. She raises two fingers to me and then holds them to her neck to mimic the pierce of fangs, one eyebrow raising in a question.

Vampire.

She gives me a thumbs up like we're both part of the same club and I twist toward the stage, uncertain what to do. The last thing I need is to draw more supernatural attention to myself. And yet my gaze is drawn to another set of eyes on me.

She wears a pensive look as she ponders me, tucking long, light brown hair behind her ear. Another vampire? Something stronger? I try out a tentative smile—*Vampire club! Yay!*—but she doesn't react. Her attention sweeps the stage. I follow her line of sight.

Nothing's changed.

When I turn back, the spot the girl occupied blurs in a flurry of motion as others move to fill the empty space.

Okay, so vampires are officially immune to not only incubi, but sirens as well. Sloane hadn't mentioned that, but then again, I didn't tell her about the other supernaturals in the group.

In a crowd this big, it doesn't seem farfetched to have a few creatures of the night wandering around. Vampires can love good music, too. Sloane does.

I wonder if there are any werewolves. The thought is there, creeping through my veins as my pulse starts to hammer. *Don't,* I beg my brain. *Don't think about it.*

I'm not doing this. I'm not panicking here in this crowd.

Not in the middle of a job. But I can already feel the flood of adrenaline, fight or flight.

On stage, Roanoke ducks to his knees, slamming his hands against the headphones over his ears to hold them tighter against his head. December's voice rises, sharpens. Around me, the crowd stirs as if uneasy.

The riot of movement starts slow. A few steps. A shove. Someone jostles me and I stumble, one of my arms smacking someone as I raise it to protect myself. The crowd surges forward.

If those werewolves are here, you're stuck. They'll devour you alive.

Hundreds of bodies crush tighter. The press of people jerks me onto my tiptoes, then off the ground, compresses my chest.

Don't panic, I command myself, even though I'm already there. *Don't panic. They won't let her sing long. It's a pressure valve.*

As if Roanoke can sense my distress, he rises to stand at center stage, a fist held high. He flicks up one finger, a second, a third, and then strips loose the headphones and flings them aside.

The same instant, December's voice stops. Roanoke clutches the microphone, picking up the song where he left off. Around me, the crowd explodes in cheers, surging to life again as it rolls back like a wave. My feet hit the floor and relief overwhelms me.

Not so bad, I think. *Got through it fine.*

"Get your hands up!" Roanoke commands, stomping across the stage. I stretch, flex my fingers and then wiggle them in a mimic of the surrounding crowd, feeling a little silly despite myself.

Two songs later and my cheeks are aching with the grin spread across my lips. The Raven Shakes aren't just good, they're phenomenal.

Roanoke runs a hand through his sweaty curls and ducks out of sight behind the curtain at the side of the stage. He returns with a violin tucked underneath his chin.

Violin, too? I think. *Christ, how talented is he?* I watch, enamored, as he draws the bow across the strings. A single note sears through the room. He jiggles the bow and the sound quivers.

A few steps behind Roanoke, Damien takes a spread-legged stance. He plucks a climbing scale, his face scrunching tighter as the notes rise, fingers digging hard against the neck, then the body of his guitar. Roanoke's mouth drops open in an amused look of faux bafflement. He steps aside and Damien moves into the space he occupied center stage and starts into a new song.

While Damien savages his instrument, Roanoke strides to the mic and sings. This time when December's vocals rise and fall in the background, there's not so much effect on the crowd.

The violin weeps under Roanoke's deft fingertips.

I shiver.

"Jesus," I whisper. I glance around for the girl who took me under her wing before, if anything, to have someone to share this with, but she's gone. I close my eyes, savoring the music, Roanoke's voice. The heat rising off the crowd lulls me. A languid smile winds onto my lips, grows as the violin takes over again. The note draws long and sorrowful before it fades through to the last reaches of the venue.

"Wow," I whisper.

Thunderous applause shakes me from my trance. I blink hard, orienting myself.

On the stage, Roanoke points to Carter, then Damien, and finally to December, who stands and chucks a drumstick to the crowd. I lose it in the lights, only see where it landed by the sudden riot where it fell. She hurries offstage with a last wave. Carter stoops to rip a piece of paper off the floor at his feet and passes it to the outstretched fingers grasping toward him. A setlist. That means it's over. Five songs. Too little. Far too little.

"You guys are fantastic," Roanoke murmurs, grinning, dipping low to slap hands as he moseys offstage. I mirror his sideways motion and squeeze through the crowd until I find myself at the door I originally came through. Luckily, it's manned by the same bouncer who led me to Roanoke. I smile and give him a wave as if we're old friends.

"Giving up your prime spot before the headliner comes on?" he says in an almost teasing voice.

I raise my eyebrows. "You honestly think anyone could top The Raven Shakes?" I ask, and his shoulders shrug with laughter.

"True. Your dude's got that thing. He'll be playing stadiums in no time."

Pride swells through me, but it's silly. Roanoke isn't mine to be proud of.

I roam the hall until it spills into the backstage area. The sound of laughter greets me. I hesitate, not wanting to interrupt the post-performance celebration clearly going on. I see Nigel

Lee, the lead singer of Timber Boom, with his bright shock of green hair, along with the badass girl who plays with him, preparing to take over the stage The Raven Shakes vacated. Roanoke seems oblivious, scanning. His eyes snag on me. A smile blazes across his face and he pushes through hands that clap congratulations onto his back and shoulders.

He stops shy of me.

"Well?" he asks. His chest still rises and falls with heaving breaths from performing. Sweat glistens on his skin. He licks his lips and then throws his head back in mock frustration. "Willow, you're killing me! What did you think?"

Perplexed, I laugh. "Are you kidding? You were fantastic!" I gush and then correct myself. "All of you! All of you were fantastic!"

Part of me expects the cold shoulder from Carter and Damien after the terrible introduction this morning, but Damien tousles my hair as if we've known each other for months. Carter goes a step further, scooping me into his arms and twirling me before he sets me in front of Roanoke again. Damn if the whole band doesn't seem determined to sell Roanoke and I as a couple. They must have discussed me, had a meeting and hashed it out or something, because Roanoke gives them an approving nod like this was all planned.

I meet Roanoke's blue eyes and my brain stalls.

Job, I remind myself. *This is only a job.* One of his hands moves forward to find my hip, eases me closer. Through our clothes, I feel the heat of his skin.

"So, you were saying how I was fantastic?" he teases and I

tamp down on genuine amusement as I roll my eyes.

He slips the hand that isn't on my hip into the curls at the nape of my neck. I lick my lips, my eyes on his mouth before he leans into my ear. "I sang for you."

"Yes," I whisper back. "And you should kiss me. Now. There are cameras."

"Always rushing me," he chides before his mouth meets mine.

I'm not prepared for the hunger in his kiss, the involuntary sound of pleasure that climbs my throat before I think to stop it. I clutch his shoulder. His hands leave my hair, my hip, and curl against either side of my jaw.

He presses his lips once more against mine before he moves his mouth to my ear. "We'll fool them all, won't we?"

CHAPTER 12

ROANOKE

W illow presses against my chest as she cheers on Timber Boom from where we're watching backstage. *This isn't real*, I remind myself as I drop a kiss on her shoulder, circle my arms around her waist.

I watch Nigel bob across the stage. The drum machine kicks in precisely when needed to up the fever-pitch of the crowd. The guitarist is a gorgeous femme fatale redhead named Trelliz Redux who knows her instrument like no one I've ever met. She's also the only female I know who can drink my ass under the table. She and Nigel have an on again off again thing.

Tonight, they're off again, which adds to the fire of their performance. Her guitar riffs pound through my chest, the sound hard and unnatural as Nigel bellows into the microphone in time to the drum machine.

It's almost time.

The thought claws into my consciousness and for a split second, all I feel is relief. Two more songs and we'll celebrate with drinks. Ten minutes. Fifteen max.

Except tonight, I'm not doing that. Tonight, I'm going to the hotel. No bars. No capsules. No powders. Even with Willow in my arms, I can't shake the dread welling inside me.

I'm fighting against the memory of who I slept with before her. It's a blur, nothing but shame and the bottle of Jager I split with Nigel after the show. A teasing laugh. A girl's hand on my crotch, tattooed card suites across her knuckles. The popped button on my jeans. Sensations and movement I barely remember. Is she still alive? Is her body being ditched in a place that'll incriminate the band?

Against Willow's heat, I break out in a cold sweat.

On stage, Timber Boom finishes their set and runs through a quick single song encore that has me wondering if the argument between Nigel and Trelliz isn't something more serious. The house lights cut on and Willow turns in my arms. I fight a smile onto my mouth to mirror her own.

"You were right!" she says, beaming. "They're great!" She raises her voice to be heard above the screaming crowd. "My car's here. I texted the driver. Do you want to ride to the hotel with me or on the bus with the band?"

There's a pause as I glance around to find Damien, December, and Carter, and Willow's expression goes stern. Beyond the stage, the audience files into the night. The cheering has stopped.

"It's your first night sober," she says. One of her hands is at the back of my neck, her fingernails absently stroking there like we've always been this close. I'm fairly certain she hasn't realized she's doing it. I can't concentrate on anything else.

You fuck, I think to myself. *What's wrong with you?*

"You shouldn't be alone," she says, and I don't know whether to be disappointed that she means it entirely innocently.

I shrug, unwilling to admit she's right. Already the anxiety has tightened into a ball, a twitch in my limbs, my feet shifting as if I'm tired of standing on the concrete flooring.

"So, do you want to, then?" Willow asks, biting her lip. I'm not supposed to be watching the way it pops loose. I'm not supposed to be thinking about kissing her.

"Huh?" I drag my eyes up to meet hers.

"Ride with me in the car? Or we can meet in the lobby at the hotel?"

The last place I should be is anywhere alone with her. Not with the thoughts running through my head. Too much need. The demon burrows behind my ribs, stretching, awakening.

No, I think. *This isn't right. I should have a week.* I swallow hard and my throat clicks. Willow raises an eyebrow.

"Lobby," I say, my voice cracking. "I'll meet you in the lobby."

For the briefest of seconds, concern flickers across her expression.

"Hey," she says, her tone soft. "It's going to be okay." Those fingers stroke against the base of my neck again and I'm desperate to kiss her, soft and lingering. She'd let me if there were cameras. I need to find cameras.

You're still thinking you're going to get into her pants again? Gonna let that demon chew off a little more of her life? My pulse hammers as I fight to keep myself together. *Or maybe you'll be the one to find her body a few cities up the road.*

I ache for the burn of a few shots. A slug of whiskey. Anything.

What if the demon needs more if I'm sober? What if the cycles speed up and it needs to be fed every day? What if it takes everything, draining whoever I'm with into a dead, dry husk while I'm still thrusting into them?

One of the venue's security guards taps Willow on the shoulder. Her car must be ready for her. I don't move my hand from her hip as she steps out of my hold.

Stay, I think. *Stay with me.*

"I'll see you at the hotel?" she says. It sounds more like a question than it should. Willow watches my slowly lowering hand. "Maybe I—"

"No!" I say with false nonchalance. "Take off. I'm right behind you."

She opens her mouth to argue, but then the bouncer touches his earpiece again and her shoulder again and I know she's going to leave.

Don't, I think. *Don't go. I can't do this.*

She turns to follow. After a few feet, she spins back to me. "Roanoke, are you?"

I raise an eyebrow.

"Okay?" she asks.

"I'm fine," I say. Before she can think about it too much, I tuck my hands in my pockets and head off in the direction I saw Nigel go when he finished up onstage.

Down a darkened hall, light glows from beyond a threshold.

I hear glass shattering and the heated words of an argument.

"Well, fuck you then!" Nigel barks. He stumbles out, one hand raised in protection as a bottle of amber liquid hurdles out of the room, misses him, and explodes against the cinderblock wall in a wet firework of shards.

"Love you too, Pumpkin!" he snarls in what I'm almost positive is a fake British accent, and then he catches sight of me and breaks into a sheepish grin. "Roanoke, my man. Having myself a little tiff with the lady and like a damned beacon of hope in the darkness, you show up to help me drown my sorrows, eh?"

He hooks an arm over my shoulder, the black tank top he wore on stage still sweat soaked and stinking. I'm sure I'm not much better.

"I...no," I say. "I just wanted to tell you good show tonight."

He jerks as if in shock and screws up his pale face, before snorting like I made a joke.

I brush off the hand around my shoulders. "Willow's waiting for me. I told her I wouldn't—"

Nigel grabs at his crotch and gives it an over-exaggerated squeeze. "Have any balls as long as she's hanging about?"

He clicks his tongue in disapproval, watching to decide if I'm serious or not. I'm about to protest when he grins. "You wouldn't leave me in my time of need," he says. "Me and Liz might really be done."

Now it's my turn to look dubious. "You and Trelliz will have fucked up makeup sex by morning."

Those two will literally go at it like bunnies anywhere the urge comes over them. They give exactly zero shits who's in the room, listening, watching, filming.

Nigel cocks a grin my way. "Ay, you're probably right. But that's morning. No reason me and you shouldn't go out now."

One drink to knock down this panic attack. Settle the fucking thing living inside me.

"I can't," I say aloud, and I'm not sure if it's in answer to him or myself.

Nigel's not giving up. "Then why'd you find me, Ro? You need something?" There's an emphasis on the 'something' that makes it obvious what he's implying. He taps two fingers against the tiny pocket on his pants where he keeps his stash hidden. "You want?"

My eyes lock on that pocket. "N-No. I..." Words fail me. I settle for shaking my head.

But I do want.

Just something to take the edge off. Not anything that'll fuck me up enough that Willow would notice. Not enough to matter. I'll hang out with her in the hotel lobby as planned. I'll get through it. I'll be okay.

Nigel's fingers dig into the pocket, and I close my eyes like not being able to see whatever he's offering will somehow dial up my willpower. There's a rustling noise, the pop of a Ziplock, a press against my lips.

"One last hurrah?" Nigel says again as he slips a gel cap into my mouth.

I open my eyes as I cheek what he gave me. "I'm not going out. Not tonight."

"Course not." He cups an orange pill in the center of his palm and then slams it against his mouth. When he drops it, his eyes are wide, excited. The pill is gone. "Bottoms up," he says.

I swallow.

• • • ● ● ● ● ● • •

Nigel and I are islands, surrounded by fans of our bands holding shot glasses aloft as he booms out a toast. "To the kisses we've snatched!" he yells. "And the snatches we've kissed!"

A chorus of groans fills the bar and then a moment of near silence as we all knock back the liquor. Someone tucks the next round into my hand as soon as the last glass is empty. With each swallow, there's nothing but relief.

I'm okay, I think. *I'm okay. I'm okay.* I want to believe it. Another shot and I might. With a laugh, I rock my head and the room tilts and blurs. I throw an arm around the closest shoulder for stability.

Cherries. My throat clenches as the scent overwhelms me. I already know who my arm settled around when I glance at her. "Willow."

"Hey, you," she says sadly. She tightens her hold at my waist as I sway. "You never showed in the lobby."

I want to ask how she found me, but it's not like Nigel and I were being discreet. With how packed the bar is, word got out.

She snags the shot glass I'm holding. She's going to go nuclear, smash it in a million bits, and slap me across the face. I deserve it. Instead, I watch, stunned, as she holds it up. Before she speaks to the crowd, she turns and locks eyes with me. "May none of your mistakes be regrets!" Willow yells.

The place cheers as my mood sinks.

She drinks the shot and grins at me. Has she given up on this sobriety coach angle?

"I missed you," I murmur. My body leans toward hers like a magnet. I need her touch. I want her mouth on mine. "See any cameras?"

When I go in for a kiss, her hand hits my chest, stopping me. "You come with me right now, or I'm done."

I deflate against her. "I meant to," I say. "The lobby. I meant to be there."

Willow's not hearing it. She separates from me and my brain has trouble keeping up, especially when she's laughing, high-fiving Nigel. Am I imagining things? Hallucinating? I think of the orange pill I didn't ask about and the one that came after. The third I swallowed a few minutes ago.

I fucked up.

Willow reaches for me, her fingers locked between mine. She leads us out of the bar, winding through the impossibly thick crowd until it's me and her alone on the street. As soon as we're outside, I expect her to unload on me.

It's worse when she doesn't.

A Town Car idles a block down. When we get to it, she opens the door and nudges her chin toward the gaping back seat. I slide in. The partition is up, separating us from the driver.

"I'm sorry," I say. "Starting tomorrow, I—"

She holds up a hand to silence me. I watch the muscles in her jaw twitch. Instead of a lecture, she shows me her phone. There's a picture of Nigel doing body shots off some woman I don't remember. She scrolls. Another of me, surrounded by people still wearing face paint dots on their cheeks and feathers in their hair as they hang off me.

"Do you need to see more?" Willow asks. I shake my head. Even through the spinning buzz, I know better than to plead my case. "You told the entire world we were together on that stage."

"I thought you liked th—"

"And two hours later, you're alone and fucked up on God knows what in some trashy bar. Do you grasp how that looks? For both of us? Do you care?" She turns to me, her brown eyes glittering with rage in the passing streetlights as the car drives on. "Are you even going to remember this conversation in the morning, or am I wasting my time?"

"It was a couple drinks," I lie.

Willow scoffs. Her fingers slide to my wrist, pause there. "Your pulse is erratic."

I fight against the tide of my blurring vision to focus on her face and give her my most charming grin. "Well, you're a little intimidating."

It's like she's sizing me up all over again only this time, I'm failing her test and she's furious about it. She leans against the leather of the car's seat. "Your pupils are blown and I am not a fucking idiot."

There's nothing I can say to fix this. I drag a knee up and

balance my chin on it. The air conditioner's raging in the car, but a fire stokes inside of me. Too much heat. My skin goes clammy and then hot. I lay my head on my knee and watch the city blur by outside the window. A slow throb starts behind my eyes as I close them.

My brain kicks in on the elevator and my first thought is how fucked up I look in the mirrored backing. I've got a room key in my hand, still tucked into the paper sleeve, the room number written on it smeared. I blink hard and it clears. Willow's standing beside me. The smile she wore at the bar was for everyone else. Now, there's nothing but disappointment.

The doors of the elevator slide open.

Without a word, Willow slips an arm around my waist to help me walk. Everything in me wants to shrug her off, tell her I'm fine, that I don't need her or her fucking judgment. But as we walk, I'm dragging one shoulder across the tacky wallpaper. I count down the room numbers until, by some miracle, I find mine and get the key in the card reader. It clicks, but I miss my chance to rotate the handle and have to start all over.

"We're not at your room," Willow says. "I need to change. Then we'll go to yours and get you in the shower."

"I don't need a babysitter," I say. "I've already put you through enough tonight."

She snatches the key from me and feeds hers in effortlessly, and then steers me through the door before sliding past me. "You're too drunk to be left alone." From the bathroom, her voice sounds dull and tired. She's already sick of me. "And I really can't deal with you choking to death on your own vomit."

I let out a sad attempt at a laugh. "Not gonna happen," I say. "Demon, remember?"

It needs its vessel alive. The second orange pill I took doesn't matter. Or the third one Nigel hesitated to hand over, right before Willow showed up at the bar.

Now I know why he looked nervous. The overdose comes on quick—the strange roiling through my blood, the ache in my chest like my heart wants to quit, the warmth shifting to heat, slow coals, orange then blue, roasting me from the inside out. White flickers of light pinprick through my sight. I lean against the wall, gasping a few shallow breaths, as if it'll help cool me down.

Splaying my palm, I stay upright until I can flop into a chair. My eyes slide closed. Behind my lids are flashes of color, my brain firing random synapses.

"Hey!"

Someone wrenches my chin upward. After a slow blink, I focus on her. Willow. She's taken her hair band out and the way she's standing above me makes her brown curls frame her face, ethereal and glowing in the light.

Her hands run through my hair. She catches a snarl and winces, but I don't feel any pain.

"Now you won't get puke in your hair," she says, and I realize she let hers down to put mine up. I know I'm entirely fucked up, but goddamn it if it's not the nicest thing anyone's ever done for me.

Hours ago, I swore to her I would play the game. No more drinking. No more pills. I promised. I lied. I let everyone down.

"You're figuring it out, aren't you?" I say. The words come slowly, but I enunciate each one.

"Figuring what out?" she asks, distracted. She slides her finger across the screen of her phone to check for something and then tucks it into her pocket. She's gorgeous, even as a silhouette. And kind. Sober or drunk, it doesn't matter; I'll never deserve someone like Willow.

"I'm a lost cause," I say.

My head lolls to catch the sadness in Willow's eyes as she blinks at me, startled.

"Come on, Roanoke," she says. "Don't say things like that." She squats down in front of me, her phone balanced on her knee as she takes my hand in hers. "It's my fault. I didn't realize how bad you were."

She means the liquor. Still, the guilt rolls over me and once it's snuck around the buzz, I can't shake it off. I paw a hand across my eye.

"I *am* bad, aren't I? A bad thing." Part of me realizes what I've said and winces in second-hand embarrassment. Another part is so far beyond caring that a sad laugh slips from between my lips. "God damn it."

"Hey." She's got two hands pressed against the sides of my face. There's nowhere to look but into those brown eyes of hers. They hold me steadier than her hands ever could. "I have known bad things," she says. "You are not one of them."

She moves forward and before I can react, her lips press against my forehead.

"There's so little of me left," I whisper.

"There's enough to matter," she says. "Enough to fight for."

Her arms encircle me. I'm distantly aware of her fingers stroking against the base of my skull in the same movement she'd used backstage. The soothing motion hits me like a spell. As I relax against her, I wonder if there's not something supernatural about her after all.

"Come on," she says, and even as intoxicated as I am, I hear the careful edge in her tone. "It's been a rough night. We should get you showered and to sleep."

I barely make it from Willow's room to mine, using the wall as a support while she opens the door with the key she confiscated from me earlier. An instant wave of frigid air rolls out. I must have cranked the AC before I headed to the venue.

"Sit," she commands. "I'll get a shower ready for you. Try not to pass out, okay?"

It's a big ask. My body is in revolt. The last of the drugs are hitting my system. My shiver morphs into a full body tremor and despite it, I'm on fire. I need to lie down for a minute.

The lights are off. A glow streams from the crack between the curtains to give me an idea of the path to the bed. I stagger until my thighs hit the mattress and crawl onto it, flipping to my back.

As I lay my head on the pillows, the ceiling above me starts a languid spin. I inhale, and there's a tickle at the base of my brain. *Trouble*, I think. *Danger.*

My eyes slide closed. Inside me, the demon skitters, tapping against my spine, writhing.

Am I breathing? No. I choke in a broken inhale. There's a scent, strange and cloying. The start of a gag tightens my throat.

"Still with me out there?" Willow yells from the bathroom.

I grunt in response as I fight myself conscious. Whatever that smell is, it's making me sick. I struggle upright again, and my feet hit the carpet, one hand behind me, holding me semi-upright on the mattress. The change in position amps up my dizziness. Static sounds in my ears.

I need another drink, I think. But I'm not at the bar anymore. I've lost track of where I am. How I got here.

Head drooping, I lose my balance and almost tumble to the floor. When I overcorrect in my backward lean, my fingers squish into something thick and cold and slimy.

"What the fuck?" I lift my hand and reach for the lamp. It takes two tries to grip the little screw button to turn it.

I wince against the brightness. Reddish brown discolors my palm. I ponder it for a long second, perplexed, before I turn toward the spot and freeze. I can't see whatever I touched through the pattern of the quilt.

But I'm not alone.

A head rests on the other pillow in the bed I'm on, the face turned from me, dark curly hair fanned out.

My sluggish brain spits images in reverse. The hotel key I took out of my pocket. Laughing in the bar with Nigel. Ducking out on Willow backstage.

But... I flash to Willow helping me out of the bar. Walking me in here.

December's voice whispers through my mind. *You've been blacking out, Ro. Losing time.*

I search my memory for blank spots that explain what I'm

seeing.

"Willow?" I call, her name barely audible. That weird static noise in my head hasn't stopped. Worse, the smell is stronger. I raise my palm to my mouth, sure I'm going to vomit.

I yank away the bedspread to reveal a wide swath of reddish-brown spreading out from the woman curled on her side in my bed.

"Hey, are you okay?" I ask as I reach an arm out to grab her shoulder.

The slightest pressure rolls her toward me, her arm moving. I spot tattoos on her knuckles.

Card suits.

I have a split-second memory of her lips on my neck, her hand down my pants a week ago.

Her vacant eyes stare through me.

I scramble off the bed, hit the rough carpet hard. My feet dig for traction as I backpedal from the body.

This is all some sort of fucked up hallucination. Whatever Nigel gave me. The alcohol kicked it up a notch. Or I'm having a flashback. A reaction. A freakout.

"Roanoke?" Some of the anger's gone from Willow's voice.

She's not dead.

"Are you okay?" she asks, coming from the bathroom. That static sound, it's the shower she's running for me. "Are you bleeding?"

"You can see that?" I ask and her face goes uncertain as she squats next to me.

"Look at me," she says, staring worriedly into my eyes.

153

"Where is this blood—"

My vision tunnels. My heartbeat stops, starts again, chugs twice hard. A palm taps against my cheek, rousing me from the black.

"Come on. Wake up," Willow says, and from the slightly desperate note in her tone, I'm sure it's not the first time she's tried. "Please, don't do this to me."

Slumped against Willow's side, I settle for unrolling my eyes from somewhere within my skull. When I struggle a desperate breath, the air is thick with blood and death. I gag hard and halfway through it, the sound changes, echoing. Willow has the small trash can in front of my mouth. My guts empty.

Soon, I'm spent, half-heartedly dry heaving. After a few false starts, she lowers the makeshift bucket to the carpet.

"We gotta go," she says. There's no room for argument, no pity for me. One of her hands rubs my shoulder blade. "Come on, Roanoke."

"Wait," I mutter as I crawl myself onto all fours. "Wait. The demon. A week ago. She..."

A voice murmurs my name, but it's not Willow. *Let's not talk about that with her*, it says.

Though my brain is muddled, those words hit crystal clear. I give my head a rough shake to cast them off. "She was...she..."

She was with me a week ago, and now she's dead. I can't get the sentence out.

Aren't you tired? that soothing voice croons. The cadence lulls me away from consciousness. I have to focus. I have to fix this. Those bodies, the dead and the missing, they're all women the demon fed from.

And Willow is next on that list. I have to warn her. Save her.

Shh, the voice whispers. *Your body is shutting down, Ro. Let it happen. I'm right here with you.*

"Roanoke?" Willow's fingers press against my neck to take my pulse, but her touch only serves to shove me loose of myself.

Help, I think. *Call me back. Keep me here.* But it's already too late. I'm gone and ghosting into the silent dark.

CHAPTER 13

WILLOW

Fourteen hours into my easy babysitting gig and Roanoke is overdosing, there's a dead body in his hotel bed, and I'm fucked.

Totally fucked.

I have no idea how to fix any of this.

"Jesus Christ, please don't die on me," I beg as his eyes roll into his head. His pulse stutters against my fingertips as I tip him until he's lying on the floor. That demon he insists will keep him alive had better not pick tonight to quit. He's breathing in uneven gasps, but he *is* breathing.

"Fuck!" I stand to pace. "Okay. I need a second to figure this out."

The dead woman's raised tank top exposes her stomach. Scrapes and cuts cover her arms, but they're superficial. I can't tell at a glance what killed her, but this room isn't our crime scene. The swath of gore on the sheets shows they placed her here after.

Roanoke didn't do it. The thought hums through me, my only comfort.

Someone knocks on the door.

"Shit," I chirp and then, horrified, clamp my mouth shut. What if it's the front desk with a noise complaint? What if this dead girl was screaming ten minutes before we walked in here? What if they called the police?

The knock sounds again.

I glance at Roanoke long enough to watch his chest rise with an inhale, at the body on the bed, at the door. "Yes?" I call as I creep toward it.

No answer.

My palms press against the cold metal. My eye finds the peep hole. Ice blond spikes and colorful tattoos walleye in front of me as Carter, the bass player, lifts his head.

"Oh, thank God," I whisper. Before he raises his knuckles again, I open the door a crack. "Hi. Not a good time."

His brow furrows. "Where's Ro?"

"Uh..." I glance behind me and swing the door open for him to glimpse the scene.

He surveys, eyes ever widening. A smirk ticks the corner of his mouth. "Sobriety's going well, then?"

At my pitiful sigh, he squeezes my shoulder and brushes past me into the room. "From personal experience," he says as he kneels. He tilts Roanoke's head to the side. "It's messier if he chokes on the vomit."

I should have thought of that. Why didn't I think of that? I need to calm down, but fight or flight keeps trying to kick in.

"Willow?" Carter points a finger at the corpse on the bed. "What happened?"

"We got back from the bar. I went to run him a shower. Someone dumped her before that." I'm too focused on Roanoke. "He's not good, is he?"

Carter notices the change in me. "Make sure she's really dead, okay?" he says.

I nod, turn my attention to the body and move toward the bed again. Bloody doesn't mean anything and with supernaturals, I know not to accept lack of pulse as definitive proof of anything. Still, her eyes are fixed and dilated, and while rigor mortis hasn't fully set in, it's starting.

"She was here when you walked in?" Carter asks.

"Yeah," I say, my voice tight with nerves. "Roanoke found her." *I missed it*, I almost say.

There's a pause. "Where'd you find *him*? Closest bar?" he asks. When I don't answer, he chuffs an annoyed sound. "Was he with Nigel?"

I nod as I roll the woman's hand and snap a picture of her tattoos, then several of her face and profile. I riffle through her pockets, but there's no ID, nothing.

"Fuck Nigel," Carter growls. I startle at the vehemence in his voice and glance to find him scowling at an unconscious Roanoke.

"I'm sorry," I say. The words are out before I can stop them. When the Winnebago parked and the rest of The Raven Shakes came into the lobby, they walked past me without a word. My first test, and I failed them. It won't happen again. "He said he was right behind me, and I left with my driver and—"

Carter's bitter laugh cuts me off. "You can't think Ro hasn't given each of us the slip at some point." He gives his head a slow shake as the faux amusement falls away. His voice lowers to a hurt whisper. "Please don't give up on him, Willow. I know you didn't sign up for this."

My first impression of Carter at breakfast was pure judgement based on his looks, the edgy tattoos, his bleached hair, the snarly disposition. But he'd been the first one to admit he worried about Roanoke. And he'd been the only member of the band to come check on the singer tonight.

"I'm not going anywhere," I promise.

In the silence that follows, I don't know what to say. It's Carter who finally speaks. "He's going to get worse. That girl," he says, pointing to the dead body behind me. "God, he..."

"He didn't kill her," I insist.

"Of course not, but whoever did? Whoever put her here? They're doing this to torture him. He'll blame himself. If he found her, he'll put it together." He groans in frustration and pinches the bridge of his nose. "I should have known Ro was at the center of this."

"Carter," I say. "Do you know who's doing this?"

He shakes his head and I slump. "I've racked my brain. Everyone loves Ro," he says. Another long moment passes. "What happens? To her?"

"I'm going to handle it," I say quietly. "I'm going to protect your band from the fallout like your label hired me to do, and I'm going to stop whoever did this."

"How?" he asks.

I ignore his question. "Can you move Roanoke to my room next door? Stay with him until I can get there? It could be a while."

He rises. "I don't want to know what's going to happen in here, do I?"

I sniff a discouraged laugh. "Nope."

I help Carter lug Roanoke onto his shoulder. He jostles his weight and staggers toward the door. "Open that for me," he says with a grunt. "And yours if you could?"

"On it." I brush past him and use the keycard to open the door to my room.

"On your bed, cool?"

I nod. "I need to make some phone calls."

With a groan, Carter plops Roanoke onto my bed. "Go do your thing. I've got him."

Roanoke doesn't flinch as he bounces roughly before settling on the quilt. I'm furious with him, but I'm more furious with myself. It takes everything in me to not reach out and stroke his cheek. "You're sure he's safe?" I ask Carter.

His brow furrows and I resist breaking his gaze as he studies me. I expect him to call me out on my confused feelings for Roanoke, but he stands to run a hand through his hair.

"If you hadn't tracked him down..." he starts and then trails off. The intimidating tattoos on his arms fade to their black outlines as if briefly forgotten in his distraction before they flare with color again.

If I hadn't tracked down Roanoke, there were two probable

outcomes. One, he never made it back and housekeeping found that body in the morning. Or, two, he came back here alone and crashed out, oblivious, in the bed. Woke up to her cold and stiff beside him. *That would've been some trauma*, I think indignantly.

At least with how fucked up he is, Roanoke likely won't remember finding her. I shiver. "I'm going to go get whatever clues I can from that poor girl," I say as I make it to the door. When I reach it, I turn to him. "Carter? Thank you."

He juts his chin at me, settles into an overstuffed chair, and slings a leg over one arm of it. "No rush," he says as if organizing a body disposal and watching his wildly intoxicated bandmate is a normal day. "Hey, Willow?"

I raise an eyebrow.

He reclines crosswise in the chair and knocks his interlocked hands behind his head. "Don't take off on us, okay?"

Two hours later, a tiny tap rips me from my fugue state. I snap alert and open the door to find two extremely normal looking teen girls, all white teethed smiles and polite hellos.

Confused and still not fully awake, I zone out as they lug a plastic tote into the room.

The taller blonde wipes her forehead in mock exhaustion with a laugh while the other pops the lid off the tote and then pauses with it lifted. I glimpse chemicals and solvents and what I think is...an ax?

She raises an eyebrow at me and lowers the lid. "Is there something else you need?" she asks.

"Uh...did you...shouldn't I help?" I ask.

Her face scrunches as if I'm being adorably naïve. "That is the sweetest!" she says, her voice pitching higher. "No, honey, we've got this. It's why we're paid the big bucks!"

"Oh, that's right! Pay," I blurt. "Do you need cash or?"

The blonde waves me off, grinning all the while. "It's taken care of."

"Taken care of," the other echoes.

When I look over at the corpse in the bed, a strange fuzziness creeps through my brain. "She...can you get her home to her family?" I ask.

A hand touches my arm and I startle. Part of me forgot they were here as impossible as that sounds. Before I turn toward the two girls, I can't picture them. Their features skate through my memory like skipping stones. "You should go," one of them says, her voice soothing.

I have the presence of mind to know she's using some sort of supernatural sway on me, and they're overpowering the protection of Sloane's blood. Whatever they are and whatever they're going to do, I don't want to be a part of it. Plus, if I piss them off and they leave, what do I do then? Or what if they decide I'm a problem?

"Thanks," I say as I grab Roanoke's suitcase. I repacked his things early on during my wait, not wanting to abandon his stuff for him to collect tomorrow.

When I unlock the door to my room, Carter is where I left him, draped across the armchair, and now asleep. I'm surprised to find he looks exactly the same as he did awake. With the way his tattoos occasionally falter in and out of reality, I attributed other elements of his appearance to shapeshifting. His cheek-bones *must* be a mirage. Yet everything about him holds steady though he's snoring.

"Carter?" I whisper.

He bolts upright, sights me and grimaces, rubbing at his neck. "Fuck," he groans.

A split second later, he glances over to check on Roanoke, who doesn't look like he's moved an inch since I left.

"Thanks for staying," I say.

He grunts in response and struggles to his feet. "Everything good?"

"Yeah," I say.

With a sleepy sigh, he leans forward and tips his phone on the side table toward him. "I was only out five minutes. I set an alarm to check on him every fifteen." He yawns and stands. "He mumbled your name half an hour ago."

My attention flicks to Carter. "What?"

He smirks. "I won't rib the shit out of him about it *if* you keep your mouth shut about me coming here." At my confused look, he runs a hand through his haphazard blonde spikes. "Everyone knows I'm an asshole. Can't have that jeopardized."

A surprised chuckle breaks from me. "I can do that."

"Morning's gonna be rough," he says. "He's gonna feel shitty for ditching you and shittier about that girl."

"He won't remember."

"He will," Carter insists.

I cock a hand on my hip. "So, you're asking me to go easy on him?"

Carter moves to the door. "Fuck no," he says. "Might be your only opportunity to get through to him. Make it count, Willow."

Long after Carter's gone, the click of the automatic lock engaging behind him, his words sink in.

Exhaustion flickers at the edges of my consciousness. I've been running on fumes since the adrenaline of the concert wore off on the car ride back to the hotel alone. I could probably get away with passing the night scrolling through my phone or watching late night television, all the things I normally do until the sun rises and I muddle through a couple broken hours of sleep.

Fucking Blake, I think. I haven't had a decent night's shut eye since I walked through the werewolf's door for the last time.

That's not true though.

I glance at Roanoke's unconscious form and remember how disoriented I'd been to wake up and find him missing in Austin, not because he ghosted, but because I actually slept deeply enough for him *to* ghost me.

I wonder if it's a habit of his leaving like that. Being an incubus doesn't exactly lend well to relationships. This one has written songs about cutting ties before dawn.

I creep around the other side of the king-sized bed. If I'm going to be checking his pulse every few minutes, I may as well make things easy on myself.

Climbing in fully clothed, I leave a careful distance between Roanoke and I and stretch out, staring at the ceiling.

In the silence, I realize I can't hear him breathing. "Are you awake?" I ask.

It's not like I expect him to answer. It's a 'Who's there?' shouted into a dark room.

"Roanoke?" His name escapes me in a hush as I nudge closer. "Are you alive?" I snake an arm over his ribs, scooting forward to get the angle I need to press my hand against his chest.

His heartbeat pounds against my palm, too hard, but steady. I slump in relief, my head falling to rest against the other half of the pillow he's lying on. I don't move my arm.

I haven't had time to check the internet and see what sort of damage his little romp around town caused. Or what his declaration onstage trended for hashtags. Or to figure out the identity of the dead girl.

It was pure chance that I ended up in his hotel room. At least I handled it. In the silence, I listen for any noises from next door. Running water. Body dissolving sounds. Chopping.

My imagination spits horrific images, scared away by the bump of Roanoke's heartbeat against my palm. It soothes me. Slowly, by degrees, I relax against him, time my breathing to his quiet inhales and exhales.

It's hours until dawn. I have no hope of sleep. All I can do is wait until morning and pray I can pass his last wild night off as planned to the record company.

Because there's no way in hell the entire world won't know about us being together at that bar come morning.

● ● ● ● ● ● ● ● ● ●

*B*lake's eyeing me, his hungry gaze ripping over my bare skin. *My shirt is in tatters. Blood slithers down my wounded arm to plop fast against the tiled floor. I'm cornered, exhausted from running. He knows he's beaten me.*

Fight me, *he whispers. His fingers drift through my sweaty hair as he brushes it away from my cheek.* I love it when you fight me, Willow.

I inhale through my clenched teeth, blood bubbling in one of my lungs. On the floor behind him is the dead girl with the tattoos on her knuckles. She winks at me.

One chance, *I think desperately.*

I slam my head forward. Blake's nose collapses in a crunch of bone under the crown of my skull. Where's his cry of pain? Why isn't his hold loosening?

I glance up at Blake's quiet laugh. There's not a mark on him.

I told you I'd find you, *Blake whispers. His fingers grind my bones where he has my wrists pinned against the wall.* I'm going to finish the job.

In the hazy distance, I hear the far-off echo of my name. My eyes flash to the dead girl, but she's gone. Blake's lip lifts in a snarl as his chin lengthens into a muzzle, shifting into a wolf.

But someone's searching for me. Someone's coming.

Damn him, *Blake says, the words garbled in his changing mouth as he turns toward the sound.*

I'm here! *I scream.*

Blake's yellowed eyes flicker across mine, cold and calculating. His hand drops from my wrist and fists. Whatever he plans to do next is going to hurt.

You think that incubus can keep me away? *he asks.*

"Roanoke!" I call.

Shut up, Willow, *Blake demands.*

"Roanoke! Please! Help me!"

"I've got you," Roanoke whispers in my ear.

Blake dissolves. The kitchen cabinets melt. The cool tile below my feet is gone as I ease into the empty space, my toes leaving the ground. The scent of citrus and sweat twinges at a memory that won't come. *Safe*, I think. *I'm safe.*

I'm enveloped in Roanoke's muscular arms. His hand rubs up my spine and cups against my neck, drawing me nearer. "I've got you," he murmurs.

The dream shifts from terror to temptation. And then I'm kissing him. My mouth finds his, a slight bite of his lip enticing him to open to me, kiss me back. He tastes like fresh toothpaste. The carnal craving I've been warring against wins out. "Touch me," I plead, edging one of his hands to the waistband of my shorts. "I need you to touch me." I nip at his jaw. "I need you to fuck me."

His entire body goes rigid, including the part of him pressed against my leg. I grind against it because I can, because in dreams there are no consequences and even if this is only a dream, I want him so badly that I'm already slick with need, achy.

He grips my hip, the fabric of my shorts bunching under his touch. "You want me to fuck you?" he asks, his tone strange.

When I nod, his mouth finds mine. His kiss isn't a question anymore. I match his hunger with my own, throbbing with relief as his fingers edge between my legs, my own hand delving into his boxers to his thickening cock. "I thought you'd never give in," I murmur as I stroke him.

And then as quickly as it vanished, his control snaps into place. "Wait," he chokes, rearing back from me as he shoves my hands off him. "We can't do this. Christ, I've never wanted anything more but I—"

My eyes pop open. Reality slams into me. We're in bed together, my legs still entwined with his.

"What?" I blurt as I take in the room, frantic in my attempt to orient myself. Hotel. Not Blake's kitchen. Hotel with Roanoke. "Oh my god, I thought I was dreaming."

His blue eyes skip over mine. "I should have known," he says finally as I move to the edge of the mattress, clawing my fingers into my hair. "You were having a nightmare. Before we—"

"So, you cuddled me?" I sound absurd.

"You were flailing, and I couldn't wake you up and you said my—" He cuts off abruptly.

I said his name. In the dream, Roanoke was my only chance to save myself. I untangle from him, suddenly aware of all the places we're still touching. The throb between my legs betrays me, wet and longing for every inch of his cock.

"It's fine," I say. Foggy details drift through my mind. Blake. The scent of blood and terror. "You're right. I was having a nightmare."

His touch drifts over my shoulders before he squeezes my upper arms. "What was it about?"

The answer's obvious, at least the last part of the dream. But I'm too embarrassed, the closeness of him too intimate. Instead,

I lie. "That you took a handful of pills and blew everything we were supposed to be working toward together." I force my mouth into a snarl. "Oh wait," I say, my tone thick with sarcasm. "That was last night."

Roanoke sighs and then goes quiet. "It won't happen again."

I sniff a dismissive laugh. "Right," I say as I rotate to him. "Because you promise?"

He winces.

"Do you remember the body, Roanoke?" I ask. I'm hurting him because *I'm* hurt and ashamed and scared of how much I want to kiss him again and I'm afraid if I stop the words spilling from me, I'm going to, which is entirely fucked up considering what I'm saying. "The dead girl you found in your bed?"

He's saved from answering by a volley of pounding sounds from the door. We both turn. I climb up and over him awkwardly, desperate to get some distance between us. My feet hit the floor and a second later I'm clutching the knob. I pause.

"Who is it?" I ask as my eye nears the peephole.

"It's December. You didn't answer your cell."

My phone's tucked in the pocket of the jean shorts I'm wearing, on silent since last night. I crack open the heavy hotel door. "Hey," I say, my voice still raspy with sleep.

Her arms cross over her chest, but not in a hostile way. More like she's trying to hold herself together, her fingers gripped tight around her upper arms. "Is he here?" the siren says.

"Who?" I'm not sure how I want to play this yet.

She stares at me. "You...don't remember what happened last night?" Her eyebrows raise as if to prod me. "With Roanoke?

What he did to you? I saw the pictures."

I freeze. Shit.

"What did you see?" I ask. I need to know what hit the press, what rumors circulated while I slept wrapped in his goddamn arms.

While I slept.

I glance back at the bed in disbelief. At the edges of the blackout curtains, there's sunlight. It's well into morning. I slept for *hours*.

December fidgets, one hand delving to tug at the pleats in her skirt as I fight my attention to her. "He hates using his sway," she says finally, the words bleak and clipped. "No matter how fucked up he is. Still, I should have gone with you." She presses her lips together, distress blooming in her expression. "I never thought he'd do that to you."

My mind spins through last night. Discovering Roanoke's location through the photos posted on the Timber Boom account. Catching an Uber from the hotel to the venue and walking the block to the bar.

December's voice lowers as she leans closer to me. "There's a video, too."

"A video of me?" I repeat. For a split second, I'm afraid Roanoke did somehow wipe my mind clean. But that's impossible.

"Of you at the bar," she spits out. "Doing shots. Toasting." The last word bursts from her like a curse.

Relief spills through me. "December, it's not—"

"He made you drink." Her gaze flickers across mine, a terrible fear in her eyes. "What else did he make you do, Willow?"

In December's expression, I watch everything she knows of Roanoke dissolving into chaos.

I have to fix this. He made a mistake going out last night, but everything after is snowballing in a direction he doesn't deserve. "If you'd let me explain," I start.

"Explain?" She exhales, her brow pinched. "You were at the bar with him. I saw the video. The entire internet is freaking out about you two being together and—"

The door yanks out of my hand as I struggle for words. Roanoke leans against the edge.

"Hey, December," he says. He sounds utterly broken. Some of his hair has come loose from the tie I gave him last night, wild wisps and flyaways surrounding his head. A dark shadow of stubble hardens the line of his jaw, but despite it, I see the splotch of red where I nipped him minutes ago. Heat flushes through me.

December flicks back and forth between me and Roanoke before a sound of utter contempt breaks from her. "Wow," she says.

Roanoke stands silent.

I resist the urge to take the lead. Honestly, I'm curious to hear what he remembers about last night. December's eyes blaze a pale green that almost glows in the dimly lit room.

"You promised me," she snarls at him. "You sat in that bunk, and you promised you were going to get your shit together. Is this what you meant?" She draws a breath. It's not because she's done. This girl is a hurricane, and Roanoke seems aware he's caught in the center. There's nothing to do but brace. "You *asshole*."

She smashes past me. I close the door and lean against it, unsure if I should step in as she follows his retreat. When he hits the wall, her palm splays against it at his side.

"How fucked up was he?" She tosses an angry sneer at Roanoke, though her words are meant for me. "When you tracked him down in whatever shithole Nigel was posting from?"

"Dec, please," Roanoke whispers.

Fury sharpens her features. "I don't know you anymore," she spits. "Did you black out? Do you even remember feeding off Willow?"

"It's not like that!" I cut in.

December holds out an arm to point a shaking finger at me as she glares him down. "Do you know what she said yesterday? She said you were a good guy," she says, emphasizing the last two words. "She was determined to get you clean, to help us, and hours later, you expect me to believe Willow fucking Taverson one-eightied? Doing shots with you? Spreading her legs for you? All of her own free will?"

The accusation hangs in the air between the three of us.

Her gaze strays to me again and pauses, waiting for a reaction to what she thought would be an epiphany.

"You think I forced her?" He says it so quietly, I barely hear him.

December's face falters. "No, that's not what I—"

"That's exactly what you meant." Roanoke's tone is heartbreakingly matter of fact. "You can call me a drunk. A liar. A selfish fuckup. I am *all* those things. But don't you ever call me a rapist."

The snarl uncurls from December's mouth. "Ro, I didn't mean.... You wouldn't." Her attention flicks my direction, a question in her expression.

The confusion on her face only grows as I shift a step closer to Roanoke. It might look subconscious, except it's anything but. Despite our rough awakening, I want him to be aware I'm on his side, that when it comes down to it, I'll choose him. He has to trust me to lean on me for support.

"There were a lot of cameras at that bar," I say. "After the concert last night, everyone thinks he and I were out being public about our happiness for the first time. I had to play along."

December's brow furrows. What I'm saying makes sense. She knows it. And then that hard snarl returns. "And then you two pounded a couple of drinks and scurried here for a romp in the sheets?"

Roanoke opens his mouth, and I can see the denial forming.

"Christ, Ro, you're really going to let her believe she had a say? Look at her!" she snaps, one hand gesturing toward me as an afterthought. "I knew she never had a chance. How is some normal human supposed to control you when you bat your lashes and get whatever the fuck you want?"

For the first time since her accusations started, Roanoke lifts his head. His gaze steels. *Welcome back*, I think.

"You know damn well," he grinds out. "I don't use my sway like that."

The side of my body closest to him breaks out in goose-bumps, a visceral reaction to the power rippling under the surface of his skin.

"December," I say. She tears her attention off Roanoke. I'm expecting anger in her eyes, but there's only sadness. "Sing."

The siren freezes. "What? No!" she says instantly.

Roanoke turns to me in surprise. "Her, too?" he asks.

I nod.

"Do it," Roanoke says to December, almost as if daring her. "Try to lure Willow to you. Try to get her to do anything."

Her head tilts, considering.

After what I saw in the crowd last night, she has the potential to be the most dangerous person in this room. Still, his challenge and my permission give her the okay.

She licks her lips and parts them. A single note drifts from her mouth, subdued but so pure I'm almost certain I can see it, a mist, tangible. It's beautiful, and sorrowful, and so, so quiet, and then it falters.

"Keep singing," Roanoke demands through clenched teeth.

December's eyes go pained. She picks up the note again and I catch a movement. Her gaze shifts there, too. It's Roanoke. His head bobs. It reminds me of his drunken stupor last night and then he snaps straight. His face relaxes as he locks on her, one hand reaching for the siren as if asking her to dance.

"Roanoke?" I manage.

He doesn't blink. Doesn't acknowledge me as he stumbles toward her. I reach, intent on stopping him, but he slides through my fingers in a lurch.

"Stop," I beg December. "What are you doing to him?"

Her song swells.

"How much proof do you need?" I ask, exasperated.

December slams a hand over her mouth, staring at me in shock. "How?" she blurts around her fingers, but I ignore her.

Roanoke shivers and seems to come into himself. I press my hands on either side of his jaw, using my touch to reassure myself he's okay. His eyelids flutter and then he focuses on me.

"You back?" I ask.

He squints, blinking before he nods.

It's unsettling, the way he became a puppet for her. I wonder what December's capable of. My brain catches on religions, devoted cultists following her blindly for a few hummed bars. They could destroy the world, this band, if they wanted.

Roanoke's fingers slide between mine on his cheek. "Are *you* okay?"

I nod, lowering our clasped hands. When I turn, December's focused on them, her expression tight as if she's trying to puzzle out a riddle.

"You've got some kind of immunity to me?" she says, slowly, testing the idea. Understanding dawns on her. "You're immune to *him*. Holy shit."

December leans from me. I'm not sure if she wants to process me in this new light, or if some part of her fears me now that she knows she has no control over me. I don't want her to see me as a threat, but I won't back down either.

She bites her lip and that wrinkle to her brow returns as she lifts her face to Roanoke. "So, you going out with Nigel? That was..."

"Me fucking up," he admits. "For the last time. I swear."

There's a subtle change to December's expression, a hardening. I wonder how many times he's offered that excuse.

"When I got him to his room, there was another body," I say. She freezes.

"It's taken care of," I tell her. "And I will loop you in on everything, I swear. Just give me a couple of hours to sort this out."

"But—"

"One hour," I compromise.

She makes a small noise of acceptance as her gaze drifts downward. I'm still holding Roanoke's hand. I should drop it, but I don't appreciate the implication she caught me at something. He's a friend—no, a client—I'm comforting. I'm not doing anything wrong.

December's eyes flick from Roanoke to me and back. "You two really haven't—"

"Get out." Roanoke's tone is sharp enough that I startle alongside her.

She winds her fingers around a lock of her blonde hair. "Ro, what's—"

He smirks. "Oh, we're all cool again? You forget I couldn't handle a single night in and I forget you accused me of being a fucking rapist?"

The little color in December's face drains. "After the show, you disappeared! I was scared for you." With each word, her tone becomes more urgent. "I was scared for her!"

He winces at the last sentence, and his fingers flex between mine before his grip tightens. It's only then I feel the tremble in his touch. I squeeze.

"Get out," he says again.

This time, December listens.

CHAPTER 14

ROANOKE

The door closes solidly behind December. The finality of the thud cuts through me. *You know me,* I want to scream into the hall after her. *You fucking know I would never do that to anyone!*

"Roanoke?" Willow's hand still clasps mine. There's trepidation in her tone.

She is *afraid of me.* My jaw aches, clenched tight. I blew it. Everyone's writing me off.

"Ro? Are you okay?"

It's the first time she's called me by a nickname. Coming from her, the familiarity of it snakes through me, coils around my chest. Without a word, I drop her hand and bolt for the bathroom, twist the sink knob onto full cold and jam my face under the stream. I stay there until my cheek numbs, waiting to see if my stomach revolts and I need to throw up. When I don't, I swallow a few mouthfuls of the icy water and finally slide free, gripping the edge of the porcelain, dripping on the white tiles.

I strip a coarse towel off the bar and dry where the water flowed across my face and into my hair.

Willow's immune to December.

My brain feels like it's been paused and is skipping frantically to catch up, missing big chunks of information. Nothing about Willow makes a damn bit of sense.

I hear a door close.

For a second, I think maybe she wised up and took off, but her suitcases are on the floor at the end of the bed, open and overflowing with colors. Mine is beside them, zipped shut.

I don't remember how I got here. Blinking hard, I struggle for memories. Snapshots. Anything. A voice tumbles through my mind. *Shh*, it whispers, and I remember the slip of the quilt across the sheets of my bed.

Clouded eyes and card suits.

Adrenaline flushes my system. What happened next? What happened after I found her? I don't know. I don't know, I don't know, I don't—

A click sounds from the locking mechanism and Willow elbows the door open. In her hands are two cans of soda from the vending machine a few doors down.

She holds one out to me. "Ginger Ale?" she asks.

"Yeah," I say, grateful as I take it. "Thanks."

We both stand in silence for a long moment before Willow speaks. "December talked to me a bit yesterday," she says. "She's really worried about you. After she saw me at the bar with you last night, she must have thought—"

"She knows what it means to be an incubus." I shrug a shoulder, as if I'm not bleeding out from the betrayal of December's accusations. "She assumed the worst."

A bead of condensation slides down the metal of the can. I think briefly about running it over my forehead. Instead, I crack the top, cold fizz spraying across my knuckle.

"But...why?" Willow presses. "Consent seems like it's a sticking point for you," she says and quickly adds, "Not that it shouldn't be. It's just, most guys aren't so careful."

I scoff. "Don't give me credit for bare minimum humanity." My throat is suddenly parched. I take a swig of the soda straight from the can. "But after what was done to me? Yeah, it's important." The nausea in my unsettled gut is growing stronger. "There's a reason December jumped to the conclusion she did."

Willow sits at the table and cracks open her drink, pouring half of it into one of the glass tumblers after removing the paper cover. Her eyes flash pointedly to the chair across from her. I sink into it, my can making a sad little clink as I touch it to the table.

"Can you tell me?" she asks.

I move a hand absently to my ribcage, not sure exactly where the damned thing is. "I have seven days, eight max, before it has to be fed. Because I know the cost, I hold out as long as is safely possible."

The rare others I've met revel in what they are. Permission is a thing of the past. They fuck who they want, where and when they want. A bit of sway, a bump of power, and 'no' means anything they want it to.

But that's not me. "About day five, I get the shakes. I can't focus. It *claws* at me, Willow. From the inside. I feel everything."

I watch the color drain from her cheeks.

"After about ten days..." I wipe my palms against my knees. "The demon takes over my body and it *will* feed. Consent or no." I lift the can to my mouth and take a hard, quick swallow. The carbonation burns, but not as much as the shame. "I've never let things go that far," I say, because despite everything, it's important to me she knows that, too. "I never will. That's why what December said was so fucked up. She thinks I'm spiraling. If she thinks I'd *ever*..."

I can't make myself say the words.

"You said consent was important after what was done to you?" she asks before her voice falls quieter. "What was done to you, Roanoke?"

When I don't go on, Willow does. "Does it have to do with how you were made into an incubus?"

A picture of Cassandra flares in my brain and I can't stave off my instinct to recoil. "She singled me out at a gig," I say. "Some shitty dive outside Chicago, near where I used to live. Drew me off the stage mid-song. I never had a prayer of escaping her."

I've got glazed memories of those months. Flashes of need so intense I thought I'd turn inside out like a salted slug. "I gave her everything I had, more, while she let that thing eat me alive." I can't look at Willow. If I do, I'll never finish. "I thought that's what love was supposed to feel like. Intense. All-consuming."

The words are all wrong, too little to make Willow understand. I try again.

"I would have swallowed acid if my voice fell short of pleasing her." I drill a finger against the tabletop. "If she had hinted," I say slowly. "That it would have made her happy, I would have cut off my hands."

Twin lines dig between Willow's eyes, and I wonder if I've taken the explanation too far or not far enough.

"I've never found a high like being with her and believe me, I fucking tried." I let out a soft sniff of embarrassment. "I thought it was real. I thought—" The word chokes off. "I thought I wanted it."

"Jesus, Roanoke," Willow whispers.

"She spent months preparing me, though I didn't know it. I was so sick and growing weaker. I barely noticed. All that mattered was her. And then one day, she explained she'd taken every bit of my life force. She laid out my choice," I say, emphasizing the last word. "I take in the demon, and become an incubus, or I'm dead in a couple of hours."

Willow raises her elbows onto the table, one of them bent, her palm supporting her head. "And you chose to live."

"Fuck yeah, I chose to live!" I say incredulously. "What would you have done?"

Her mouth opens. She hesitates.

For a heartbreaking second, I expect her to tell me I made the wrong choice. That I'm evil. Wicked. All the thoughts that run constantly through my head, worsening as the demon's hunger grows.

"It's not a fair question to ask me," she says. "I've seen the dark side of the supernatural world. That's what I help you guys come back from."

"How?" The word escapes, raw and ravaged. I lick my lips and press them shut before I make things worse.

"Well, I'll start with the guilt you're—"

"No," I snap, cutting her off. "How are you not getting this? I can't be fixed!" My voice raises. "Even if I didn't force you into the sex, I helped this demon rip years from your life." I stab a finger against my chest. "I'm fucking complicit! I'm a monster, Willow!"

Her expression eases into pity. "You're not a monster. You're surviving."

A chill rushes through me and at first I assume it's goose-bumps, some bodily reaction to her words being truth. Then, I feel the pinpricks of claws as the demon skitters up my spine from the inside.

An image swims through my mind. The wriggle and shudder as it crawled from Cassandra's mouth to mine, the choking fear as it slithered down my throat. And suddenly in front of me sat a sunken-eyed girl a year or two younger than me. She looked worn through, a war zone, her dirty hair lank and dull. In most of my memories, her eyes shine electric blue. In this one, they're a pale smudge. She must have seen the shock roll over me, the confusion. Without the demon's sway, I felt nothing for her.

Only then did I realize the extent of what she'd done to me.

She never explained why she chose me. She never apologized. She simply plodded away to suffer through the last minutes of her life alone.

"Ro?" Willow says. Her voice drags me to the present as she leaves her spot to kneel in front of my chair. "You are not a monster."

Except she's wrong.

"Card suits," I say. "Across her knuckles."

Willow blinks before she catches onto the subject change. "You remember last night?"

She's half right. "I remember the tattoos from Denver. From a week ago."

"Oh," Willow says. Her throat bobs as she swallows hard. "She was the last one you—"

My dread wells. "No."

"She wasn't the last girl you were with?" she says, confused.

I lock eyes with her. "You were the last."

"So that means," she says. She's still kneeling in front of where I'm sitting on the chair. "I'm next, then."

"Fuck," I whisper, my voice all shock while the truth of my statement sinks in. Willow's next. I mean, I knew. On some level, I knew, but... "That's not going to happen to you."

She sniffs as if in disagreement. What can I say to a person who's been poring over pictures of murdered and missing women for the last day and just discovered I unintentionally set her up to be one of them?

"You weren't at our show," I remind her, aware of how panicked I sound. "I rode to the hotel with the band that night and that's where I left from. No one followed me. I made sure. You weren't at the show, so no one knows about you. Right?"

She pauses. "You *made sure*." Her tongue flicks to wet her lips. "You knew this was tied to you then and you didn't tell me?"

"No," I say, adamant before I backpedal. "I mean, maybe I... I thought if there was a chance..."

She nods abruptly and stands. "Don't sweat it," she says. "This is the opposite of a problem."

I watch her in disbelief. "How do you figure?"

"Leaving that corpse in your bed was personal. You recognized her tattoos. This wasn't random. They're not after December or Carter or Damien."

"And they're what, trying to get me busted for murder?"

Willow shrugs. "If they can't kill you, they're killing the women you're with?" she guesses.

"Why?"

"Jealousy? Someone you were with who's jealous of the women you sleep with?" she offers before her face scrunches. "Could it be your ex who—"

"She's not my ex," I say. "We were never together. It wasn't real."

Willow watches me.

Eventually, I shake my head. "She's dead. She passed the demon on to me. It, uh..." I hesitate as my voice falls to a strained whisper. "It does a lot of damage, making a home in there for itself. Once it's gone, things fall apart. No one survives without it."

I don't have a way out of this alive.

"As for someone being jealous?" I go on. "There's a reason I didn't remember any of them were with me until I spotted her tattoos." Humiliation slows my words. I have to clear my throat before I can go on. "Look, I have to keep the demon fed.

It uses my body to make that happen. But me? Whether I'm coherent? Hell, whether I'm conscious? It's never been a deal breaker. Everyone takes what they want. End of transaction."

For a long moment, Willow says nothing. "Me," she whispers. "I did that to you, too, didn't I?"

"No," I say instantly. "You were different."

"I bet," she mumbles. From her tone, she doesn't believe me. She paces, head down. "Once we got to the hotel, you started in with the coke, the whiskey. You were fucked up. I should have stopped things before we—"

I get to my feet and slide myself into her path. She stops a few inches from me. "You said for this to work, we have to be honest with each other, right?" I ask.

She won't look at me. I tuck two fingers under her chin and lift her eyes to mine. At the shine in them, I frown. "I get that this is a job for you. That I'm a paycheck. But that night, I wasn't, so it's okay for me to tell you, I didn't want it to end. When I said I wished I could see you again? I meant that. Maybe not like this," I add with a halfhearted chuckle. "But I meant it, okay?"

"Okay." The word leaves her, barely a breath.

I say her name. "What are you?"

She meets my eyes again. "What do you mean?" she asks.

"December went siren on you, and you're immune to me," I venture, because it seems as good of an entry point to this conversation as any. "What are you?"

She tilts her head and I drop my fingers from underneath her chin. "If I tell you this," she says. "It stays between us."

I nod.

"I needed to be at one hundred percent for this job, and I wasn't," she says. "I had a wound leftover from a fight."

Someone hurt her. My stomach clenches at the thought of anyone leaving a mark on her that she'd use the word wound to describe.

I can't help the sweep of my gaze over the parts of her I can see. "But you're okay?"

"Yes. Vampire blood healed it. The protection against you was a carefully considered bonus," she adds.

Ouch.

I tap the sweating can beside me on the tabletop and swivel my finger through the wet ring it's left on the table. She's human. She's mortal, with an asterisk.

An urge to keep anyone else from ever laying a cruel hand on her overwhelms me. Rich promises coming from a guy who nicked a few years of her life. I might not leave scars, but I do damage just the same. I need to be sure I won't do more.

"Can we test it? Your immunity?" I ask. "Like you had December do?"

She considers me before she nods. I blow a slow exhale, unsure how to start.

"Look at me," I command.

Her eyes lift. It's almost instant, her reaction. I should have known. I don't know why I'm so disappointed. "Damn it," I manage.

There's a sudden confusion at my expression before she gets why I'm distressed. "Oh! Shit!" she says. "Sorry! That was me.

Totally me looking up and not me reacting to your incubus juju, promise."

I can't bring myself to return her smile. She watches me with a sort of removed curiosity before she clasps my hands. "I'm ready," she says. "Do it."

A rush of goosebumps prickles across my skin as I dial up the power until it radiates like heat waves surging through the air between us.

"Kiss me," I say, my voice deep and seductive. "I can't stop fantasizing about the taste of you, that sweet slit between your legs. I'm going to take my time getting there. Torture us both." I stroke her thumb the way I want to stroke her inner thigh, but don't dare. "Kiss me, Willow, and I'll make it happen."

Her focus breaks to flick down to my lips and she licks hers. I tense, sure she'll rock forward, meet my mouth. Every part of me craves that kiss, but not like this.

Willow shakes her head so slightly I almost miss it. "No."

The demon dredges its claws across my stomach. I stumble back from her in agony. I slam into the bathroom door frame and grab for it, steadying myself. Groaning, I clench my teeth, wait for the pain to subside. She ducks under my arm to stand in front of me.

"Do you believe me now?" she asks.

Her fingers tighten on my shoulder. The motion crackles across my skin like an electric volt. She knows what I am, what Cassandra did to me. She's immune to this monster inside me that colors every other interaction with doubt. Every kiss, every slip of my fingers against her skin and then inside her—she wanted it. Two nights ago in the hotel, Willow wanted to be there. One hundred percent.

And I can never have her again.

"I believe you," I say, struggling to find the words to make her understand the enormity of what she's shown me, but there's no time.

"Then believe me when I tell you that me being next on this serial killer's list is the best thing I could ask for."

When I cock my head to disagree, she ducks until she's in my sightline again.

"If it's jealousy, nothing will stoke that more than us announcing we're a couple. And if not, I'm still on the chopping block. We have almost a week to figure this out. We'll set a trap," she says. "We can stop this."

"No." I won't argue about this. "I'm not making you bait."

Willow winces, her mouth opening and closing as she hesitates before she finally says the words. "You already have, Roanoke. It's okay," she promises. "This part isn't your fault. It's helping me do my job."

I don't speak, lost in my own thoughts, the memory of those milky irises burned into my brain.

"You're helping others, too," she goes on. "December and Carter and Damien. You brought the Raven Shakes together to support each other."

Except I hadn't. I brought in December because she ravaged the drums, and her voice struck me as a dark mirror of my own. Carter's bass lines kept the crowd bouncing and his looks helped, even if sometimes keeping up with his tattoos slips his mind. And Damien. Where the hell would we be without Damien?

"I wanted you to know..." Willow falls silent.

"You can tell me." I watch her expression, surprised when it clouds with trepidation.

"I called in reinforcements. A friend of mine." Her hands raise to my shoulders as she speaks, her fingers toying with my curls like it's the most natural movement in the world. "She's meeting us for the show in New Orleans tomorrow."

"Why?" I say, distracted. The light catches the edge of Willow's cheek. I watch the glow, the way it traces her skin in all the ways I can't.

"My immunity to you isn't permanent." Her words are thin, hesitant. I almost don't register what she's said. "Sloane's going to help me with that." There's a pause. "With her blood."

"Wait." I blink. She's got to be joking. "Sloane is the vampire? Sloane Marquette?"

The laugh she lets out is almost sad. "Yup. And a fan of your band. She jumped at the chance to come hang out for a city or two."

"She listens to The Raven Shakes?" I ask, baffled, as I struggle to keep up with the conversation. "Sloane Marquette knows who I am?"

"She knows." Willow contemplates me for a long second. "She knows everything."

The words are heavy with implication.

"Oh," I say, not sure if I'm supposed to feel shamed, only that I do.

Her voice drops low. "You are...not a typical client." She pauses. "I've already crossed so many lines with you, Roanoke," she murmurs. "I can't seem to stop."

The moment feels delicate and dangerous.

"Like this morning?" I ask. When I heard her cry my name, I was brushing my teeth with a hotel toothbrush. I only wanted to comfort her, hadn't expected the kiss. Or the impossible temptation of what she begged me for after.

She nods slowly. "When she gets here, I think Sloane will be a voice of reason we both need."

"And until then?" I ask.

It's a challenge the way I say it. I want more of this liquid warmth filling my gut every time she's close, and the thrill that ran through me when she called me fantastic. I want to be fantastic for her. Maybe I could be.

I could try.

My eyes slip shut. The slightest creak fills the silence. It's the sound of her shifting. I swear I feel her, close, closer, her breath reaching out to mix with mine. She has to be the one to move. It has to be her.

Willow takes a step back from me, another. "We should check what made it online about last night. December mentioned pictures," she says quickly.

I open my eyes as she crosses to the table again. "Right," I say.

She scoops her glass of Ginger Ale up and gulps the contents. I watch her throat convulse as she swallows. When she's done, she presses the back of her hand to her mouth for a long beat. "Right," she says finally. "Let's check."

I sit down as she goes into one of her suitcases and tugs out a laptop. Once it's connected to the hotel wi-fi, she types for a bit and then waves me over.

She's not smiling.

"How bad is it?" I ask.

My hungover brain fights through the last few hours of memories before Willow got me from the bar. Shots, fun. Nothing incriminating. There aren't any gaps in my memory. Then again, one photo of me leaning into a fan's ear to be heard and they could make an exaggerated angle look like kissing.

What if I've destroyed this before it started? I glance at Willow, bent over the laptop in concentration.

End this. The thought whispers through my mind, only a smear of words across my consciousness. *Before things get more complicated.*

I think of the blues bar where I first laid eyes on her, her head thrown back with laughter she shared with no one, and the tug of curiosity drawing me toward her. The second time I saw her, in the Winnebago, when those same brown eyes that devoured me the night before shoved me out of her orbit. Backstage, the pull of her, and our kiss. Last night when I broke her trust. Push.

And here when I was so sure we were going to kiss.

Pull.

Willow glances up at me and the smile that lights up her face sends a shiver of nerves through me. *Am I alone?* I wonder. *Is she feeling any of this? Is it all in my head?*

"What'd you find?" I ask.

She spins the laptop. "Perfect," she gushes.

I'm utterly unprepared to see myself on the screen. I'm on-stage, the smoke machine's haze giving me a whole-body halo. Whoever shot the still used a long-distance lens from somewhere deep in the crowd. I grip the mic stand in one of my hands, my head tilted up slightly, a wide smile on my lips.

Inset is an oval picture of Willow in a red gown, her hair a pile of curls. She's stunning. She'd been looking at someone to her right, and the two pictures are arranged to make it look like her adoring gaze is meant for me.

Shaking Off the Blues, screams the caption in bold, black letters.

I swipe my finger across the touchpad to scroll down to the article.

The smaller subtitle reads, *Willow Taverson moves on with the swoon-worthy singer of The Raven Shakes.*

I skim the rest. There's mention of me having a wild side and a veiled reference to alleged drug use. Arguments about me being a bad influence on a grieving celebrity. Her ex is still missing.

I zero in on the last paragraph.

While her relationship with Blake Brennan was anything but drama-free, friends are rumored to be worried Taverson is going off the rails with this bluesy bad boy rocker leading the way. Not that we can blame her. We'd follow that gorgeous ass anywhere.

"Did you actually read this?" I ask quietly.

"No, just the headline." Her smile fades as she takes me in. "Why?"

"It's not good, Willow." I twist the laptop to face her. "Apparently," I start, my voice sarcastic and cold. "I'm out of control, you're slumming it, and your Hollywood crew is scared about the gutter I'm dragging you into by way of my, and I quote, gorgeous ass."

I'm utterly unprepared when Willow bursts into laughter.

"What the fuck!" I yell, frustrated.

She reads the article as I pace, her lips moving along. When she's done, she shrugs. "Well, you do have a gorgeous ass," she says.

"So, you agree with them?" I demand. "That I'm bad for you?"

The smile fades from her mouth. "You are bad for me, Roanoke," she says. "You *are* out of control. That's the reason I'm *here*."

The truth of it sucks. "Is that right," I say, more heat in it than I intended.

"You have no idea what you took with Nigel." Her arms cross over her chest. "Do you?"

I scoff, but she's right. I don't have an answer for her.

"You were worse than in Austin. It scared me." She licks her lips. "Without that demon, you'd be another body I got stuck cleaning up."

"What do you want?" I yell. "Another apology? Another promise?"

Her posture tightens. She closes the computer.

You're a predator, that voice in my head snarls. *That's why every person you're with leaves as soon as the act is done. That's why you're so caught up on this one. Immune or not, her instincts are finally kicking in.*

"Tell me what you want," I say. I can't push her away. There's a rough edge to my words. "Anything."

Willow doesn't answer.

I try something else. "What happened last night? You said you took care of the body?"

"I'll ride in the Winnebago with you guys on the drive to NoLa," she says and tucks her laptop into her bag. "There will be paparazzi outside. Count on them being around twenty-four seven. You and I will walk out of the hotel together, holding hands."

"Got it," I say. If there are cameras, she'll kiss me. I'll win her over. *I've got to find more cameras*, I think.

"We'll have to figure out a low-key way for you to feed." Willow's eyes meet mine, expressionless. "There's time. We've got six days to figure it out, right?"

My mouth is dry as dust. The thought of having sex with anyone but Willow turns my stomach, except if I'm with her, I'm siphoning her life as the demon feeds. "Technically five," I whisper.

"Are you good?" she asks suddenly.

"Am I good?" The question throws me off in its directness. "You know all about me now. What do you think?"

A flare of color starts at the base of Willow's throat and rises until her face burns red. "I meant, are you going to puke?" She hooks a thumb over her shoulder toward the bathroom. "I need to jump in the shower."

"Oh, fuck," I blurt. "Sorry. Am I... Should I wait out here? I mean, not like I'm gonna join you or..." My brain catches on an image of Willow under the spray, soap rolling over those perfect breasts and I—

What the fuck is wrong with me? Why can't I shake loose of her?

She points to the tousled sheets on the bed. "Sit. Don't move," she says, ducking down to go through her suitcase to choose her outfit. "I'll be out in three minutes."

I raise an eyebrow. "How will you know if I move?"

She frowns. "You almost blew everything yesterday. For yourself and for me."

Dropping onto the bed, I nod. "Yes, I did."

I don't know what penance will make what I did better. Maybe there isn't one.

Willow drapes a white sundress over her arm and stands. "Don't make plans for when we get to New Orleans," she says.

"Got it," I say. "In for the night."

"Nope, out for the night. Whatever daylight we have left, too," she says, stripping off her socks with a hop that sends her curls cascading to bounce against her back. She launches the socks toward her suitcase as she heads to the bathroom. "You're taking me on a date."

CHAPTER 15

WILLOW

"How do you not have any presence on social media?" I ask, my shoulder nudging into Roanoke's. I tilt my head into his and angle the phone to hide the shine of sweat on our foreheads.

It's abysmally hot in New Orleans. The wooden bench we're seated on scalds the back of my legs. I imagine a metal one would give me blisters.

After the drive from Houston to New Orleans, once we were all checked into the hotel, Roanoke and I made it to the Audubon Zoo with two hours to spare until closing. Plenty of time to get in some cute pictures I can post later tonight. In order for our ruse to be successful, we've got to keep feeding the flames. People need to be rooting for us.

I've already decided on how I'll spin the scene at the bar last night. The article Roanoke read earlier on my computer talked about how my friends were worried about me going off the rails. With Roanoke's history, it fit. Which is why he'll be the one to initiate both of us sobering up and moving past our separate traumas. He'll be my post Blake Brennan redemption.

And I'll be his.

"Move your hand to my shoulder," I tell him.

Roanoke's fingertips slip into the dip of my collarbone, his palm resting near my neck.

"Just not my thing," he says. The rough timbre of his voice rumbles through the side of his chest where I'm nestled against his ribs.

Behind us are deep green plants amid a sea of pink flamingos. My arm aches, shaking. I raise it higher anyway and reframe the shot.

Roanoke gazes into the screen of the phone with wide, un-certain eyes. "Good?" he asks.

"Yeah," I lie and snap the picture.

I haven't been able to loosen him up since breakfast this morning. The band and I pillaged the continental assortment on the way to their Winnebago, though I'm ninety percent sure Roanoke didn't touch his before he tossed it. Only Damien had greeted the two of us, a warm hello in a sea of silence.

Once we were on the road, I updated the rest of them on what happened last night and the plan going forward. With the tension, recruiting his bandmates to search the vehicle for drugs and alcohol seemed like an asshole move, so I did it myself, Roanoke watching and clearly miserable from his spot at the small booth-style table. An hour in, my legs aching from strug-gling to find equilibrium as the Winnebago swayed down the highway, he stood, crossed to me, and unhinged a tiny drawer next to the bathroom that I missed.

He didn't say a word as he swept his hand inside and came out with a fifth of whiskey. He held it in his palm as if reading the wrinkled label before he passed it to me and trudged to the table. As I watched him, I noticed December tracking him across the space. She moved into the seat opposite him as we crossed into Louisiana. By the time we pulled into the hotel we'd be staying at, I caught them laughing at some shared joke.

"Okay, one more," I say. I expect Roanoke to roll his eyes or make some snarky comment. Instead, he tilts his head against mine, posing without complaint. Sighing, I lower my phone. "Look, imagine each of these pictures as a gift."

"A...gift?" He tilts to glance at me.

"Yeah," I say. "That's why people follow on social media. We're letting them in. Sharing our secrets. We have to let them see us falling in love, so they'll get emotionally invested. We want them rooting for us."

I pause, unsure if he's understanding me.

"Listen," I say finally. "I need 'cute date', and you're giving me 'hungover and nervous'. It's just us, Ro."

It's a long moment before he nods. One of his arms cocks around my neck. His lips press against my temple as he nestles me closer. I raise the phone, the screen showing the lopsided grin I whip into existence the second before I snap the shot. My lashes are black against my cheeks, my expression slightly overwhelmed and yet there's the barest hint of bashfulness.

Perfect. Totally perfect.

His lips hold warm and steady against my skin, before he leans away. His fingers run over the ruffled strap of my white sundress. "Do you want to take another one?"

I nod, solemn. *It's always one more with him.*

I'm studying his irises, a smile in the blue rings that doesn't reach his mouth. Most guys are all fake grins and dead eyes that give away their feigned interest. Roanoke's the opposite—always interested, pretending he's not.

Between us the air shifts, thickens with nervous possibility. My tongue flashes out to wet my lips. His eyelids fall to half-mast as his head tilts. I lean forward.

A flamingo gives a sudden sharp call and we jolt apart at the violent ruffle of wings right behind us.

A shocked laugh bursts from me, embarrassment quick on its heels.

"Cockblocked by a flamingo," Roanoke whispers with a smile as he turns toward the bird.

As I stand, I ignore the fluttering in my stomach. That wasn't a for the camera kiss we were both leaning into. Judging from the way Roanoke's avoiding my gaze, he knows it too. Still, he risks taking my hand as we stroll the walkway, stopping to see the gorilla exhibit and continuing on.

The humid air is perfumed with the stink of wild beasts and urine. I can't help scrunching my nose.

"Anything else you want to check out, or are you ready to go?" Roanoke asks.

I check the time on my phone. "We've still got an hour to kill before they close the zoo. The park is open later. Did you have somewhere in mind?"

He ducks his head under the guise of checking out the next exhibit. They made the building out to look like a cave, walls wavy and splotched in uneven brown paint apparently meant to mimic an animal den, though for what, I can't guess. "This morning you said I was taking you on a date. So, yeah, I kind of planned something."

"You did?" I can't help the stunned sound of the words. Roanoke whips toward me as he holds the door to the building we're headed into.

"Of course," he says, confusion drawing lines between his brows and then that splash of a smile lightens his blue eyes until they twinkle in the sunlight. This time his mouth follows suit with a grin as he moves forward to make room for me in the enclosure. "Tell social media I'm keeping you on your toes."

Airconditioning slams into me as the door shuts behind us, locking out the light. After the bird calls and crowd sounds outside, the silence is deafening. We appear to be alone. I blink hard as my eyes adjust.

There's a smell. I suck a lungful of air to place the scent. Musky. I tense. Wet fur.

Wolves.

"Willow?" Roanoke's tone is cautious. "What's wrong? Are you claustrophobic?"

The textured ceiling is low, but it's the picture window running the length of the room that has me frozen. Behind the smoked glass, a shadow lopes. Its lolling tongue slips over teeth meant for tearing meat. I swear I can hear the wolf's paw pads on the trampled earth, nails clicking on tiles.

Adrenaline floods my system—too much, too fast. I can't get air.

I squeeze my eyes shut. Not tiles. Not Blake. "No," I get out.

A phantom pant on the side of my neck sends me reeling. I grope my way across the uneven wall as panic pulls me under in one swift tug.

Blake's voice echoes in my mind from the dream—*I love it when you fight me, Willow*—and a scream breaks from my throat. I trip on a dimly lit plaster stalagmite and my legs go out. I ball up on the crushed and dirty carpet. Claws. Next come claws.

A tight band encircles my abdomen, my knees scraping as I catch air. I'm flipped into a cradle hold. Curling against the soft cotton of Roanoke's shirt, my inhale shudders his citrus scent into my lungs until I can't smell the wolves anymore.

"I've got you," he murmurs. He boot kicks the bar handle on the door and whisks me into the light. He hesitates and then carries me a good distance to a bench partially hidden behind a tree draped in Spanish moss.

He keeps me tight in his arms as he sits. I cling to him, trembling. He doesn't ask what's wrong. Instead, his arm comes around me, one hand slipping through my curls in soothing strokes. "You're safe. I won't let anything happen to you," he says.

It feels like an eternity before I can speak. "I'm sorry," I get out through a throat thick with embarrassed tears.

"You have nothing to be sorry for." Under my cheek, the muscles of his chest twitch as he adjusts me against him. "Panic attack?" he guesses.

A denial springs to my lips but I swallow it down. "Yeah," I say.

"Can I ask what brought it on?"

I should separate from him, but I don't. Instead, I tuck my head under his chin. "The dark?"

I wince as I say it. The lie is so obvious.

"The dark," he repeats.

"You said you had somewhere else for us to go?" I ask and like a goddamned saint, he takes the cue.

"Yeah," he says, following my lead as we both stand. "If you're sure you're okay."

His palm finds the small of my back, as if he doesn't want to let go of me yet. To be honest, having him near is keeping the last dregs of my anxiety in check. I nuzzle myself under his arm and he lifts it around my shoulders, drawing me in next to him as he starts us moving down the walkway toward the entrance of the zoo.

"We're gonna need to grab a cab," he says.

We follow the sidewalk until we get to an area where several yellow cars wait along the curb. Roanoke chooses one, opens the door, and waits until I've slid in before he follows.

"Café du Monde?" he tells the driver.

We pull into traffic as I lean against his shoulder.

"Beignets, huh?" I say after ten minutes of comfortable silence.

"Have you ever had them?" he asks and when I shake my head, he gives me a small smile. "Perfect. I figured if you've been to New Orleans before, you'd be craving one. And if not," he adds as his fingers stroke down the soft skin on the inside of my arm. "Then your first time will be with me. If you venture back, maybe I'll cross your mind."

My gaze flicks to the driver. I'm not happy to find him watching us closely in the rearview mirror. He obviously knows who we are. And what Roanoke said implies an ending.

"Hey," I say softly as I lower my voice. I drop a quick kiss on the corner of his mouth. "I'll always think of you."

Roanoke doesn't say anything.

When we part, the cab driver isn't interested in us anymore. This isn't L.A. where everyone has TMZ on speed dial.

I glance over at Roanoke. He's peering out the window at the passing scenery, one knee pulled up and close to his chest to balance his chin on, his brow furrowed. The dark of a five o'clock shadow races across his jaw. Those lines in his forehead only deepen.

Is he thinking of me? I wonder. *Am I the reason for that strain?*

Three years he's been an incubus. I know Roanoke well enough to guess he hasn't dated in that time. He wouldn't dare let the demon feed more than once. Which means he's been alone.

Is that why he seems to soak up my touch? Seek out my kiss?

He's just lonely, I tell myself. Like I tried to convince him, he could have picked anyone at the bar that night. It had nothing to do with me.

Maybe I'll cross your mind....

I warned him at our first meeting in the Winnebago not to

catch feelings. It's what I have to remind myself every time I kiss him, every time he touches me. Does he really think it'll take traveling to this city for him to cross my mind when this is over?

You're torturing him. Hot on its heels is another thought. This one cuts through me, too honest. I'm torturing myself.

Roanoke shifts and I drop my eyes before he catches me watching him.

The cab crawls to a stop. "Here good, man?"

"Yeah," Roanoke says, digging his wallet out of his back pocket and handing over some bills.

I don't wait for him to come around and open my door. Instead, I step out onto the sidewalk and post myself by one of the pillars holding up the roof of the building.

I watch as he hurries, casting quick glances in my direction as the driver passes change over the seat, those lines of concern cutting between Roanoke's eyes again.

I need space from him to get my head straight, but that's not an option.

So many nights I've woken up screaming. Passed the hours that followed in a dazed blur spent praying for sunlight and the illusion of safety. Days of faltering concentration and the twitch of my nerves firing at a loud noise or a sudden movement in my peripheral vision.

And twice now I've slept in Roanoke's arms. The panic attack in the wolf enclosure isn't the first I suffered in the last three weeks. Not by a long shot.

It was the shortest.

Roanoke covers the steps that separate us in a light jog and offers me an uncertain smile. "Everything okay?"

Yes, I think. *No.*

The words stall in my mouth.

Sensing my anxiety, he ropes an arm around my shoulders and uses it to draw me against his side the way he did on our walk out of the zoo. His lips press against the crown of my head. "We can get our beignets to go," he offers. "Or we can go to the hotel without them. Whatever you need."

It's so kind I almost tear up. He planned this for me, something he wanted to share with me so we'd have a memory. The truth is, when this is over, I want Roanoke to remember me, too. So far, death and liquor and fear tinge all of our memorable moments.

"Willow?" When I don't answer, his fingers slip between mine. "Your call," he says.

Flashing Roanoke a smile, I tug his hand to move us toward the insanely long line. I tell myself it's the anxiety that has me threading my fingers between his. Except I don't feel anxiety. Not here with him.

"Are you kidding?" I blurt as we take our place at the end. "Wouldn't miss this for the world."

We face each other.

With his free hand, he gives the strap of my sundress a gentle tug. "Wearing white like an old pro," he says and then snickers at my confusion.

Only when we get to the counter and order, do I understand. The squares of fried dough are absolutely piled with powdered sugar.

He carries our tray to a table and sets me up with three beignets and a coffee so strong I can smell it wafting off the cup. I take a tentative sip and instantly fall in love with the potent brew.

"What is this?"

"Chicory coffee," he says. "With a ton of milk and sugar. Only way to drink it."

He digs into his plate of beignets. White powder drenches his fingers, more tumbling to land on his chin, dusting the front of his white t-shirt.

"You weren't kidding," I laugh as I lean forward across the table. "Come here."

He holds still as I smudge away the worst of it before I take a bite of my first beignet. It's like a combination of a doughnut and a pastry, the sugary topping making my mouth water. The coffee goes perfectly with the sweetness. I notice a few crumbs of powdered sugar spilled on the table and sweep at them.

"You're fighting a losing battle," he assures me before cracking up and using the side of his palm to wipe my chinful of powder. He drags out the chair beside him. "Come here," he says.

A half-second of hesitation holds me before I give in and go to him. Ever so slowly, he raises a fingertip to my nose and dots the tip in white. "Your followers deserve another present," he teases as he tugs his phone from underneath the table and snaps a quick picture of me.

"Take one with me," I say.

I fumble my phone out of my bag and hold it high, grinning

into the screen. The moment before I snap the shot, Roanoke's gaze shifts to my face. I tap the screen to bring up the shot.

I've faked so many smiles in the last three weeks, but the one mirrored back at me is genuine. And then I notice the way Roanoke's looking at me. If I didn't know better, I'd think it was love in his expression.

"That work?" he asks.

"Yeah, it's good," I say. I tuck the phone away before he can ask to see it.

"Aren't you going to post it?" He polishes off another beignet and brushes his hands together.

"Later," I say. "If I post it now, people will show up."

His expression is blank. *Oh God*, I think. *To be that innocent.*

"If I tell people where we are, they'll come," I say. "We'll be mobbed. We have to wait until after we leave to post it."

As if on cue, there's a tap on my shoulder. I turn to find a teenager shifting from foot to foot behind me. "Um, hi," she starts. "My mom said not to bother you, but I wanted to tell you I love you and you're the coolest person I know, and I'll probably never have this chance again, so yeah." Her cheeks blaze. "Hi!"

I hold out my hand for her to shake, instantly slipping into publicity mode, radiating excitement to mirror her own. "It's great to meet you!" I squeal. "Do you want to take a picture together?"

Her phone's already out. I wait while she unlocks it and then I hold it out to Roanoke. "Do you mind?" I ask.

"'Course not," he says, jumping up. He takes a few and then

returns it to the girl.

"Thank you so much!" she says, sounding vaguely dazed.

"Absolutely!" I say and then, as she walks away, she pauses.

Her mouth opens, closes again.

"What is it?" I ask, prodding her. Sometimes they ask about Sloane. Sometimes they ask if I know various Hollywood people. I give her a nod of encouragement.

"I'm really sorry about Blake," she blurts.

The smile on my lips freezes and falters.

She slinks into the crowd, back to her mother, as I sink into the seat next to Roanoke. With shaking hands, I raise my cup and choke down the last of my coffee.

When I lower the cup, Roanoke's expression is curious.

"The missing ex," he says, and I'm worried I'm going to have to give him that same canned speech I gave at Sloane's movie premiere. I can't stomach it. "Something made you think of him at the zoo," Roanoke finishes.

Perceptive bastard.

"Why?" he asks.

I bite my lip. Blake's demise isn't a secret I dare share. It's too risky.

Around us, conversations are falling to whispers behind hands. Attention shifts to me, to Roanoke. Once one person recognizes me enough to call me out, others instantly place my face.

"Let's get out of here," he says, his chair clattering as he stands. He doesn't wait for my answer, tossing a couple bucks onto our empty plates before he smuggles me out of the open aired seating of Café du Monde and into the anonymity of the crowd bustling on the street.

It takes a full block before my heart settles into its normal rhythm.

"She asked about Blake?" Roanoke says quietly. "And you got weird again."

It's a gentle nudge at all the doors I've kept shut over the last month. They need to stay locked tight.

"Willow," he says. "Tell me about your ex."

I can't. Words spill out of me, anyway.

"We weren't really together," I say. "He was a job."

Roanoke jabs his hands into his pockets as he walks beside me. "He's missing, right?" he asks, but by the inflections he already knows the answer, so I don't bother. "You worried about him?"

Maybe it'll be like drawing out a poison, I think. *To get it out of me.* He opened up about the terrible things Cassandra did to him before she stole away his mortality. *It's okay to trust him with this*, I promise myself. *Two words, a secret between us.* "Blake's dead."

Shock flickers across his expression and then disappears as quickly as it came. "I take it there's a good reason you know that?"

"He was a new werewolf," I confess instead. "He didn't take to the change well." Everything about Blake is a black spot in my brain. A hole threatening to swallow me piece by piece. "He pummeled some poor guy at an art show."

"Who the hell gets violent at an art show?" Roanoke interjects like he's hoping it'll break the tension, but his tone is off, and I can tell he regrets it.

I raise an eyebrow and offer a sigh. "Blake apparently. It was a mess. The guy pressed charges and the guy's girlfriend recorded the incident. Blake got court-ordered counseling." I pause, the fingers of one hand wrapping around the wrist of my other, worrying the skin there. "Blake's costar got word to him about what I do, the services I provide. It seemed like the perfect time for me to swoop in and prove to the world he'd changed for the better. Behind the scenes, I was supposed to help him with control, but what he needed was a pack, guidance, discipline."

A sinking feeling fills my gut. I can't explain why I glance to Roanoke for comfort. For a brief second, I'm lost in his blue eyes, and a new calm rolls over me. I want to go on, get these awful secrets out of me.

"We didn't exactly hit it off," I say as I walk again, hoping the forward motion will keep me talking. "He had a temper."

I fall silent as we pass a group of drunk friends staggering along on their way to the next bar. I wonder if we're heading toward Bourbon Street, if we should turn around and catch a cab to the hotel. Roanoke shouldn't be near this element.

"I saw a picture," he says slowly. "Yesterday after the Winnebago, I googled you and there was a picture of you and him, on a beach."

He cuts off when I nod along.

"Things kept going south while we played our rolls for the cameras," I say. "We were at the beach, on the dunes and he made some cutting remark. I told him if he didn't want to

211

change, I couldn't help him. I tried to leave. He grabbed me." The story comes out mechanically. "I tried to rip away. He latched on."

Roanoke's eyes flick to my wrist as if checking for the bruises so long healed.

"He didn't let go," I whisper, my voice shaking with the memory. I roll my shoulders. The motion helps break the shell of anxiety rippling across my skin. "He shook me. Violently."

"So, it was true what the articles said?" Roanoke asks, shock and anger tightening his tone.

Little bits of me wonder what would have happened if that moment hadn't been captured. Would I have kept trying? Would Blake have come around? Bigger bits of me know it wouldn't have mattered.

Blake was rotten.

I remember watching the purple marks shade to green and yellow as the days passed. "I told him I was done. He called me weeks later. He wanted to apologize. Begged me to help him. To come over, talk it out."

"Willow, no," Roanoke says, as if he'll change the past. I can hear his pity, though I'm not looking at him. I hate it.

"He was the only black mark on my record," I say like it'll explain.

"What happened next?" he asks.

I bite my lip. Once I say this, there's no going back.

"What happened?" Roanoke asks again. The care in his voice wriggles in to form cracks in my hesitation. "You went over. I'm guessing he did more than talk."

I nod slowly. I remember the sound of breaking plates, though that can't be right. The tightness in my throat as Blake choked the life out of me.

"He started to shift. It happened so fast. I could smell his fur." My free hand falls to my abdomen, fingers curling. I trace where the marks were, my gaze unfocused, caught in the past. I swallow, willing away the lump. "There were claws."

Across the street, someone screams.

I startle and stumble sideways into Roanoke even as the sound fades to a drunken giggle. Without a word, his arm circles around my waist. He studies me to gauge if I'm okay before he starts us walking again, turning us down a side street. I'm not sure how well he knows the town, but he seems to have a destination in mind. I don't care where we're going.

"Claws?" he prods after a block. "When you said the vampire blood healed a wound…"

I nod. "He almost disemboweled me." My voice trembles so hard I'm not sure Roanoke can make out the words. I remember how I struggled a hand free, ripped aside the billowing fabric of my skirt and grabbed my blade from its sheath. Blake's claws made one swipe as my knife rose. A race.

We tied.

"I had a knife. I cut him. Here," I say as I draw a line with my finger on my own neck where I stabbed him. I remember the sluice and crunch as it passed through the gristle and bone of Blake's throat. The sudden gush of warmth. "He bled out on his kitchen floor while I called for help."

Roanoke stops us, leaning against the old wood of one business lining the sidewalk.

"Hey," he says. His thumb moves under my chin, and he tilts my head until I'm forced to look into his eyes. "That dude was unhinged. He had to be put down. If it wasn't you, it would have been his pack."

"But it *wasn't* his pack," I argue.

He hesitates. "Do they know?"

A huff breaks from me, the sound rough with nerves. "If they did," I say. "I wouldn't be here."

"It was the smell of the wolves," he says. His fingers skim across my cheek, tucking a curl behind my ear, but I'm not ready to lose the crutch of his touch yet. I lean into his palm and he takes the cue, his thumb stroking the edge of my jaw. "At the zoo. It reminded you of him."

"I'm sorry," I say, too quickly. "I shouldn't put this on you." He looks at me like I've lost my mind and so I babble an explanation. "I've been having...issues. I don't know. I might have a touch of PTSD." The admission brings heat to my face. "Anxiety. Insomnia. I haven't been sleeping."

"But..." he starts before I give him an uncertain shrug. I can't explain what lets me drift off in Roanoke's arms when nothing else helps. I don't understand it myself.

"It seemed like a good idea to get out of L.A. for a while," I say. "That's why I took this job with you. The wolves, they were stalking me."

I start walking again but he draws me up short. "I thought you said they didn't know it was you?" When I glance at him, the concern in his eyes is almost too much to bear. "Are they after you?"

"If they want to find me, it's a Google search," I say, trying to sound nonchalant.

"Any city we're playing," he adds and frowns.

"Paparazzi find me anywhere. Touring with you keeps me moving, gives me time to come up with a plan. Besides," I add, my tone growing more serious. "I'm not leaving you."

He's slightly in front when he turns to face me and walks backward. I expect him to tell me he's fine or argue that he doesn't really need me.

"Cathedral," Roanoke says instead, and lifts a hand and points to our left. There's a gorgeous white church with pointed bell towers bright against the blue sky.

"I'll show you this whole town," he says. "We'll get dinner. We'll talk. Explore." His voice quiets again and it's only now that I hear the slight nervousness in it. "And when we get to the hotel, I'll be too tired to do anything but sleep. You, too. Okay?"

"I'd like that," I say.

And so we do.

It's long past sunset when we make our way to the hotel and check into a shared room. Once we're ready for bed, Roanoke crawls under the covers and I force myself to tell him I'm going to stay awake a little longer and settle into a chair.

I need to get my head together, but I can't leave him alone.

An hour passes, then another couple, before Roanoke drifts off mid-conversation. I watch him from across the room, willing myself to let the thought pestering me fade.

But it won't.

I play the memory again. My panic attack at the zoo. The way he cared for me after. How I changed the subject from Blake. After our beignets, he asked me about it, about Blake, about that night. I wasn't going to tell him. I couldn't risk it. I decided not to say anything.

I stare at his sleeping form, waiting for answers I'm not ready to face. I can't figure out who the truth will hurt more, me or him.

At two a.m. he stirs. The bed creaks, his feet hitting the floor before I realize I haven't slipped into some sort of half-conscious dreaming.

"Roanoke?" I say as he sits up. There's no reaction. His eyes are open, unblinking. The hand I can see fists the bedsheet as he stands, dragging the fabric behind him like a tether.

I get to my feet, my leg muscles screaming from hours of disuse. "Ro?"

He crosses in front of me with no acknowledgement of my presence.

Is he sleepwalking? He never mentioned doing that. No one in the band had. But is it something they'd bring up?

I pace him and then slide ahead to wave my hand in front of his face. "Hey," I say, louder. The bedsheet snags where it's tucked into the corner of the mattress and he stops, stalled, before his fingers slowly uncurl and he's free to move forward again.

Like everyone else, I spent my life being told not to wake a sleepwalker even if it's a myth. Still, I let this play out, glance to where he's focused.

The door.

A series of quick footsteps and I'm there, my back against the metal as I watch him make his slow, stiff-legged progress. His eyes are open wider, tearing up to glisten in the low light of the single lamp I left on.

"Roanoke?" I try again. "You're kind of freaking me out a bit."

I snap my fingers in front of him as he approaches. He doesn't flinch. Doesn't blink.

His hand nudges past me to find the knob.

"Wake up!" I yell loudly enough that he should. He has to. "Hey!"

He's turning the knob and so I do the only thing I can and slide the chain lock into place. He yanks the door open as I stumble out of the way, the metal giving a sharp rattle as the chain goes taut and stops it from opening.

I watch in stunned horror as he jerks hard against the lock, once, twice, again, each time more violent, the corded muscles of his arm straining.

"Stop!" I beg, going for his wrist, moving to loosen his fingers from the knob. I can't get my nails under his skin. His grip won't budge. "Wake up, Roanoke!"

I hear a thump from the hallway, maybe someone slamming a hand against the wall to tell us to shut up, and then the rush of footsteps.

Fuck, I think. That's all we need is a complaint to the front desk. If a rumor gets started that we're fighting, goes public, Blake will be brought up again and some reporter will put it out there that Roanoke's hitting me. I can't have him come out of this job looking worse.

Lowering my voice, I brush my thumb across his cheek. "Hey," I whisper soothingly.

He freezes.

"Are you awake?" I ask.

Silence.

His head tilts ever so slightly, as if he's listening to me or trying to.

December, I think suddenly. This is how he acted when she was singing. Can he hear her through the walls? I go still, ear cocked toward the two-inch gap in the door. It's quiet.

Roanoke's hand falters on the knob, drops to his side. The door falls instantly shut with a loud *thunk* as the automatic lock engages. Slowly, he turns, crosses the room, and crawls into bed as if nothing happened.

I stand where I am, unnerved and shaken. What if I wasn't awake? What if he wandered out into the night? Into traffic?

Into a bar. Is sleepwalking a symptom of alcohol withdrawal? I tell myself I'll look it up in the morning. As the buzz of adrenaline fades, I decide to climb into bed, sliding in behind him.

Adjusting, I lay on the pillow and then scoot closer to him. With a sleepy groan, he rolls over. Before I can react, one of his arms drapes to draw me into his embrace. His nose brushes mine as he settles in, our foreheads touching, exhales mingled. I stiffen, unsure of what to do.

As the minutes pass, despite everything, I relax against him.

I've got a long night ahead of me, I think. *Might as well get comfortable.*

CHAPTER 16

ROANOKE

C herries.

It's my first conscious thought. It drags me from the start of a dream involving Willow that has my cock twitching to attention. I stretch and hit skin, and I figure out where the scent came from.

Willow is in bed with me.

Her head nestles into the space between my neck and shoulder, tucked in under my chin, clicked into place like a puzzle piece. I've got one arm around her, the other bent awkwardly under the pillow. Ever so carefully, I stretch out my arm with a wince.

She's dreaming, her eyes darting behind her closed eyelids.

I remember what she told me yesterday about that fuck, Blake, and how she hasn't been sleeping. And yet...

Three times we've woken up in the same bed. Every one of them, we've been tangled around each other as if even asleep we're desperate to get closer.

She was in the chair when I passed out. After we took separate showers and got ready for bed, she'd been almost cold toward me, stand-offish.

This is a job to her. She'd reiterated that yesterday. I'm a job. I wonder if that's why she got cagey. Maybe I put too much into our kiss.

Maybe she knows I'm falling for her.

How she ended up in my arms is a mystery I don't really care about unraveling.

How the fuck do you think this is going to play out? my conscience snaps and I flinch. *You can't have her. You can't make her happy. You can't be with her.*

Truth. All of it.

God, Willow came here because she thought she'd be safer, and I screwed her literally and figuratively. No more days off. We need to figure out who's behind the killings and get her safe. Then, maybe...

No, I think. We solve this and then Willow can jet off to Europe. Somewhere those werewolves will never find her. My fingers raise off her hip. I run them across her cheek, the dark curl framing her face. She sighs at my touch.

The twitching under her eyelids settles and then stops. She tenses, her eyes opening. She blinks in surprise when she sees me.

"Get lonely in the chair?" I ask. I smile, hoping it'll set her at ease.

"I was fine in the chair until your moonlight escape attempt," she says, her voice gravelly with sleep. She rubs her face and then rolls away from me with a heavy sigh. She crosses the room to the little sink beside the bathroom. The tiny shorts she wore to bed aren't helping me any. I shift the sheet she left behind to cover the bulge in my lap as I sit up.

"My what?" I laugh.

She turns on the water and cups her hand under the faucet, swallowing down a few gulps before she twists to me again as she rebinds her curls with the hairband around her wrist. "You never told me you sleepwalk."

"Because I don't," I say. I'm not sure why I sound defensive. Maybe because she sounds like she's pissed about it.

"Well, you do now," she says, sounding weary.

"Did I..." I don't want to ask, but there's a sinking feeling in my gut. "I didn't do anything bad, did I?"

"To me? No!" she says as if the suggestion is ridiculous, be-fore sitting cross-legged at the end of the mattress. "I was still up. But you got out of bed and tried to open the door."

I glance over at it like it'll unveil some sort of memory before I raise an eyebrow at Willow. "Where was I going?" I ask. "Did I say anything?"

She shakes her head. There's a haunted look in her eyes as she takes me in and I can't shake the feeling something happened she's not telling me. "I slid the chain," she says. "Eventually, you went back to bed on your own." She shrugs, and her smile's al-most apologetic. "I didn't want you sneaking off again, though, hence the unexplained cuddles."

"Yeah, well, it's not all on you," I admit. "I woke up first. Gave me a chance to look all innocent."

I catch sight of the doorknob from the corner of my eye and I swear a memory tickles at my brain; me using every bit of my strength to grip the sheets as I'm dragged forward toward a whisper I can't ignore.

Despite being awake, the nearly forgotten nightmare casts spider web threads that stick to my bones. I shiver, run my hands over my arms as if to dislodge whatever hold they have on me.

"What time is it?" Willow asks, and I grab my phone off the nightstand to check.

"Not quite nine," I say. I poke around in my suitcase and take out yesterday's jeans, slipping them on over the boxers I slept in. "You hungry?"

She's lining the entire sink with her makeup and hairbrushes and lotions. My stomach gurgles, the etouffee I ate for dinner a memory. Willow looks like she's settling in for the long haul as she shakes her head. "Not really much of a breakfast person." She pauses. "Um...I need to talk to you. About yesterday."

Here we go, I think. "Cool if I grab something to eat first?"

I'm not sure if I'm supposed to ask permission. Yesterday, I didn't have a drop of alcohol. Nothing. And while I'm not exactly freaking out about it like I did backstage before I left with Nigel, I'm aware. My bones ache, weirdly fragile, like they'll crack apart.

Kiss me, Roanoke, whispers a dream voice I can't quite place.

"Why don't you order room service?" Willow glances up at me and pauses. "Are you sick?" she asks.

My skin prickles as every hair on my body stands on end. I grab the edge of the nightstand. A second later, Willow's there, gripping my forearm to hold me steady.

"Sit," she demands, and shuffles me toward a tacky, over-stuffed armchair in a corner. Her wrist presses against my clammy forehead.

"Incubus," I remind her. "I'm not sick."

Not from germs.

I do the math in my head, counting. It seems like so many days have passed, but tonight will mark three since I slept with Willow. Three days since I fed the demon. I have more time. How much does *she* have left, though?

Before we reach the chair, I twist free of Willow's grip, barely stumbling before I take in a cleansing lungful of air and straighten.

"I'm fine." I say. "I need something in my stomach, that's all."

Willow doesn't look convinced. "I can go with you," she offers. "Give me a minute to—"

"No," I say, cutting her off. "You do your thing. I'll get some toast in me. We'll talk when I'm done, okay?"

A war plays out in her expression as to whether or not she's going to let me go. I can see it, the way she wavers. She doesn't trust me.

She'll never trust me. But then what do I expect when I royally fucked her over less than thirty-six hours ago?

Those soft brown eyes go steely. "This is withdrawal, Roanoke."

She's wrong. I know she's wrong. "I will be right back," I say, as much honest as I can muster poured into the words. "Ten minutes. Let me go, Willow."

"Okay," she says, as if she's come to a decision.

It seems too easy. I pause, uncertain, while she returns to the sink and counter. "Okay?"

I don't wait for her to change her mind. Instead, I take a room key and without looking to see if she's watching me, I grab a key ring off the tv stand. I tuck both into my pocket.

Then I stroll out of the hotel room, alone, in the clear, and already guilty as hell.

Every step I take down the hall to the elevator, I expect Willow to yell after me, ask what I picked up, call me out.

The second the doors slide open on the main floor, I smell pancakes and eggs, that weird ever-present hotel lobby scent of burned coffee. I don't glance in the food's direction as I dart toward the building's entrance.

My feet hit the asphalt. I follow the sidewalk around the front of the building, cross its side, and stumble into the rear parking lot. I spot the Winnebago.

Digging into my pocket, I yank out the key ring, stick the silver key in the Winnie's lock. None of the windows in mine and Willow's room face this lot, but I hurry anyway.

I need two minutes. Less. I can be in and out. Get breakfast and go to her. Ten minutes total. I didn't lie.

Inside me, the demon stretches as if in sympathy. An uncomfortable gurgle sounds from my abdomen. It's fluids and organs being shoved and prodded as the thing crawls around.

This is only going to get worse. It's what I tell myself as I walk toward the rear of the Winnebago. It should be another three, maybe four days before I have to feed the demon. It's riled up.

My fingers skim the ancient, stained paneling and snag on a small, nearly hidden drawer. I showed it to Willow. I handed her the fifth I'd stashed in there months ago. I gave it over as a peace offering.

I gave it over because I didn't want her to search the drawer.

I send up a prayer that what I'm looking for is there. I send up another that it's not. Either way, I'm pretty sure it's useless. I've got a demon living inside me; something tells me no one in Heaven is listening to the likes of me.

My fingers scrape the back of the drawer, out of sight, and then I find it. A small baggie. I palm it, not bothering to check that the bars are still in there. Five Xanax. I tuck them into my rear pocket.

It's backup, I promise myself. *I won't take them unless I need to.*

If Willow knew what it was like, the scratching, my wounded organs leaking blood from pinprick claw tracks, she would understand. She would.

On my way out, I grab the case that holds my acoustic guitar. The show's not until later tonight. I'll play for Willow. Strum all her favorite songs. I lock the Winnie up and cross the parking lot.

This is withdrawal, Roanoke.

But she's wrong. I'm not that bad.

"Hey."

My head snaps up. Carter leans against the pillar near the entrance of the hotel, next to an ashtray full of stones. Of the four of us, he's the one who most looks like a rockstar. His shock of white-blond hair battles with his tattoos for attention.

The smile I grapple with doesn't fit my mouth, so I drop it. "Checking up on me?" I ask. It sounds guilty. Accusatory. "I was getting my guitar."

I hold up the case I'm carrying as proof.

He gives me a long look before his eyes slide from mine. "Sure, Ro," he says, his tone ambivalent. "You and Willow have fun yesterday?"

"She's never been to NoLa. I showed her around." The taste of bile rises up my throat and I swallow hard, willing myself not to vomit. "What'd you guys get up to?"

Carter shrugs. He doesn't usually do small talk. "Dec said we got a shit-ton more followers on everything. Whatever Willow's doing with you seems to be working."

I'm not sure what I'm supposed to say, so I don't say anything at all.

"Is it?" He glances up when I don't answer. "Working? You make it through yesterday?"

Without drinking. It's unsaid, but it's there between us, deadweight.

"Yeah," I say.

"Figured," he says as he pushes off the pillar with the sole of his shoe. "You look like shit, man."

And then Carter smiles.

Carter doesn't ever smile.

"Seen a lot of friends through the dregs. Couple more days you'll be through the worst of it," he says over his shoulder. The doors slide open for him. "You eat?"

I shake my head though he can't see it and follow him as he crosses the lobby and leads the way to where the food's set up. I catch sight of Damien, of December, in the same booth, a dirty plate where Carter clearly sat.

And an empty fourth spot.

For me, I realize. I wonder how many of these band breakfasts I slept through, passed out in the Winnebago. Have they always saved space for me?

Damien sees me first. His face lights up in a way I don't deserve. "There he is!" he says as I walk toward them.

December's smile is cautious, but there. All of them, waiting for me, like they were hoping I would show. I lean the guitar case against the booth.

"I..." My throat tightens and I hook a thumb over my shoulder toward the food.

In line, I grab a plate and then drop two pieces of bread into the toaster. There's a hole in the metal counter near a straw dispenser, a hidden garbage can to dispose of wrappers. In one quick movement, I dig the baggie out of my rear pocket and toss it into the hole.

The toast pops.

I join the rest of the band.

Five minutes later, as I head toward the room, I grab Willow an apple and a wrapped Danish. I juggle them and the guitar, slide my key into the reader and open the door with my elbow.

Willow's sitting on the edge of the bed as if she's been waiting like this the entire time. She doesn't return my smile.

"Apple?" I say and gently lob it toward her.

She snags the fruit overhand and then sets it on the nightstand without a word.

"Everything okay?" I ask her.

She stands. Her lips press into a tight line. "Empty your pockets."

My good mood disintegrates. "Willow, I—"

That gorgeous mouth twists into a vicious snarl, and she crosses to me. Her hand shoves roughly into one front pocket of my jeans, then the other. I hold my own hands up, off balance with the ferocity of her search. The cellophane-wrapped Danish hits the floor. She checks my rear pockets and my swell of relief is so strong it almost brings tears to my eyes.

She steps back and studies me. "Take them off. Your shoes."

I dig with the toe and scrape the heel of first one, then the other of my sneakers off. She squats and shakes them both out before swiping around the tongues. Standing, she tosses the sneaker to the side. It tumbles to settle against the TV stand. I tug off my socks and make a big show of turning them inside out for her.

Willow's tongue flicks across her lips, wetting them. "Your pants."

I smirk and give my head half a tilt as I unbutton my jeans and then slide down the zipper. "All the way?" I ask.

She rolls her eyes and tears the jeans past my hips until they're crumpled at my ankles. I step out of them. Her fingers slip inside the waistband of my boxers.

"Willow," I say, hoping she catches my warning. Instead, she doubles down, her warm palm wrapping around my dick.

I can't help how I stiffen at her touch even though she's all business.

Her hands tug free and then slide across my shirt as her expression grows perplexed. "I thought…"

You were right, I want to tell her. I pick up the pastry. "I brought you breakfast."

"Can I search the guitar?" she says.

"Can I eat your apple?" I counter.

As if to spite me, she unzips the case. I grab the apple off the nightstand and crunch off a chunk. Juice runs down my chin. I palm it dry.

The tiny, zippered pocket holds a couple picks that she returns. She handles the guitar as if she's afraid of it.

"Make it easy on me, Roanoke," she says. "Tell me what I'm looking for. Or did you already take it?"

"I did not take anything." I sound out each word.

"What did you go downstairs to get?" she prods. I eat another bite of the apple, stalling.

"My guitar," I insist after I've chewed and swallowed. "Breakfast."

"And?"

I wince.

"And?" she repeats, quieter this time.

I wait a beat.

"How did you know?" I ask.

A muscle twitches in her jaw. Her tone is so hostile I flinch. "You lied to me."

"No." I reach for her, but she steps away. "I didn't lie. It was a bad idea, I know that. I thought about it," I admit. "I did. But I tossed them before I came back up. I didn't take anything. I didn't drink anything."

The disappointment in her look crushes me. She's going to walk out on me.

"Please, Willow. I can't do this without you." I'll beg her to stay. Promise her whatever it takes. "Listen," I say. "I know I've only been sober for like thirty something hours and that's probably nothing to you, but it's been over three years since I had that much time under my belt. I am not fucking this up. I'm in. I'm with you."

She wraps her arms around herself.

"But we're not together, are we?" she mumbles, half under her breath as if trying to convince herself. I'm not sure I'm supposed to hear it. I don't understand what she's questioning. Does she not want to do this anymore?

When I try to reach for her hand, she jerks free.

"What, did I not play pretend lovers good enough for you yesterday?" I say, my tone too harsh, but I dare another step toward her.

"Stop trying to touch me," Willow blurts. There's panic in the sliver of her face I can see. "Stop talking."

I pause, doubt ricocheting through me as she retreats. I've seen her mid-panic attack and what's in front of me doesn't match, but something's very wrong. My thoughts run again to how she said I sleepwalked. Did I do something? Scare her? *No*, I realize. *This started last night.*

"You wanted to stay in the chair," I remind her. "Once we

231

got back here, it's like you shut down on me. Now, this. What's going on?"

"Nothing," she says, too quickly. She returns to the sink and starts to brush her hair as if she's mimicking normal behavior, except she's not even close to nailing it. Her reflection makes methodical strokes, her brown curls springing with each pass.

"What happened to being honest with each other?" I ask.

For a long time, I think she won't answer, and then she sets the brush down and turns toward me. Her eyes hit mine, defiance in them.

"I didn't know what to look out for," she starts. "The signs."

"I am not," I say emphatically, "using anything."

She goes back to her makeup, dotting lotions onto her skin and rubbing them in with careful fingertips. The scent of cherries fills the room, stealing my attention for a brief second. Then she speaks. "I should have known yesterday at the zoo. No one knows about Blake. If what happened that night gets out, I'll be killed."

"Now you don't trust me anymore. Is that it?" I drop what's left of the apple into the garbage can, my appetite gone again. "I told you, I'm in this!"

"'Willow', you said. 'Tell me about your ex.'" Her brown irises flick across mine as she waits for me to figure out whatever has her so twisted up. As the seconds pass, she only grows more desperate. "'I can't,' I remember thinking. 'I can't tell him.'"

"But you did," I say. She trusted me. I opened up to her about my past and she did the same. It brought us closer.

"But I did." She catches my eyes in the mirror before she

uncaps a mascara and blinks her lashes against the wand. "It's like a glitch," she says, pointing to her temple.

"No," I get out. My stomach drops. "No. That's not why you told me."

She stands and slowly moves toward me. "Ask me." Her hands find my shoulders. "Ask."

My tongue flicks across my lips. She's giving me permission.

I don't want to do this. I want to beg her not to make me, but we both have to know, and so she nods again. The air around me tingles, the hair on my arms standing straight. I cup her cheeks in my palms as my forehead knocks against hers. Before I can talk myself out of it, I speak a sentence I never thought I'd dread. "Kiss me, Willow."

A puff of air slips out of her, the tiniest resistance, and then the warmth of her mouth meets mine, the kiss soft and sweet and wrong.

I almost give into it before I twist my head away to break our touch. "It's wearing off. The blood," I say. My hands still press against the sides of her jaw. "It's wearing off."

"What?" Willow asks, her voice dazed. "No. I wanted to kiss you." She nods as if convincing herself. "I just..." She trails off and then glances up at me with too much trust after what I've done. "Didn't I?"

"No," I say, my voice shaking. "You didn't. You said Sloane was coming to give you more blood?"

She stares at me, wide eyes blinking as if she's gone slightly unsteady. I brush at a loose curl by her cheek, unsure if I should touch her at all, but I'm terrified once I let her go, it'll be forever.

"Right," she whispers. "Sloane. Tonight. For the show."

"Okay," I say, fighting off the nerves rattling through me. "Okay, we stay apart until then."

"Apart," she echoes.

How many tiny decisions have I already influenced, I wonder. *Tell me about your ex*, I said.

I will be right back. Ten minutes. Let me go. And she said okay like it was the most natural thing to let me out of her sight.

I release her and grab my socks off the floor. Stepping into my jeans, I turn away from her to button and zip them.

"I'll get a new room. You keep this one," I say as I tuck my bare feet into my shoes. "You'll come to the show separately."

I glance up at her to make sure she's listening.

"I'll come to the show separate," she repeats, and I jam my palms against my eyes, rubbing hard.

"Damn it! Stop!" I demand and she flinches.

"I don't understand why you're so mad at me!" she says, as if this is somehow her fault.

I kneel, zip my suitcase, and yank the handle. It clacks upward as it extends.

"Roanoke?" she whispers. She sounds hurt. Scared. "Whatever it is, I'm sorry."

I did this.

I wrap her in my arms, one hand on her back, the other gently gripping the nape of her neck. My lips find her ear. I concentrate on the sway, turn it up to kill whatever resistance she still has. "Nothing is wrong," I murmur, and she instantly relaxes against me.

234

I'm going to have to have December come sit with her. I can't leave her alone. If she trusted me with her secret, the least I can do is use that to keep her safe. I'm pretty sure December's siren abilities will be stronger than any werewolves. She'll protect Willow from them.

From me.

"God, I'm sorry." My voice breaks and I swallow hard and start again. "You're going to take a long nap until December wakes you up, okay? You'll come to the show with her. You're very tired, Willow."

She sighs. "Stay with me?" she whispers against my neck.

Her fingers curl around my shoulder. I scoop her as she droops and carry her to the bed, lowering her onto the pillows. I don't linger. There's no moment where her hair fans out and I kiss her gently to bring her back to me.

I'm not part of anyone's fairytale.

At the door, my suitcase in hand, I pause. "Willow?"

Her eyes are already closed. She stirs with the slightest moan of consciousness, moving one arm to curl it against herself.

"Dream of beautiful things," I command, as I let the door between us shut.

CHAPTER 17

WILLOW

I watch the phone in my hand, the screen lit, the battery slowly draining. It's dark here, backstage, the area cut off by crates and the detritus of past shows until it's almost like its own little room. My texts to Roanoke are there on the screen, single lines with no replies, black and white against the cool cream of my palm.

An image flashes into my mind, Roanoke's crestfallen expression when I'd told him what I suspected, that the immunity the blood gave me was wearing off. I remember kissing him, wanting to, wanting more. It's such a clear memory. As is our entire conversation until I'd grown suddenly exhausted and decided—myself—to lie down. It makes perfect sense in my head.

And yet, I can't trust it. I know what happened doesn't belong, but I can't seem to find the edges to peel it up and see what's underneath.

Earlier, I spent the better part of an hour trying to decide what to send to him.

Are you sober?

Are you safe?

I would have trusted you to stay.

Instead, I screwed it up.

I dreamed about you, I sent, not sure why it seemed so important until the second it was done, and a memory wriggled out of my brain of Roanoke standing in the doorway.

Dream of beautiful things.

Three little dots popped up, showed he was typing, and my heart leaped into my throat. They blinked on and off, lines composed and then deleted, until they disappeared without an answer.

Sloane will be at the show, I texted him finally. *Which means more people watching us. We've got to keep playing our roles. Nothing's changed.*

No answer. Nothing. Not even a clipped 'k.

December was in my room when I woke up, waited while I got ready, rode with me in my hired Town Car. She stayed as long as she could before she had to prep for their concert but made me promise to stay in the public area backstage before she left.

It's another half an hour before Sloane shows up. I don't have to turn around to know it's her. A sudden hush falls through the area followed by a collective shocked silence and then every groupie, fan, roadie, band member begins quietly chattering in surprise.

I spin, sight her instantly, and wave. When she spots me, her entire face explodes with joy. She's utterly oblivious to the wake of stares as she crosses the space between us.

"Hi, Gorgeous!" she squeals and wraps me in a hug. She's in tailored jeans, her skimpy, draped-fabric top looking like the upper half of an Oscar dress.

I'm not sure how a vampire always smells like sunshine, but Sloane does. Then again, just being around her warms me. "Hey, Love!"

"This is the best call for help I've ever gotten!" When she separates from me, her eyes are absolutely sparkling. "The Raven Shakes and Timber Boom? These are the circles you should run in, Wil. Ones that have a fantastic soundtrack."

I snort a laugh to hide my contempt at hearing the name Tinder Boom. I have half a mind to claw out Nigel Lee's eyeballs next time I see him. "Like you couldn't get passes to any show, anywhere, with a single phone call?"

Sloane shakes off the comment. "What fun is that?" she whines before she squeezes my arm. "How are things going?" she asks.

I lock eyes with her.

He almost slipped up again today. And when he admitted it, when I should have been reassuring him, helping him, I had to let him know my defenses were failing.

Sloane frowns. "Happy for the cameras, Willow," she warns.

My cheeks stretch tight. "I'm so glad you're here."

My genuineness seems to deepen her concern. "Is the blood wearing off?" she asks, her voice low enough to only be heard between the two of us.

"Spotty at best," I say. "Started sometime yesterday afternoon."

"Two days before you can't trust it," she says, her voice thoughtful. She wraps her hand in mine and tugs me off into the shadows. We tuck down behind a crate. "Okay, a dozen drops of my blood bought you two days," she says. "Let's see if increasing the amount will increase the duration you're immune."

"Okay," I whisper, as if we're about to be caught.

Sloane twirls the ring she's wearing. It's an overlapping double band of rubies, but as I watch, one section comes apart and swings open like a miniature pocketknife. Sloane pauses. "You're sure you want this, Willow. We can leave. You and me. Right now. I'll call in every favor I'm owed to protect you from those wolves. You know I will."

I glance down to where the point of the blade indents against the pale flesh of her wrist. The night before last, when he snuck away to that bar with Nigel, I found Roanoke shaking and red-eyed. Damaged in a way I'm still not sure I can fix.

And then I remember him on our cab ride to get beignets, and how he'd wanted me to have a memory of him not tainted with all the drama surrounding us. Something for me. A reason to smile later. I think of today in the hotel room. His careful wording when he realized what was happening.

Dream only of beautiful things.

I can't afford to cut myself on that boy's broken edges.

He'd never forgive himself.

"You were right," I say softly. "That first morning, when I called you and you said I was compromised." I watch, entranced as she lowers the miniscule blade to her skin. "But I'm in this.

I'm seeing it through."

There's a sick pop as her skin breaks. Sloan widens the slice with a wrinkled nose.

"Don't make a mess," she warns. She pulls the point from the puncture and then her wrist is at my mouth, the warm taste of her blood spurting against my teeth, salty and metallic.

I gag before I can help it, my eyes watering as I fight a swallow that only makes me retch harder.

"Good girl," Sloane coaches even as I thrust my tongue to block the flow.

I feel like I've taken in mouthfuls, but in truth, it's probably no more than a shot glass. Finally, she moves her arm away, locking her palm over the wound.

"Christ," I say with a grimace. "I don't know how you stand that." I lick my teeth, hoping to get rid of the cloying taste as I dig my phone out of my pocket.

Sloane's voice is so quiet I almost don't hear her. "It's different for me."

I grunt in response, my concentration on the single word I type.

Done, I send to Roanoke. I tuck the phone into my jeans without waiting for a reply.

Sloane raises an eyebrow. "What's he like?" she asks. "Do you make him serenade you? I'd have him singing me to sleep every night. His voice is like lady porn!"

She's not *wrong*, but I still stumble over the mental gymnastics my brain has gone through in the last two minutes when it comes to Roanoke.

When I don't laugh along, Sloane's tone goes sharp. "Are you sharing his room, Willow?"

I roll my eyes. "I'm keeping him sober. That means watching him. Closely. I can't screw up again."

Sloane releases her wrist. The wound is sealed. She dips her fingers into her cleavage and comes out with a single wet wipe in a foiled paper packet. "Willow," she says carefully as she rips it open and wipes any traces of blood off her palm. "Are you sharing his bed?"

Despite my best attempts to avoid it, my cheeks blaze. "Not like that," I promise. "It's...I..." I give up and shrug. "We just sleep."

"Wait, you're sleeping again?" There's so much relief in Sloane's words that my implied cuddle sessions with Roanoke might be forgiven after all.

How do I explain what's happening between Roanoke and me? How can I trust it anymore?

Because it's not new.

"I don't feel fragile with him," I say and then tilt my body to lean against the crate we're huddled behind. "I feel...like myself. Like how I used to, before Blake. But better."

Sloane frowns. "Are you falling for him?"

I shrug, miserable. "Falling would imply it hasn't already happened."

Sloane doesn't react. "Yeah, well," she says. Her expression grows serious. "If that's the case, there's something you need to know about vampire blood."

Sloane leans in, her voice a whisper as she tells me what

she learned and in a few short sentences, everything between Roanoke and I since the moment we met shifts violently. I lead us back into the light, my mind spinning, my entire world thrown off its axis.

"You're sure?" I ask her again. "Positive?"

Sloane nods. "The vampire who told me, she's been around a long time."

"Holy shit," I whisper as we walk. And then a wave of panic rolls through me. "Don't tell him. Not yet. I need to think this through."

"That," she says. "Is the smartest decision you've made since you got off that plane in Austin."

We're barely out of the shadows when a heavy arm drapes over my shoulders. Roanoke's kiss presses against my temple. I should tense. I should be freaking out. But the second he's at my side, everything raging inside me twitches into normal nerves.

How does he keep sliding himself into this role so easily while I'm fighting the flutter in my stomach every time he touches me? Is it the incubus influence? Maybe Sloane's blood hasn't kicked in yet. These butterflies I'm feeling aren't real.

I glance up to meet Roanoke's blue eyes and find them locked on mine.

"Hey," he says carefully. So much in the single word goes unsaid, but it's all there. "December stayed with you?" It's not really a question. He already knows the answer.

I give him a slow nod. *I'm okay. We're okay.* Even though I'm not. Not after what Sloane told me.

His thumb traces my jawline. "I was with Damien all day. I

told him you were sick. Oysters, yesterday. I never left his sight, Willow. Ask him."

I don't realize we're leaning into each other until my forehead knocks lightly against his. When I speak, I attempt to work a teasing edge into my words so he knows I'm not mad. "I would have much rather spent the afternoon on research. Strategy for when this serial killer makes their move. Searching for patterns in their behavior. Anything besides napping the day away?"

Despite my tone, Roanoke looks crestfallen. He winces. "I panicked. I'm usually so careful not to use the influence. I let my guard down with you," he says and then hesitates as what he said sinks in. "When I realized that I was—"

I silence him with a quiet kiss on his lips. "It's okay," I whisper.

A throat clears beside us.

Embarrassed, I turn. I forgot where we were, who was watching. "Roanoke, meet Sloane Marquette. Sloane, this is.... This is Roanoke."

She's not at all bashful about the once over she gives him. "Can I just say I am such a huge fan?"

My gaze flips to Ro. An adorable flush colors his cheeks.

"I appreciate that," he says. He hesitates. "And I appreciate you helping Willow out. I couldn't do this without her." And then he adds, "Should be a good show tonight," as if to cover the awkwardness.

I'm waiting for what I'm sure will be a snarky little flirt of a comment from Sloane, but nothing comes. When I turn, she's watching me. "Willow is important to me," she says, as her gaze drifts to him. "I will always have her back. No matter what that means."

Ro gives her a nod. "Same team, Sloane," he says quietly.

Annoyance ripples through me, and I have to fight not to roll my eyes. I'm not exactly a helpless human here. Roanoke needs to remember I'm in charge. Since this morning, our power balance is all screwed up.

More like since you showed up in that Winnebago and realized you slept with him...

A sudden cheer goes up from the curtained off area that keeps us out of view of the stage and Roanoke jolts from my side. "That's my cue." His expression turns serious. "I will meet you right here. Hand to God, okay?"

"Go make me proud!" I yell after him for the benefit of anyone listening. I lace my fingers together and point after him. He blows me a kiss and spins toward the stage.

"Jesus," Sloane says. "Do you two script this shit out?"

Confused, I shrug.

A bouncing blonde head flounces past us as December starts for her drum kit. She gives my arm a squeeze on her way by. Damien's behind her, his attention on the guitar slung over his chest as he tunes a string in a last-minute adjustment. Carter must be on the other side of the stage.

"Willow," Sloane says, stretching out my name as her head tilts. "Their drummer...she's..." She pauses as if searching for the right word. "Off."

I paste on my most apologetic expression and sigh myself into what is going to be a hot mess of angry Sloane in about twelve seconds. My answer comes out more question than anything else. "Would that be because December's a siren?"

A roar fills the auditorium as December bounces onto the stage and does her customary curtsey.

Instead of anger, Sloane gapes open-mouthed as December finds her seat behind the enormous and complicated-looking drum set. "Wait, but she sings. She sings on the album."

"Her recorded voice doesn't have any effect. She sings live, too, though," I say, watching her expression.

"I've never known one," she says. A small smile breaks across her face. "A real siren. I mean, that's as close to being a mermaid as you can get. Minus all the murder."

"She keeps it in check." I'm not sure why I want to defend December. The girl's worked hard to kill off her nature. And so far, it's working. "She sings during the second and fifth song. Low dose of siren vibes to a high number of people. It's pretty brilliant, honestly."

"My blood protects you from her too, then?"

I nod.

"But the rest of them aren't—" She rips her curious gaze from the silhouetted outline of December under the stage lights and turns to me.

I must give something away because Sloane's jaw goes tight. "You've got to be fucking kidding me, Willow." Her hands drop to her hips as she huffs a frustrated breath. "Spill it."

With each member of The Raven Shakes that walks on stage, the crowd grows louder.

I lean into her ear and cup my hand around it. "Bass player's a shapeshifter!"

Carter sways into his spot.

She screams at me, probably asking about Damien, but I shrug and point. It's no use talking anymore. The audience is in a frenzy and Roanoke hasn't even taken the stage yet.

"NoLa!" he teases from offstage. The noise is so loud my ears ring. "Anybody out there feeling a bit tingly?"

I whoop in answer, clapping as he goes through his intro. My smile is so wide my cheeks hurt. But when I glance at Sloane, she's fixated on the crowd.

I clutch at her arm, but she doesn't react, doesn't move. I get in front of her and she tilts around me as if I'm some random object blocking her view.

"Sloane?" I yell, her name lost in the driving beat of the music. "Hey!"

I grab her shoulder and give it a shake. Her lip curls, one deadly fang glinting in the stage lights. Under my fingers I hear the rumble of her warning growl. I stumble back a step in my shock and it snaps her out of her fugue. Something has her spooked. It's been so long since Sloane's control slipped a fraction. And never toward me.

"What's wrong?" I demand, mouthing the words.

"Vampires," she mouths. "Other things. Things I don't even—" Her gaze flicks to the crowd before returning to me. There's a subtle glitter of silver shine around the pupils of Sloane's gray eyes, like they're lit from inside and dancing through the cracks. "Lots of power."

"Shit," I whisper. After seeing the two vampires in Houston,

I had a hunch The Raven Shakes were drawing a significant supernatural element to their shows.

Sloane loops a protective arm through mine. Uncertain what else to do, we watch, both a bit unnerved as December sings harmony and the crowd goes vacant. Just like last time I saw them play, it's not as pronounced during their fifth song. I'm learning snatches of lyrics, singing along with Roanoke as I can. Twice, he looks over and I'm almost positive he's searching for me in the shadows behind the curtain.

I have to tell him, I think. *I have to tell him what Sloane told me about the blood.* But what if it changes things?

What if it doesn't?

Sloane and I dance backstage. Once the Raven Shakes finish, they head offstage to the right, opposite of where we are, and a nervous energy blooms inside me.

He's leaving, I think. *He's going to ditch me again.*

I must tighten my grip on Sloane. "Listen to that crowd," she marvels, yelling to be heard above the near riot in front of the stage. "They're going to sing another one!"

I'm about to tell her she's wrong when Damien takes a wild running leap and drags a hand across the strings of his guitar. He drops to his knees on the stage, the instrument wailing as he leans nearly flat, his legs bent awkwardly to the side behind him.

December follows, laughing as she walks beside Carter and his surly grimace. Finally, Roanoke reclaims his spot to a wall of screams and cheers.

"One more," he says, panting into the microphone. He gives a nod to Damien, who crawls out of his squat to start into the surprise song. It's a dirty jam, dark energy and brooding beats.

"He's got a crush on you," Sloane says. "Roanoke. Did you know?"

I scoff. "It's not real."

She seems to weigh my words. "His pulse," she says. "It sped up as he approached you."

"Probably because he saw you," I say. This is not why I brought her on. She's my voice of reason. I needed her to meet Roanoke, to see him, judge him, pick him apart in a way I can't. "First impressions of him? Other than his impressive pulse rate?"

She gives her head a thoughtful shake. "He's captivating," she says. "Like a supernova. I don't think half his charisma has anything to do with that demon. It's just...him."

I nod in agreement.

And then she pauses. "But there's something...a vibe..."

"What do you mean?" I ask.

"He feels...very off limits."

I stifle a chuckle. "Cool, so you won't be taking him to bed, then?"

I expect her to laugh. Instead, she turns away from me, her strawberry blonde bun catching the dim light. *It was a joke*, I want to say, but I know it's not my lame attempt at humor that has Sloane unnerved. Prodding her won't help. My best bet is to wait her out.

In silence, we watch the last song.

CHAPTER 18

ROANOKE

I'm dripping sweat when we finally finish our set and stumble off the stage. A roadie lobs me a bottle of water and a towel. I drape the latter over the nape of my neck and chug the bottle in four long swallows, then toss it into a garbage can.

I run the towel over my hair before I head for the spot I left Willow. Tonight, I'm keeping my promises.

Damien catches up with me and squeezes my shoulder. December and Carter will come from the other side of the stage, using the backdrop curtain as a private tunnel.

"Did you love that fucking slide thing I did?" Damien asks. The guy is pumped, but then again, all of us are after a show.

"Everybody freaked," I say. It's a good crowd tonight, rowdy. Timber Boom is going to have them raging.

Damien is in front of me, hands flying as he retells the whole story of the slide from start to finish, as if I wasn't there. I'm laughing, half of me positive he's going to trip walking backward like he is, but I'm barely paying attention to him.

I can't find Willow.

She's not where we agreed to meet. I sweep the pile of crates and speakers along one wall. Nothing.

"Hey," Damien says, grabbing my shirt sleeve. He gives me a knowing look and hooks a thumb over his shoulder. At this angle, I can see Willow behind one of the side curtains that had blocked my view of her when I came offstage. Relief courses through me, knocking down the adrenaline rush from playing.

Willow's facing away, watching the crowd, one hand sliding across the bottom hem of her red top over and over. She's put her curls up into a messy bun. I let my eyes meander the curve of her shoulder. The stage lights send a knife-edge of a glow racing down the side of her neck as she leans to whisper to Sloane.

The temptation to touch her is almost too much and then I realize I can. We're acting like a couple again. But after what happened today, the rules have changed; I need to be sure she wants my hands there. I have to talk to her alone, somewhere quiet, figure out where we stand.

I can see Sloane beside her, still staring out at the crowd. What's out there that they find so mesmerizing? As if she senses my gaze, Willow turns. The second she spots me, she lights up in a way that makes me uncertain again.

"Hey, hey!" Damien says, pawing at my arm to get my attention as he leads, walking backwards a few steps in front of me. "Could we work the extra song into our normal set? And I can do the slide?"

I give him a token laugh, my attention on Willow when Sloane whips around to step accidentally into Damien's path, catching him by the shoulders.

Sloane's foot tangles with his. I reach, but it's too late. Damien's quick on his toes, grabs Sloane by the shoulders and twists his body enough that he hits first, a loud 'oof' escaping him before Sloane lands on top of him, cradled in his grip.

There's a good three second pause before Damien grins. "First that slide, now a gorgeous woman throwing herself at me? I am having a *night*!"

Sloane flings her head back and laughs as Damien gives me a wink.

"You okay?" he asks her, and she nods and climbs off him.

"Damien," I yell over the noise of equipment breakdown going on. "Sloane. Sloane, Damien."

"How dare you!" Damien says, as he clambers to his feet. "What the hell am I supposed to start off with for small talk?"

"How about that amazing slide thing you did?" the actress purrs and I know Damien is utterly and truly fucked. About six months ago, he tucked a few pictures of hot girls from magazines on the bottom of the bunk above him, and I'm ninety percent sure one of them was Sloane Marquette. I spent the whole day with him and never warned him she would be with Willow tonight.

I'm a very bad friend.

"Right?" he manages before he turns to Willow. He hooks an arm around Sloane's shoulders like they're old friends. "So, Sloane votes we add it to the show. I'm clearly a mark in the yes column. Willow?" He shoots a finger gun in her direction. "I need your vote, girl."

She waggles her hand and grimaces. "It was a little showy," she says, and I burst out laughing.

Damien finally releases Sloane to clutch his heart in mock devastation.

Sloane's expression fills with amusement, but her pale eyes bore into mine. I'm strangling in them. I give my head a shake, willing the feeling away even as it intensifies. I don't want her anywhere near me.

It's only when I step back a bit from Sloane that it dispels. I glance at the actress. She raises an eyebrow, an uncertain smirk playing at her lips as confusion cycles over my face. Sloane's giving Willow protection against me. If she thought I was dangerous, all she'd have to do is *not* give Willow her blood, and Willow would have to leave. So why is my skin crawling the closer I get to the vampire?

Sloane smiles sweetly, looking from me to Damien and then utters the least likely sentence I would have predicted to come out of her mouth next.

"Can I please meet December?" she asks.

• • • ● • ● • • •

Willow said she needed a few minutes in private with Sloane, time for me to rinse off the sweat from the show, get some hot water running over my sore muscles.

I put everything in tonight. My body paid the price. Since I didn't tonsil-fuck a bottle of whatever was closest the moment the show ended, I've got to deal with the pain.

The hurt I can handle. But I'm staring at a popcorn ceiling, one arm cocked under my head on my pillow as my heart races. Outside, I can barely hear the buzz of highway traffic over the noise of the air conditioner. There's no mini fridge in here. Not a single tiny bottle.

Don't think about it, I will myself.

My mind won't stop. The hum of the air conditioner kicks on and off. I'm wondering about our Winnie parked outside behind the hotel. If, when Willow went through it, she truly found everything. Every pill. Every bottle. The couple minis we had stashed in with the knives and spoons.

There must be something left.

You could go check. That way you'll know. Just in case. You don't have to take it.

My skin crawls with the compulsion to move and so I toss the sheet aside, lower my feet to the carpet and start pacing. I can't get my heart to stop hammering.

One drink.

One drink and this will stop. One drink and I can fucking relax.

I have to get through tonight. Willow is putting her career on the line to help me and the band. Tomorrow will be easier. And the next will be a piece of cake. I swallow hard and my eyes flick to the clock. The hotel bar should still be open. It's not quite midnight. If it's closed, I can go for a walk. Burn off some of this energy. Last call isn't until two.

One drink.

I crouch on the bed again. My fingers touch the phone, the handset. I could call room service. I wouldn't even have to leave. I lift the handset, hear the slow click of the line connecting. No one would have to know. But it's not what I want. It's not what I promised.

A sharp knock sounds from the door. Startled, I drop the receiver into the cradle.

Willow, I think. *Thank God.*

In my rush to the door, I trip over my shoes and almost send myself sprawling. When I answer the door, my surprise is obvious.

"Sloane? Hi." I stand awkwardly in the door frame. She's wearing the same draped top and jeans she had on backstage. In the stilettos she's got on, she's a few inches shorter than me. It's weirdly unnerving how the fame radiates off her. She's taken her hair down so it bounces against the top of her shoulder like a shampoo commercial in slow motion. Willow's gorgeous, and Sloane's in the same category, but there's this pedestal feeling to her. Being in the same room as her only amps it higher. I don't like it.

"Hey, so…" I run my palm over my damp curls and then drag my hand to my shoulder as if having my arm between the two of us will help. "What's up?"

She watches me, silent, clutching the handle of her suitcase. A weird disconnect starts in my brain. She's known. More famous than I could ever hope to be. But she's standing at my hotel room door with a sheepish expression. Her gaze holds quiet power, not right in someone as slight as Sloane. Not right in anyone human.

"Hi," she says, her voice low as if she's afraid of being over-heard. Her gray eyes flick down the hall toward Willow's room. "You and I need to talk. Privately."

No isn't an option. I'm guessing Sloane Marquette isn't a person who hears that word often, and I'm not about to risk pissing off Willow's best friend despite my uncomfortableness so I throw open the door. I'm wondering if I'm supposed to officially invite the vampire in, but she steps past me. *Good to know*, I think to myself.

Drawing out the desk chair, I collapse into it and swivel to face her, eager to get this over with. "What's up?"

Sloane's hand tightens around the handle of the suitcase, worrying it. She steps toward me and I retreat before I think better of it.

Her head tilts ever so slightly. When she speaks, all traces of the power that overwhelmed me have fled. "You can feel that, too, can't you?" She considers me, her mouth pinched into a frown. "Roanoke, have you ever hooked up with a vampire?"

The shocked horror in my expression seems to win her over, because she winces and blows out a long sigh that seems to be more out of annoyance than necessity. "Bad phrasing. Not an offer," she clarifies. "I mean in general."

"I'm an incubus. I don't know how to say this without sounding like an asshole, but the women I sleep with aren't exactly the type who trade secrets with me."

Get her out. The thought in my head is scrambled. Comes in from a wrong channel. Too loud. I raise a hand to cup over my ear and hide the motion by tucking my hair behind it.

"Is Damien then?" she asks. "Is he a vampire?" She pauses. "He didn't smell like one."

"Damien?" I almost laugh at the suggestion, though I'm more caught on the imagery of her scenting him. "No."

"The band you opened for, then?" she pushes. "Someone in their road crew?"

The more she talks, the more desperate she sounds.

"No? I mean, if so, they never mentioned it." I hesitate. "They don't know about us in The Raven Shakes though, so it's possible. What's going on?"

"And you haven't done a blood exchange lately. You remember *nothing* like that? Freaky shit one night with some groupie?"

I stare at her. "Are you being serious?"

"Never woke up from one of your benders with fang marks? The taste of blood on your lips?" Her hand slips off the suitcase handle as she starts a slow saunter toward me across the room.

"No," I answer, my tone definite. "What's going on?"

Her fingers raise to stroke my cheek. I cringe at her touch.

"Don't move," Sloane tells me. She grabs my chin and gives my head a soft wrench to the side, as if she wants to get a better look at my carotid.

My heart leaps to double time. Sloane leans closer to the pulse in my throat. I'm sure she'll sink her fangs into my neck. Inside me, the demon thrashes.

"Relax. You're fine," she says. It's an odd sensation, to have her mouth so close to my skin and not feel the heat of an exhale. "These two freckles. How long have you had them?"

"My whole life, I imagine. Isn't that how freckles work?"

"You specifically remember having them when you were little?"

"Well...no?"

My muscles strain. Sloane presses closer. Her fingers stroke through my hair as I hold the uncomfortable angle. My entire body shivers, as if trying to wriggle away from her. "What the fuck are you doing?" I ask through clenched teeth.

"You feel that too, don't you?" she whispers.

I break. We jolt away from each other like two magnets repelling.

Sloane straightens and nods grimly, apparently satisfied. "You're definitely marked."

I'm hoping it sounds more ominous than it is. "What's that mean, marked?"

"Vampires mark those close to them. It means you're off limits. Taken. Protected. Think of it like a force field."

I grab the television stand for stability. "What?" I ask, exasperated.

"I've never seen another supernatural with one," she adds. "Maybe it's left over from before you took in the demon? I can't..." She fades off, studying me. "I can't figure out how they got past the demon to make the mark stick, otherwise."

I raise a hand to my neck, touching the places Sloane couldn't. My skin's still crawling. Someone marked me. Someone claimed me. Someone had teeth in me. I don't remember any of it.

A dirty feeling crowds into my throat. I'm never drinking

again. "Can I get rid of it?"

"They're really not meant to be removed." She shrugs. "You'd have to cut it out of you. Then I'd have to put my mark overtop. Without it, you're like an open doorway. Too dangerous."

"More dangerous than keeping it?"

"Yes. Honestly, it could be as simple as a fan who gave you a little extra bump of protection. There's strange power in your crowds."

I fight the urge to retreat as she approaches. "Did Willow let you do it to her? Mark her for protection?"

Sloane scoffs. "Have you met the girl? She'd never give up control like that," she says. "Word of advice? Willow doesn't deal well with anyone having influence over her."

I drop my eyes. "Which is why I'm out after this morning, yesterday."

"It's why you *should* be," she says carefully. "You're a bit of a wildcard."

I decide to switch the subject *off* Willow for now. "So should I be worried about mind control with this thing or?"

"It's not mind control so much as a nudge in the direction I want. A hard nudge," she amends. "Plus, whoever gave you that mark would know when you were hurting, in danger. And like you saw, there's protection against other vampires. I couldn't bite you. Neither can anyone else. Well, except the one who made that mark. Could I kill you another way?" She shrugs. "If you were mortal, probably. Trying might draw out whoever put that on you, but it could mean a lot of trouble for me. I'd think damn long and hard before going after anyone marked. Then again, whoever did it is most likely half a country away. Very curious though!" she says as if she hasn't dropped a bombshell.

"Wait," I say. "You *were* trying to bite me?"

She doesn't look particularly guilty. "Trying," she says as she gives me a once over. "Like I said, having that mark protects you. It's weird you don't remember getting it. You must have been pretty fucked up to forget something like that."

The judgement in her voice is clear. But how Sloane Marquette feels about me doesn't matter.

"Me having this," I say. "Does it put Willow in danger?"

Her expression goes odd. "No," she says. "Would you care if it did?"

"Of course," I answer instantly before I back off it. "Look, I know what I am to her."

Sloane's eyes narrow.

"I get it. I'm a job." It hurts to say it out loud, to acknowledge it.

"Yes, you are," she says. "And me? I was Willow's *first* job. I almost lost her to her *last* job."

"Blake?" I say, because some vicious part of me wants to win the point. *I know her secrets*, I want to argue.

"She told you about Blake?" she starts, the words easing out of her like cold molasses.

It's a completely innocuous sentence, but my skin prickles, every tiny hair on my body standing straight. Willow told me people could die over that secret. It could get her killed. I wonder if I should deny everything, but then guilt gets the best of me.

"It was my fault. Your blood was wearing off, and I told her to tell me about him. I didn't know what I was asking." A hot wave of embarrassment rushes over my skin and I kick my toes into the carpet. "I assumed she trusted me because I trusted her with something. But yes, she told me he's dead."

"Did she say how?"

I won't betray Willow by answering, so I rub my jaw and shrug.

"She can't go home," she says, and it's so insistent that I look back up. "You've got to keep her with you."

"She's in trouble, isn't she?" The ground seems to drop out from underneath me. "Bad trouble?"

Sloane nods. "Those wolves want answers, and they think Willow is the one who has them."

What battles out of me is much rawer than I intend. "I can't lose her."

Her lip curls in a silent snarl and the tip of a fang reveals itself against the deep red of her lipstick. I'm not sure if it's meant to scare me. "Don't think this is some verse chorus verse meet-cute," she snaps. "Creatures like us don't get to fall in love, Roanoke."

My arms cross over my chest before I can stop myself. "So, I'm the villain in this story?" I ask.

Her expression softens. Her sad smile flares and fades. "No. I'm here to ask you to be the hero. Let Willow do her job. Keep her occupied and keep her safe for me. You two have to get close. I understand that. But keep it professional."

"I'm trying," I grind out. "I am. But—"

Now it's Sloane's turn to scoff. "Don't be dramatic. She can't mean that much to you already."

Three years. Three years without affection, without a touch that meant more than a goal of pleasure. Until Willow, I starved for a brush of nervous lips, for a laugh not brought on by whiskey and bumbling sex. I ache when her hand's not in mine.

"We're doomed," I whisper. "She and I, we can't..." Sloane knows what I am. "We can't be together long term. But I never expected to see her again and when I did..."

I flick my eyes to Sloane's, hoping what she sees in them will explain when my words can't. Every moment I'm with Willow is like a salve to a burn.

"Roanoke," Sloane asks. "Do you love her?"

I don't answer, crossing to the room's sole overstuffed chair and dropping into it.

"Are you falling in love with her?"

"Should I lie?" I ask.

She frowns. "It's too fast."

My head starts a slow shake. I try to keep the words in, but I can't. "You don't know what it's like to doubt every human connection. I influence everyone around me. I don't have a single friend I can't be sure isn't there because of this thing inside me. You don't understand," I say, "how lonely it is living like this."

Sloane wilts, her shoulders drooping like a flower starved of water and sunshine, and though her voice is light, it's thick with sadness. "I do, though," she says.

She's won damn near every award statue in existence. Faking emotions is her literal job. But those three words aren't lies.

Sloane Marquette has secrets.

I sigh. "Then you get it. How she can mean so much to me, so fast. But I'm not going to talk about this with you. Whatever this is, whatever's happening, it's between me and her."

Sloane paces the section of carpet at the end of the bed a good ten feet from me. "And the bodies, Roanoke?"

I flinch. "We're going to figure out who—"

"You're distracting her!" Sloane argues. "She's next on the list and instead of working on solving this, she's rolling you over in her thoughts, having to chase you down in bars—"

"I won't let anything—"

She holds up a hand to shut me up as the fire of her anger burns out. "I know you'll do everything you can to protect her. But what if it's not enough?"

My voice lowers to a snarl. "Are we talking about whoever's stalking the band, Sloane?" I ask. "Or are we talking about me?"

She doesn't respond.

"Do you think I don't already hate myself for what I did? Do you think I could ever live with myself if this demon in me took a second more of her life?" I pause to get my emotions in check, but the silence only makes things worse. "I hate what I am. I hate that if she cares about me a fraction of how much I care about her, even in the best-case scenario, this is going to end in pain for her." Shaking my head, I bite my lip before I force myself to go on. "I can't walk away, but if she can? Take her. Right now. Get her as far from those wolves, from whoever's killing our fans, from..." I hesitate. "As far from *me* as possible."

She stares at me, stone-faced. The awkward moment stretches into a minute, more. And then Sloane moves to her suitcase where she left it standing near the door.

"She has a few extra doses of blood," she says. "Go talk to her."

The effects of the vampire blood last two days before my influence breaks through. I've got four days until the demon will need to be fed again, and during that time, if the pattern of disappearances stick, someone's going to come after Willow. "I thought you were staying to help?" I ask. "You're not leaving, are you?"

"Gotta be on set early," Sloane says breezily. "I chartered a plane. Go to her. She's waiting." Her head tilts to the side as she studies me across the room. "Welcome to your new life, Roanoke."

"What's that mean?" I call as she opens the door. "Sloane!"

"You're taller than I thought you'd be," she says without turning around, her voice thoughtful. "And you're fucking great live."

The door shuts.

I stand there for a long second trying to process what the hell happened. I grab my sleeved room key from the nightstand, running it across the tips of my fingers as I go to find Willow. My bare feet squish against the hallway carpet. Outside her room, I realize I'm only wearing my boxers and a t-shirt. I hesitate.

You can still leave. Find that bar. Find that drink.

Instead, I knock on Willow's door. There's a rattle as she unlocks the chain and opens it.

"Hey," she says, as if she's been expecting me.

"Hey," I say.

She turns, revealing a room setup exactly the same as mine—King size bed, TV directly across from it, dark maroon blackout curtains drawn closed. She points to her bed where one of my flannels is carefully folded. "You left that in my room today when you…"

She trails off and stops near the table in front of the window. I must have missed the flannel in my rush to pack when I forced her to sleep and abandoned her. "Thanks," I mutter.

She's facing away from me, the long t-shirt she's wearing brushing the backs of her knees, oversized sleeves belled around elbows in motion. She clearly caught a shower earlier; her brown hair drags two dark splotches across her shirt near her shoulders. I wonder if the skin underneath is damp, warm.

"Close it," she says, and I realize I'm still standing in the open doorway.

I can't see what she's doing at the table. I step closer. The door clicks closed. She turns, sees me frozen in the entryway and raises an eyebrow.

"What, do you need a written invitation?" she jokes.

"Yeah, I mean no…I wanted you to know it's my fault. All the stuff that happened and I should have been…it's just you didn't want me to leave that first night and it's been so long since…" I bite my lip and she shoots me a look of concern.

"Shit," Willow murmurs. She drops whatever she's fiddling with at the table and makes her way to me. "When did this start?"

"Huh?"

She reaches forward, her fingers prying open my eyelid. "The confusion," she says, scrutinizing.

I wince away.

"Huh?" I say again and then grab at her hand as she goes for my eyeball a second time. "Stop that!"

"Let me do my damn job, Roanoke," Willow commands.

Perplexed, I stop fighting her. She takes my hand and lifts it to hold out in front of her.

"Hmm, slight trembling. Not bad though," she says. "Any other symptoms of alcohol withdrawal besides the confusion?"

Her grip slides to my wrist, our pinkies resting together as she counts.

We're both silent as the seconds tick by.

"Your pulse is high." She glances at me. Those chocolate brown eyes meet mine.

"I'm not confused," I tell her. "Not anymore." I catch her cheek, my thumb shivering over her blushed skin. "Willow."

Sloane's warning flickers through my mind. Be the hero.

But I'm not, I never have been.

"You're all I think about." I don't break her gaze, not even when the surprise jolts through her. "You're all I want. It'll be complicated. Impossible maybe. But I—"

"Stop," she says.

My chest clenches in anticipation of her rejection.

And then her lips hit mine, the sweet taste of her reawakening my lust.

What the hell are you doing? my brain spits. *What the fuck's wrong with you?*

Her hand flexes against my abs and then presses flat there as if to shush me. Tension tightens my shoulders even as Willow relaxes into me, her mouth skipping across my jaw to my neck. There's a fumbling at my waist as she tugs at my boxers.

I can't help myself. My mouth finds hers again, desperate and searching. Everything in me rages against stopping her. I'm mostly certain it has nothing to do with the demon and everything to do with Willow.

Finally, I break the kiss, my forehead leaning against hers, afraid to pull away completely, not sure if I want this to end, not sure how far I dare let it go. I just want a few minutes more to pretend.

Our breaths mix in the scant space between us, desperate gasps of air before our mouths meet again. This time, when we move apart, reality creeps in around the edges of whatever fantasy we're caught up in. I watch her pull her lip between her teeth, bite it softly as she struggles for words. Everything in me wants to kiss away that hesitation, which means I need this to stop. I need to walk away. Leave. One more temptation—an opened zipper, a flash of skin, the skitter of a touch—and the last of my willpower will slide through my fingers like sand. I won't risk that.

"Roanoke, we need to talk," she says, but her mouth finds mine again, moves along my jaw to my ear. I don't stop her. Her whisper is warm. "Sloane's blood does three things. It heals."

I groan in response, distracted.

"It makes me immune to the incubus sway."

"And the third?" I ask, lost in the sensation of her touch on me.

When my lips find her throat, she swallows hard. "It gives me extra life force," she says.

My mind stutters to a stop as I draw away from her. Willow's eyes hopscotch across my gaze. I fight to catch up with what she's saying. "I don't understand."

"That night at the hotel, the demon didn't take anything but the extra," she says. "Sloane gave me the amount of blood needed to do the healing, and between that and what went to the demon, I had about forty-eight hours of immunity to you left."

I picture the pearl of her life force that night, shining too bright. Electric wattage when there should only have been a glow. I'd noticed it.

She kisses me once, hard. "Today, we upped the dose. I'm expecting four days of immunity and a little extra to burn," she says. "You thought you stole years from me in Austin. Let me give them to you here."

Her fingers stroke the side of my cheek.

"You mean I don't have to—" My throat catches halfway through the sentence as the hope breaks free. I didn't shorten her life.

"And as long as I keep dosing up—"

I can be with her. Only her. I cup her face. "You swear. You're sure?"

"Yes," she says as she nuzzles into my touch. This time, when I meet her mouth, there's no hesitation, no guilt, no second thoughts. I kiss Willow, real in my arms, here and with me by choice, aware of what I am and what that means, and it's Sloane's words that echo in my mind.

Welcome to your new life, Roanoke.

CHAPTER 19

WILLOW

Roanoke's touch steals under the bottom hem of my T-shirt, his mouth on mine. *Are you falling for him?* Sloane asked me backstage before Roanoke joined us.

Falling would imply it hasn't already happened, I answered.

The need I've been swallowing down for days erupts, unstoppable, untamable. He lifts my shirt over my head, my hair swinging, wet and heavy.

"Willow," he whispers and goosebumps pepper my flesh, run up my arms as his fingers chase a fraction of an inch behind. His voice brims with uncertainty, like he can't quite believe he's not dreaming. "Are we doing this?"

"Please," I murmur instead of answering him, not sure what I'm asking for. Something. Anything. Everything. My memory flashes to the end of the nightmare when I woke up in his arms. I move my frantic hands to the spot between my shoulder blades where my bra fastens, undo the clasp, drop it. "Touch me."

At the demand he leans, his forehead meeting mine as he

palms my breast. His thumb circles my nipple. It pebbles at the brush of contact. "Until you beg me to stop," he says.

The aching need inside me swells. Between my legs, I grow slicker. I knock a knee to the side, spread to give him the access he needs as he moves one of his hands there. His fingers hesitate close to my mound. The slightest twitch would have him touching me exactly where I want. Neither of us moves, lost in the exquisite power of our shared temptation.

Roanoke breaks first, two fingers sliding past my thong and into my heat. I grab his shoulders, clutch him to me. His stiff cock presses low against my belly. I'm torn between which I want more as his fingers slide in and out, find my clit, circle it slow.

I'll never get enough of him. It should scare me, this thought, the sheer desperation in it, but then Roanoke's kissing me, lowering me onto the bed and my brain skips into pleasure. He's drawing down my panties, and then his tongue is between my thighs. I tilt my hips. His fingers curl deep, hit a spot that sends a keening noise up my throat and out into the silence of the room. His mouth works with the same glorious talents he used in Austin. I remember what came after, what's coming soon, and my body thrums.

"You swear this isn't a dream?" I get out.

He leans back for a split second to strip off his shirt and toss it away. His lips skim my nipple's puckered tip, the contact tightening it to the point of pain. His breath skates across my skin. I draw my hands around the base of his jaw and haul him to my mouth.

Our kiss starts gentle, a press of his lips before his tongue darts forward to circle mine. He cups my cheeks like I'm precious to him. "Everything changed the night I met you. See where this takes us," he says. "That's all I'm asking of you."

"Roanoke," I say quietly. I move my touch over his biceps, down his arms, to where he pins my shoulders against the sheets underneath us. My fingers curl under his. "I'm not going anywhere."

His inhale is shaky. He gives me a stiff nod. "Okay."

"I'm not going anywhere," I tell him again, only this time it's heavy with my promise. "When I'm with you—" I cut off and swallow hard. "I really like who I am when I'm with you."

"The moment I saw you in Austin—" He falls silent, abandoning whatever he'd been about to say with a flurry of kisses. "I don't want to put too much on you, too fast," he says, even as I melt under his mouth.

"You're not," I say. "I'm right with you." I take his hand and slide it between my legs. "I want *you*, Roanoke."

A sound breaks from him, somewhere between a sigh and a moan, the last of his walls crumbling. His tongue flicks across his lips. "Remember how I said that thing about not rushing?" he says with a wince.

Nodding, I tilt my head to expose my neck, let him find the spot he's learning I like. "Second thoughts?" I guess.

He nods. "Overrated."

His fingers linger at the dip where my hip bone meets my upper thigh. His touch makes me ticklish, but he seems stuck there, hyperfixated.

"What are you doing?" I ask with a giggle.

"Nothing," he says, too quickly.

I raise an eyebrow when he squeezes the rounded edge of my hip and then looks up at me. His expression fills with wonder. "It's just," he starts before his voice goes serious. His thumb strokes the same square inch of skin. "I remember this spot."

Before I can process his words, he lines himself up between my legs, the head of his cock sinking into me an inch, no more. Clinging to him, I tilt my hips in anticipation. How many times have I fantasized about this since Austin? I will my body to relax as I stretch around him, try to concentrate on him, not the demon, what it's doing.

Sloane better be right about this, I think, but then Roanoke eases into me and it's worth it, worth it, worth it, anything to have him. I remember what I told him in the Winnebago that first day, that he's not worth dying over, but I would give more years if it meant I spent the ones left with him.

This is crazy, a little voice in my head yells. But is it?

Maybe part of me knew, even then, how important he would become to me.

His arm curls around the back of my neck, cuddling me close to him as he starts on a rhythm. We roll together like waves, breaking against a shared shore to tumble forward again. My cry of pleasure pierces the quiet.

Roanoke tucks his lips near my ear. "That sound is more beautiful than any song I'll ever write."

I wrap my legs around him, lock my heels above the swell of his ass to draw him deeper. With each thrust, my need grows. I want him. I want to know everything about him, learn the tiny details that make up Roanoke, the whys that got him here.

I want to know his firsts and be his lasts.

We both speed our tempo until we're slapping together, desperately inching toward a shared release. My fingernails scrape down his shoulder blades as I dig for purchase, give him the angle he needs to drive into me.

"I'm close," he warns.

I meet his mouth, kiss him hard. "I'm closer."

My core clenches around him, sends him over the edge, the sweet throb of him spilling into me as I cry out again, arch my back as the orgasm rocks through me.

After, once the pleasure fades and there's nothing but the oxytocin left, Roanoke collapses on top of me, his weight a heavy comfort. A blissed-out smile winds onto my lips as I cuff the nape of his neck and draw him into the nook at my shoulder. He rolls to the side, but his head stays nestled against me. I press my hand against his cheek and sigh happily, then slide my fingers through his curls, make the motion soothing.

Slowly, by degrees over the next fifteen minutes, he relaxes in my arms. I'm almost sure he's asleep when he speaks, his tone drowsy and quiet. "I can't wait to wake up exactly like this."

I kiss the top of his head and then nuzzle in closer as I give in to my exhaustion. I'm dead asleep when I hear someone calling me.

Willow? It's female, dreamy and soothing, the syllables of my name rising into a plea. *Can you come to the door, Willow? I just want to say hello to you.*

I'm on the brink of consciousness before I tumble back into the post-sex lull of a dream where Ro and I are cuddling in bed, and in that dream, I'm dreaming, too, the layers stacking on top of each other. *Hide*, I think. *Go deeper. Run.*

That strange whispering goes sharp and cold and cruel, rips me to the surface of my consciousness again. *Come to the door, you cunt*, she snarls. *Let me in.*

Her giggle claws chills up my spine and I wince, groan, distantly aware of the pillow under my head, the bed.

Tapping fills my ears, like nails against the wall, scraping. The rattle of a doorknob. *He's mine. He never wanted you. You're food for his demon.*

I don't like this dream anymore. I'm lucid enough to shove out of it and into the silent black of sleep.

Except something's wrong. In the dream, Roanoke's fingers wrap around my wrist.

"Help me," he says, his voice straining with the effort of speaking and somehow, I know he shudders though he's not touching me, not near me anymore.

Because he's leaving. Following the voice.

"Please," Ro gets out, the word high-pitched with panic.

There's a quiet click.

Then, silence.

Silence and warmth and I'm fading, fading, fading. That click though...my brain catches on the sound, plays it repeatedly, scrolling through hundreds of comparisons, puzzling it out until—

I bolt upright as if surfacing, covered in sweat and shaking.

My head pounds like no hangover I've ever experienced. I've got one hand on the mattress, blearily trying to sit up. The other reaches for Roanoke.

He's not there.

I didn't lock the chain on the door. The click was the door closing because I didn't lock the chain.

Whoever killed those other girls, tonight, she came for me.

Sloane's blood blocked her. My brain still feels ravaged and riffled through. And Roanoke—*He never wanted you*, she growls in my memory. *He's mine.*

"Oh God," I whisper, throwing myself out of bed. I'm topless, my bra lost somewhere in the sheets. I fumble for my shirt, give up, and lock eyes on where Roanoke's clothes should lay. They're gone, except for his battered flannel. I grab it and slam my arms through the sleeves, fumbling the buttons closed.

"Fuck!" I yell and then rub my face, twirling, trying to figure out my next move. Pants. I grab a pair of shorts. I don't bother with shoes. At the last second, I snag my phone off the nightstand and then hurry, barefoot, out into the hallway, dialing as I pick a direction.

December answers almost instantly. "Willow?" she says, her voice rough with sleep.

"Get dressed," I blurt, definitely too loud for someone who's trying to keep things discrete. "It's Roanoke. The whispering. It was in my head, and he's gone."

"The hell?" she murmurs, the words heavy with exhaustion and anger.

"His blackouts, December. You called them Band-Aids. I

thought he was sleepwalking." I'm not making sense. My panic is all-consuming. The dream is spiraling away like smoke. "She came for me. Oh God, she came for me, but when she couldn't have me, she took him instead!"

Something's festering.

Festering. Oozing into his subconscious when he's not in his right mind, when his consciousness is compromised.

"Are you having a nightmare or something?" December asks, groaning as I hear her stretch.

"Nightmare," I repeat. Everything feels strange, one step off from where it should be. "No? He was here. I heard someone else. A woman."

"Willow, take a deep breath, okay?" she asks. The sheets rustle as she gets out of bed. She's finally taking me seriously. "Is he still in the hotel?"

"Yes." He wouldn't have had time to get down the stairs unless he was running and I'm guessing, hoping, he's in more of a shamble if he's not truly awake.

"You're still immune to me?" she asks.

"Yeah. I got a booster from Sloane earlier at the concert."

"Good," December says. "Hang up with me. Call Carter. Tell him what you told me and then tell him to keep his ears siren-style, got that?"

"Ears siren-style?" I repeat.

"Tell him you're meeting me at the pool." She hangs up before I can argue, but not before I figure out her plan.

"She's going to sing him back," I whisper to the hallway.

I break out of my trance, trying not to think about what's

happening and dial Carter, relay the message.

I expect him to question it or argue, especially since I clearly woke him out of a dead sleep, but there's only a curt, "Yup," before he hangs up. There's nothing left for me to do but bolt for the pool area on the first floor.

I make it down the stairs, follow the hall, watching for any trace of Roanoke as I go.

What if that voice wants him dead and sleepwalks him into traffic?

No, I tell myself. *She wanted him for herself.* But my brain isn't satisfied. *What if he gets across the street safe and December sings and it draws him into traffic?*

My mind's a mess. I've got to calm down, take charge. The air smells like chlorine and chemicals.

"Hey," I hear from behind. Carter's jogging toward me, his white-blond hair a riot of twist on the left side of his head, blue eyes squinted against the light. His arms cross over his undershirt. Whatever's written on my face has him reevaluating the situation.

He slings an arm over my shoulder as he passes by and starts me walking toward the poolroom at the end of the hall. "No worries. We'll find him," he says, though he doesn't sound confident.

"I woke up and he was gone," I say. "Damn it, I shouldn't have fallen asleep."

"The plan was to stay awake forever?" he asks. He sounds unnerved in a way I don't like. "Dec really said to meet her at the pool?"

I nod. "That and to tell you the ear thing. What's that mean, anyway?"

For the space of a dozen footsteps, Carter doesn't answer. "On stage, Roanoke and Damien have to wear earphones when she sings to block her voice. Me?" The corner of his mouth lifting in a smirk. "I shapeshift the bones in my ears. Much more efficient. Ro said you're immune to her?"

I nod, distracted. As he's speaking, we get close enough to the door that I can see the shattered glass of the small window.

"She's in there," Carter says, his tone low and cautious. When he looks at me, I'm almost positive it's fear in his eyes before his expression goes serious. "You let me handle this, Willow. If she tries to hurt me—"

"Hurt you?" I repeat.

Carter hesitates. "She wouldn't come here if she didn't intend to go in the water," he says, each word struggling from him. His hand worms through the jagged hole in the glass. "Don't let anyone in. If anybody gets near her, she'll drown them."

"What?" I say.

"And probably eat them," he adds. "Hopefully in that order."

"But what about Roanoke?" I ask, horrified.

"I think that's what I'm here to stop," he says. At my stunned silence, Carter sniffs. "Don't worry. I'm a good swimmer."

Before he throws the door open, he moves himself in front of me.

When we enter the poolroom it's dark, save for the underwater lights and the blue glow they send wavering across the ceiling and walls. December stands near the deep end, faced away from us, her braids undone, hair running free. A long sleep shirt hangs almost to her knees. She's got her shoes off, her toes wiggling against the concrete floor.

"December?" I call. Her name echoes around the otherwise empty room. She doesn't react, doesn't respond at all.

Carter whips a finger in front of his lips and points to the door. I want to argue that I'm not useless, but there's no time. I move. No one can get in without a key, but I flick the deadbolt, the click tumbling my brain back into the dream. Roanoke, scared, fighting, failing.

And I didn't wake up.

We're getting him back, I think desperately.

Carter's voice is a whisper, but the sound carries. "You sure this is a good idea, Dec?"

"Nope," she says. "But someone's got him, Carter. Something's been wrong for a while. Long before the bodies started. I knew." Her voice breaks. "Damn it, I knew."

Carter helps her sit and then hovers nearby as she trails her hand through the water. "You don't have to—"

"Yes, I do. You don't know what I said to him. What I accused him of. I owe him this." She pauses. "The water will make me stronger than whatever that bitch is that has a hold of him," she says, and this time there's no mistaking her terror. "Just keep him safe from me." Her profile catches the blue light as she turns to look up at Carter, her expression uncertain. "Bring me back, okay? If you can?"

"Wait," Carter says. "There's another way. There has to be."

December shakes her head. "There's not."

She slides forward. Her shirt makes a soft swish against the edge of the pool. She disappears over the lip, into the water.

"Carter?" I yell from where I'm positioned against the door. He doesn't turn. Doesn't acknowledge me. *Because he can't hear me*, I realize.

He inhales a lungful of air, then another. He's hyperventilating himself. Which means he expects to go into that water with her. "You were serious?" I ask, but he doesn't answer.

December's blonde head bobs in the middle of the pool. She rises slightly, the water streaming from her as her breath blows tiny ripples. Her sudden laugh is so full of joy that I find my insides aching. Gradually, it tapers, the echo of it bouncing in ever quieter doublings.

A sound drifts from her, close to a cooing, as her fingers sluice through the water. There's a swell, and an orangish-red mermaid tail claps the surface.

"Oh, wow," I whisper.

Her attention snaps to me. Her head crooks to the side. I watch as she smiles with too many teeth, as she swims toward me. I'm afraid to move. If I do, she'll chase me. December's no storybook mermaid.

A sharp clicking sounds to my left. Carter strides to the edge of the pool, snapping his fingers. The instant she zeroes in on him, I'm left with no doubt what's in the pool is pure predator. She glides, her movements slow and methodical and calculated.

Carter saunters backward, teasing her along the edge, closer to him. Her arms lift over the rim of the pool. Water swishes

across the concrete. The puddles soak in to leave mere damp-
ness. Her eyes are unnaturally green, nearly glowing.

"Come on," Carter says, the words off-key. "Call me in for
the kill. Gotta sing, Dec."

As if in answer, the coo rolls out of her again. This time, the
note rises, holds before it settles into a melody.

There aren't words to the song, not that I can hear. The hum
of her voice crests in a syrupy wave, cool and calm as it rolls
over me. When I glance down, I'm surprised to find I've stepped
forward. Sloane's blood should have my immunity to December
stronger than it's ever been. But when we tested it, December
wasn't in the water, was still human. Now, we're more closely
matched. It never occurred to me I could be in danger.

I jam myself against the door. Carter takes a skittering step
out of reach as her outstretched hand beckons him. Her voice
rises, the notes hover and hum over each other, complicating,
replicating and a pain starts in my head, throbbing hard and fast
in time with my heartbeat.

A thump pounds against the door at my back. Then another.
I whip around to see a woman's face pressed against the cracked
glass at the top of the pane, eyeball rolling in her socket. A man
claws at her, knocks her onto the floor and takes up the place
she occupied.

There's another thump. Another. A small hand, a child's,
works its way into the jagged hole, cutting a finger, smearing the
glass with maroon and as if December can scent the blood, she
goes nuclear behind me in the pool. Her song blasts from her
throat, reverberating in the tiny space loud enough to make my

ears ring.

There's a hard thunk against one of the floor-to-ceiling windows that line the view to the parking lot and when I turn, relief floods through me at the shadowed outline.

"Roanoke!" I call and though he's caught under December's spell, he still looks at me, a split second of clarity and confusion in his features before she launches into another song as his expression glazes again. His fingers scrape uselessly against the glass.

I leave the door. It's locked. The people on the other side of it, hotel guests, more of them now, they're not trying to unlock it. It'll hold. All that matters is getting to Roanoke. I pad across the room toward the window. All that matters is—

Fingers clamp around my ankle. I have half a startled second when I realize December's song worked on me before I'm yanked off balance. My chest slams against the concrete. I grunt, stunned and in pain.

The siren drags me backward.

"Wait. No!" I scream. My fingers rake, a nail tearing. The last thing I see as I go over the lip of the pool is Roanoke slamming his shoulder against the window.

The water's freezing. I come up gasping. Carter calls my name, all his faux bravery gone. He races toward me. "Hang on, Willow!"

"Help m—" Chlorine blurs my vision as I'm yanked to the bottom. The word disappears into a cluster of bubbles. Pressing my lips together, I flinch from a flash of orange.

December's green eyes glow like the lure lights of deep ocean fish, head tilted as she stalks me, her blonde hair fanning around her in the water.

I have to be smart. I relax as if I'm passing out and curl, knees bent, the water rotating me until my toes touch concrete.

One breath. One. That's all I need.

I shove off the bottom, rocket upward. My fingers break the surface. Carter grabs my hand to haul me up, out, free, but the siren latches onto my ankle. Bubbles distort my vision. I'm inches from air.

Even over the splashing, I hear Carter calling my name, begging her to let me go. My arm muscles yank as he struggles for all he's worth, the hand in mine shapeshifting into something not human, stronger, but still not enough. His grip slips to my wrist, and then my fingers slide through his hold as December tugs me down. My lungs burn. I don't have much time.

And then she releases me.

I kick, terrified, but if she's letting me go, some part of her must have remembered who I am.

I stretch, touch the air I so badly need. Half a second and I'll be able to breathe. But before my head breaks the surface, December gives my ankle another rough yank and my fingers submerge again.

Dread fills me as I spin on her, try a different tactic. I swim sideways. She follows along, grinning. All those teeth. She's toying with me.

I grab her, the thing that almost looks like December. I search the jade irises for any recognition, for any inkling the human part of her is in there and find nothing. My hands fist her hair.

"Please." The word rises in a prayer along with the last of my air and the siren shakes free of my grip and snaps her teeth at me. *She's going to eat me alive*, I think.

A trail of bubbles erupts behind her in the pool. Another from the other side, arcing. She releases me, her attention waning now that I'm not fighting her. I sink to rest against the bottom, my arms outstretched. I blink hopelessly into the blue light far above me.

I can't breathe, I think. *I can't—*

I choke as my lungs give in to instinct. I draw another lungful of liquid, and everything goes calm, my desperate heart slowing. There's a scuffle, movement, but the siren is gone. My vision tunnels.

It's so quiet.

Roanoke, I think. I want to picture him here, with me. I don't want to die alone. But when I close my eyes, he's gone, too.

Chapter 20

Roanoke

I pump Willow's chest, count to fifteen beats, exhale into her mouth again. Her blue lips are cold. Water drips from my chin, slides from her cheeks like tears, but she's not crying. She's not anything.

"Come on," I whisper. "Breathe for me."

Time keeps passing and I can't be sure how much because I spent some of it under Dec's song. My arms shake. I'm exhausted. It doesn't matter. I rise over Willow on the concrete floor of the poolroom, my elbows locked as I drive my weight onto her breastbone again and again.

"Anything?" Carter yells, the single word broken by his chattering teeth. He's got December, the two of them off in a corner as far from Willow and I as he could get her, his arms wrapped around her from behind. She's in human form again, though mentally she's not quite right yet.

Without answering Carter, I lean, drawing in the air to give Willow another round of mouth to mouth. While he'd shifted parts of himself into something brutal to battle our siren from the water, to clamp off her vocal chords, I struggled Willow's deadweight up and over the edge of the pool, waiting for her to smile, throw her arms around me, explain what the hell happened.

Now, I jab a finger against her eyelid, lift it. All I see are the whites. She doesn't wince away, doesn't fight me. I smack my palm against her cheek lightly as if it's waking up she needs and not a miracle.

"Please, Willow." I groan, dropping my ear to her chest, telling myself I'm only listening for a heartbeat, not hugging her goodbye. "You're still in there. I know you're still in there."

I freeze, waiting.

Count.

Nothing.

Across the room, December wails and the last bits of me holding together shatter at the sound. She's back. She sees what she's done as the siren. December never gets near water. It's suicide to everything she's worked for, every rule she lives by. Why was she in the pool? Why were Carter and Willow here? What the fuck were they all doing?

As December babbles panicked denials through Carter's attempts to comfort her, I run through my memories.

A few hours ago, I fell asleep, Willow naked and warm, curled around me.

I woke up alone, outside, dressed in my boxers and T-shirt. In the past, when coming out of the thrall of December's song, I've always remembered what happened, most likely because of the incubus. Tonight, I had no memory of how I got outside, only knew that I had to get through that window, stop what was about to happen. I pressed against the glass as relief bloomed on Willow's face, watched a hand slither out of the pool to snag her ankle. I saw who that hand belonged to, understood the danger Willow was in.

Now, December draws a deep lungful of air and keens loudly.

"Keep her away," I call to Carter.

I hear him trying to soothe her, his empty promises everything will be okay. But it won't. I run my fingers over Willow's hair. They snag in the wet strands. From behind her mostly closed eyelids, the tiniest slit of white peeks through. Dark circles cloud the pale, grayish-blue skin under them. It's not going to be okay.

Through the panic, through the rage and confusion and the slow agony of loss building in me, I hear Sloane's angry words from earlier. *Creatures like us don't get to fall in love, Roanoke.*

At least not for long, I think. Scooping Willow against my chest, I squeeze my eyes shut so I won't see the diluted blood seeping from her torn nail onto the soaked concrete. She must have ripped it off while fighting for her life.

I clutch her to me, my warm air against her chilled skin. My scream grows, rips out of me in primal agony. All my heartbreak, all my dying hope, they echo through the room.

I had days with her. It took me days to get her killed. She has to come back to me. But when I let go of her, she slumps, lifeless, against the floor.

"No! You don't get to die on me!" I command as I rise into

position over her. I give her two chest compressions. I'm exhausted. I don't have anything left to give. And then I see it, that bloody nail bed pink and pale. Healing.

"Willow?" I can't get her entire name out as her ribs hiccup. "Oh fuck, please."

Water burbles from her mouth like a fountain gone wrong and she tries to cough, chokes instead, drowning all over again. I roll her onto her side. She wheezes around the fluid, too weak to clear her lungs.

"Is she alive?" I hear Carter call in utter disbelief, and I can't stop the insane laugh that escapes me in answer.

Willow gags, one palm splaying against the cement as she vomits up a stomach-worth of clear liquid.

"Easy," I whisper, stroking her hair, keeping her on her side as she empties the rest of the pool water from inside herself.

Finally, she collapses. I catch her and drag her onto my lap. Her fingers spider across my shoulder, tightening against me as if she's testing to make sure I'm real.

"Ro?" she croaks.

"Yeah. I'm here. I've got you." I'm soaked and shuddering, watching her as if this is some awful trick and she'll be tugged back into death at any second.

She clings onto me. All I can do is hold her.

"It worked," she says, and I think she's talking about the chest compressions, the mouth to mouth, my desperate attempts to revive her, until she adds, "We got you back."

• • • ● ● ● ● ● • • •

"I don't understand," I say again, pacing the carpet. We're in December's room, Damien on the end of one of the twin beds, looking almost as confused as I am. Willow is alone on the other bed, still soaked despite the towel I wrapped her in. She's drawn her knees tight to her chest, her arms wrapped around them. I pause my pacing to squeeze her shoulder. She lays her head on her knees and blinks up at me.

Against the headboard, Carter cradles December. "Everyone's safe," he murmurs, and she gives a wet shudder that only seems to ramp up the tempest of her breakdown. "You didn't do anything wrong."

She's our December, she's human, but her eyes are a startling green I don't like. Her oversized T-shirt is stretched and torn. Her blonde hair hangs in stringy clumps. "Carter, I had to do it, right?" She claws at his shirt, grabs handfuls as if to anchor herself to him. "Ro was in trouble. I had to go into the water!"

"You did great," he insists.

She gives her head a violent shake. "No, no, you don't understand," she says, the words perilously close to an unhinged babble. "What I did. To Willow. It's over. You'll never see me the same." Her voice breaks and she huffs a quick inhale between each word. "I let her out."

Carter shoots me a helpless look.

When Willow speaks, her voice comes out flat and quiet. She's not looking at any of us. "It was my fault. I thought I would be immune even when you were stronger, December."

She's in shock. Shouldn't she be shivering? Freaking out? Something? Blue veins stand out on her skin, but my memory is haunted by how gray it looked only minutes before.

"My question," I say, doing my damnedest to hide the anger threatening to creep in. "Is why were you guys in the pool-room?" It's Carter I'm watching for a reaction. He's the one I'm holding responsible. "How did December end up in the water?"

Adjusting on the bed, Carter stares me down. "You don't remember anything?" he asks, as if he doesn't believe me.

Willow pipes up from behind me. "I thought I was dreaming," she says.

I sit beside her and take her hand. She's freezing.

"I heard a voice. Female. Calling me. She wanted me to open the door," she says. She lifts her head from her knees. "I think whatever she is, she's using mind control to lure out the women, then killing them and dumping their bodies close to get your attention."

The thin ribbon of horror inside me swells, twists tight around my heart. "Jesus," I whisper. "Do you think it really happened then? Or was it a nightmare?"

I glance at December, Carter, Damien. They're all wearing strange expressions I don't understand.

It's Carter who breaks the silence. "Where were you, Ro?"

"Me?" I blurt. "I was sleeping. December's singing must have drawn me to the pool."

He frowns as he looks at Willow.

Doubt wrinkles her brow. "No," she says to me. "The closing

door woke me up. That was before I got December. She wasn't anywhere near the pool then."

Now it's December's turn to cut in on the conversation. "Who did you leave with, Roanoke?" she asks.

"No one!" I insist.

Carter's jaw tightens. On the covers, his hand fists. "You left on your own, then?"

Damien scoffs. "He wouldn't do that."

"Let him answer," Carter demands. "Where'd you go?"

"I was—" Sleeping with Willow. And then I remember seeing her through the window. And in between...

A head bobs in front of me, down the hall, past the desk, a hand reaching to snag mine. I'm a riot inside, screaming, clawing at my consciousness, but my body moves as if it doesn't belong to me, in slow, steady steps through the lobby.

Don't be afraid, *she whispers, and suddenly I'm not. My emotions deaden.*

You want this as much as I do, *she says.* You know you do. We'll go away together and never come back. *There's perfume in my nose, something tropical and cloying. The perfume's in my nose because her lips are pressed against mine, mimicking the motions of kissing, except I'm not kissing her back because I don't want this. I don't want this.*

I never wanted any of this.

I'm desperate to hold on to the wisps of memory. Down the hallway. Lips on mine but they weren't Willow's. It's a flashback, from the time before Cassandra turned me, when I was under her sway. It has to be. Because suddenly I'm placing that voice in my head. That sadistic whisper.

Cassandra.

No. She's dead. She gave me the demon and so she's dead.

"Ro?" December calls and I snap out of the fugue, blinking hard and fast.

"New question," Carter says as he studies me. "Where were you just *now*?"

"Sorry, I'm..." I wait as if the answers will pop into being between us. All three of their heads, Willow, Dec, and Damien, swivel between Carter and I, waiting to see how this is going to play out. The coral snake on Carter's arm fills with bright reds, yellows.

Red on yellow, kill a fellow, I think. A rhyme for how to tell what's venomous.

A cold sweat skitters across my skin.

"Willow called me when she found you missing," December says.

My breaths come faster. What if Cassandra's not dead? What if she's the one who's been killing those women? As what, a punishment? Denial rattles through me, the truth too terrible to face. I'm wrong. It's just terrible memories. Ghosts.

December's eyes narrow. "She said there was a voice and she woke up and you were gone. That's why we went to the pool." For a split second, she seems herself, confident. "I went into that water because I thought something had you, Ro."

I'm the reason they were in the pool. I'm the reason Willow almost died. I'm the reason December went full siren. Something did have me. Tonight. My skin crawls as I think of all the times I've blacked out the past few months, woke up missing chunks of time, never sure how I made it back to the Winnebago when I couldn't remember my own name. I stand up, cross the room to brace against the wall, bent over. "Jesus Christ."

You've never woken up with the taste of blood on your lips? Sloane asked when she told me about the vampire's mark and I'd said no, of course not, but now a dozen memories crowd my head. December, worried about me, thumbing dried blood under my nose. The times I woke up with cuts and bruises because I was wasted and fell. Or fought. But did I? Were they scrapes? Or were they puncture marks?

The obvious answer crashes over me.

Cassandra passed me the demon because she found a better offer. Then, sometime in the past few months, she found me. She's been feeding off me. Controlling me. What she did to me in Chicago, she's doing it again. She got her teeth in me again.

"Oh, God," I manage. The realization hits me. She's the one who marked me. She's—

Shh, a tiny voice in my head whispers.

The room starts a slow spin.

"Roanoke, you okay?" Damien asks.

"Vampire," I fight out. The syllables sound a little slurred even to my own ears. "Sloane...she..."

Willow gives me a confused look before she clarifies to the others. "Sloane's giving me blood. That's how I'm immune to Roanoke. That's how I'm mostly immune to December."

"Wait," Damien says. "Sloane Marquette is a vampire?"

Willow nods and I'm expecting Damien to flip out—he has

got to be at max after the shit that's gone on tonight—but Damien's response is so utterly Damien that any other time it would make me laugh.

His face screws up. "Thought it was weird that I didn't feel a heartbeat when she was on top of me earlier."

Now it's Carter's turn to look perplexed. "Why the fuck was Sloane Marquette on top of you?" His confusion deepens. "And what parts of her were you touching?"

Damien smirks. "Parts I noticed didn't have a heartbeat."

Rolling her eyes, December breaks free of Carter's hold and stands. The ripped hem of her shirt hangs near her bare knees. A shiver rolls through her and I watch as she blurs and distends, lines and colors drooping from her.

A tingle starts at the side of my neck and radiates across my body. *Danger*, I think. *Caution.* Yellow and red.

Relax, Roanoke. A strange feeling of disconnect washes over me, every limb going loose, undone.

Let's end this. Watch how they turn against you. Watch how quickly it happens.

December is the only one who seems to notice something's wrong. Watching me warily, her chin tips toward me as she crosses her arms. "What's up with you all of a sudden?"

I don't want you guys to get mad.

"I don't want you guys to get mad." The words are out before I process them.

Nevermind, I'm fine, Cassandra says in my head, her tone flippant.

"Nevermind, I'm fine," I repeat in the exact cadence she used.

December cocks her head. "Are you fucked up?" she asks.

Cold terror washes through me as I realize exactly what's happening.

Laugh at her, Cassandra demands.

My throat convulses, trying to obey the command, but I won't. I won't do it.

Laugh at her, Cassandra says again, insistent and this time a hesitant chuckle breaks from me. It sounds all wrong, fake, which only makes December's eyes narrow.

Yes, I think. *You know something's wrong here. Help me.*

"If you let us think you were in danger while you were out popping pills," she snarls. "Let me see your pupils."

Let her see them. Keep your eyes open. Deny nothing.

My heart jackhammers into double time. On the outside though, my body follows her orders, gives no reaction.

Help, I think, staring at December, willing her to see through whatever mask I'm wearing. The tiny rebellion of not laughing cost me. I'm exhausted, a headache throbbing in my temples.

Get out of my head, I think as hard as I can.

"He's fucked up on something," December says. There's no hurt in her voice, only rage.

"No," Willow says. She crawls off the bed, toward me, one finger tugging up on my lid like she'd done earlier. I keep my eyes open like I was told. Tears blur my vision.

The sting of betrayal floods Willow's face and it's wrong, all wrong on her, because I promised her I would never let her down again.

I haven't, I want to scream. *Please, you have to trust me.* But

I've given her no reason. I have a couple days of sobriety under my belt, and she's already seen me slip up once, almost twice.

"Ro?" she whispers, as if begging me to tell her what she's seeing isn't true.

Blink, the voice says. I blink. Tears wet the corners of my eyes. *Tell her you're sorry.*

"I'm sorry," I whisper.

No! My brain goes frantic. I play the conversation with Sloane at double speed. *A hard nudge,* she'd said. Which means I can beat this. If I can't beat this, I can at least fight it. I can try. I think of the quickest way out of this, of the only person I know of who can help, who would know what's going on with me without me having to explain it all.

Don't, the bitch in my head snarls. *You have to do what I say. I'm telling you no.*

"Call." I grate out the single syllable. My throat closes. Power surges through me, but it's not mine. It crackles across my tongue and the word I'm grasping for slips. I concentrate on Willow, nothing else. She's all that matters and to stay with her, I have to get out two words. That's it. I can do it.

"Call Sloane," I croak.

"What?" Willow says. She shakes her head, confusion and disgust warring across her features. "Why? What's Sloane got to do with anything?"

Call Sloane, I mouth, but I'm fighting my body and I'm sure the words are unreadable. Air rushes from my lungs like I've been gut punched. I double over, heaving, and I remember the water Willow swallowed splashed across the poolroom floor.

Maybe this is what it's going to take to get Cassandra out of my head.

I can make you hurt, she says. Pain flares through me, skating over my skin, everywhere at once. *I don't want to do this. I love you. Be good, Roanoke.*

Bring it on, I think back. I don't know if she can hear me. Don't care.

"What the fuck is happening to him?" December says as agony drops me to my knees on the carpet. If Cassandra's trying to burn down my life, take me away, I'm going to make it as hard on her as possible.

Stand up, she commands.

I revolt against the order.

We both know you can't take much more of this. Don't be stupid, Roanoke.

The demon is utterly silent. I can't feel it at all, not moving, not crawling up my spine, not tucked into the hollow behind my ribs where it likes to curl tight. *Wrong*, I think. *Something's so wrong.*

It knows her. That's why it's not fighting against this.

"What should we do?" Carter asks.

Damien throws up his hands. "Obviously, call fucking Sloane!" he says. He hands Willow his phone as my cheek rests against the hotel carpet. "Here."

Yes, I think, mentally pumping a victory fist. I remember how I fought to bring Damien into the band. How December and Carter instantly vetoed him when they found out where I'd recruited him from. How Damien won them over slowly, just by being himself, no matter the secrets that made him a gamble.

"Dial the number, Willow," Damien says, and there's no room in it for argument. God, I fucking love him at this moment.

The tingling returns, like fingers cradling my brain. The air in the room goes acrid. I smell burning, sharp ozone.

You're okay, Cassandra's voice says, only this time she doesn't sound like she's in charge. She sounds scared, her words broken as if the signal's fading.

I'm better than okay, I think as my fingers curl into claws against the carpet. *I'm winning.* My vision halos, white lights exploding around the edges of my sight. I clench, but this time it's not her. It's me. My body.

"Oh my God, he's having a seizure," I hear December say from far off and then Willow's voice.

"Sloane?" she says. "You've gotta come back. Now. Right now!"

In my head, Cassandra screams.

CHAPTER 21

WILLOW

Running my fingers through Roanoke's damp curls, I watch his eyes flicker under his lids. I don't know whether he's dreaming or overdosing or still suffering some sort of absence seizures. When he lost consciousness, Carter lifted him onto the bed and I slid under, resting Roanoke's head in my lap.

The demon won't let him die, I remind myself. It's become a mantra. *The demon won't let him die. It won't let him die. He's not dying.*

A knock sounds on the hotel room's door and before I can react, Damien's already up and crossing the room.

"Hollywood!" he greets Sloane loudly. "We meet again!"

"You could have just asked for my number, you know," she says. "Didn't have to pull this drama. We were taxiing to the runway."

She gives Damien's abs a friendly pat as she comes around the corner of the bathroom. When she catches sight of my face, the play drops from hers. "Jesus Christ, Willow."

I offer a weak smile. Her eyes flit from me to Roanoke and back to me. I'm shivering, my clothes still wet from the pool, my drying hair hanging in clumps. I feel like death. Roanoke doesn't look much better.

Sloane turns to Damien. "Turn up the thermostat," she commands and then she moves to me, laying a supportive touch on my shoulder before her attention goes to Roanoke.

"Do you know what happened to him?" I ask. The hope in my voice isn't fair. I don't mean to put more pressure on Sloane. I've already outed her as a vampire to the band. She should be furious.

"Someone thought marking him meant mind control," she says. "My guess is he fought it and she pushed until she fried him."

"He's marked?" I blurt, trying not to concentrate on the fried part. Sloane had begged me to let her put one on me and I'd very clearly assured her it would never happen. Every couple of months, she tries her luck again.

"I thought it was old." She winces. "I played it down to him," she says, giving me a frantic look. "I got caught up on the extra life force thing. The second I knew, I should have told you about it. I'm so fucking stupid."

"Hey, no," Damien murmurs.

"What do you mean, fried?" December asks. "He's going to be okay, right?"

Carter stands, waiting for the answer.

"Tell me what happened," Sloane says as she sits on the sliver of mattress available beside Roanoke. I start from the voice, finding him gone when I woke up, all the while watching Sloane brush her fingers down his cheek, wiping at a line of blood I hadn't noticed leaking from his ear. I lose my place at the sight of it.

"Now that he's getting all the shit out of his system," she says, "he's not the easy toy she's used to playing with."

Across the room, Carter shivers.

"She's going after Roanoke the only time he's vulnerable. When he's sleeping." Sloane brushes at his curls. Roanoke doesn't respond.

"This isn't the first time," I confess, and all eyes swing toward me. "I assumed he was sleepwalking. He got out of bed once before and was pulling at the door." I swallow hard at the memory. "I locked the chain. When he couldn't get out, he wandered back to sleep like it was nothing."

Sloane nods. "When he left, he probably thought he was having a nightmare if he realized anything was wrong at all. But here, awake, he knew someone was trying to control him. He fought it." Her voice drops low, quiet with threat. "She did not like that."

"Can you tell who it is?" I ask because I'm too scared to ask her if she can help Roanoke, wake him up.

"No," she says instantly. "But I'd like to try to take that mark off him."

"Of course," December says, her words rushed. "Whatever you need to do to make that happen."

"Wait," I say.

"No offense, Willow," December snaps. "But I know Ro way better than you, and I know he wouldn't want some vampire bitch having control over him."

I glance at Sloane. She twists to face December wearing an apologetic smile. "Well, better a vampire bitch you know than one you don't."

December blanches.

"Always ask for the details," I say. "December, you're supernatural yourself. You should know that."

"She's upset about Ro," Carter snarls. "She doesn't need a fucking lecture."

"Easy!" Damien yells. "Everybody take a breath!" He points to Sloane. "Except you, Hollywood."

She rolls her eyes. "He's lucky he's fucking cute," she mumbles, but it's low enough that I'm the only one who hears her.

She lifts Roanoke's eyelid. His pupil is blown wide and black, the iris jerking from side to side. "His brain's healing itself," she says. "If it weren't for that demon, he'd be dead." Sloane hesitates. "Disorganized electrical firings brought the seizure on. Her versus him. She might have given him a stroke."

"But he'll come out of it, right?" December whispers. She takes a step toward Ro and then stops herself as if wary of Sloane.

"He should," Sloane says. "I don't know much about incubi."

December swallows hard. "How do we protect him from this happening again?"

"Earlier, I couldn't get near him without being repelled. I

think she blew the mark, damaged it by pushing him too hard against his will. Which means," Sloane says carefully. "I can try to get it off him and put mine overtop. Like covering up an old tattoo. Two things though." She releases Roanoke's eyelid and sighs. "I think if we're going to do this, we need to do it *now* while the damned thing's occupied healing him. If we lose our chance, we might not get another." She pauses and her gray eyes lock on mine. "Two, I'm not guaranteeing an outcome here, Willow."

My jaw tightens as I feel my panic flare.

"Talk it over, but don't take too long to decide," Sloane warns, as her attention flicks pointedly at Roanoke. His head is heavy against my legs, warm as if he's feverish.

"Well, we can't leave him like this!" December argues.

"Better than being dead," Carter points out.

We swivel to Damien where he leans against the wall, looking more serious than I've ever seen him as he stares at Roanoke's unmoving form. Finally, he shakes his head. "I'm not deciding that."

Which means one vote for and one vote against. Roanoke's fate shouldn't be in my hands. What would he want me to decide?

I think of our conversation, about Cassandra and how she took his consent away from him and the awful consequences that affect him to this day. He wouldn't want anyone to have control over him. Not even Sloane.

"You can't just take it off?" I ask her again, already knowing the answer.

Sloane shakes her head. "But I won't try to change his will, and I'll stay out of his head as much as possible. You have my word."

"And if we do nothing?"

"Her connection to him could heal." She shrugs. "Honestly, I don't know."

"Do it," I tell her.

Behind me, December lets out an audible exhale.

Sloane nods once. "Get him in the tub," she says.

• • • ● • ● • ● • • •

"Christ, Sloane, I don't think I can do this," I whisper, my words thready with nerves. The handle of the knife is slick. It's one of mine, silver bladed and weighted perfectly. It's also honed to split a hair. I switch hands and wipe my palm on my shirt before I switch the blade back again.

"It's got to be you. Until that mark is totally gone, I can't hurt him." She casts a pitying look at Roanoke's unconscious body. "And getting that off his neck is definitely going to hurt him."

"Okay," I say, adjusting in the bathtub on top of Roanoke. It's a tight fit, his torso in the tub's bottom and his legs raised against the wall. I've got a knee on either side of him. There's a pillow under his shoulders, his neck bent with the heaviness of his head where it's resting against the drain. "You're sure we have to do this?"

"Willow," she says softly. "I'm not sure this is going to work.

Marks aren't meant to be removed, plus with what he is…" She gives me an uncertain shrug.

I shake my hands out one at a time. "Okay," I say. "Okay, I'm gonna do it."

I touch the knife to one of the two small freckles on the side of his neck. I've kissed those freckles. I never had a clue what they were. "How deep?" I ask again.

She peels up her lip to show me how long her fang is. It's no bigger than a standard human canine in her mouth, but carving two holes that size in Roanoke's neck…

"Don't hesitate," Sloane says before her voice raises. "Do it."

I slice. The tip of the knife filets his skin as I twirl the blade. Blood drips in a rivulet and then in steady plops when it reaches the back of his neck. I pop out the plug of skin and move to the second. Under the blade, Roanoke groans.

"Shit," I whisper as I cut. "Shitshitshit." *Please don't hate me for doing this to you*, I think desperately. No, strike that. *Please come back. Hate me, just come back.*

I carve out the second spot, and revulsion skitters over me. I remember how the knife felt sliding into Blake's neck and suddenly I'm in that kitchen, too many emotions flooding through me. "I'm gonna puke," I say.

Sloane and I switch places, her in the tub on top of Roanoke and me at the toilet. Instead of sitting on it, I flip open the lid and gag into the bowl. Nothing comes up. I heave again and again, my stomach empty and aching, and I remember it's been thoroughly washed out with pool water.

When I come up for air, Sloane's got her teeth buried in

Roanoke's neck, draining him to start the process of laying her own mark overtop of the old one. I take a second before I realize his eyes are open, gaped in horror. His arm wraps around her, his fist pounding weakly.

"Ro?" I manage, my voice shaky from being sick.

His eyes fly to me, wide and frightened. His fingernails claw and Sloane arches away from him. "Run!" he rasps.

Only then do I understand his terror. The last thing he probably remembers is being controlled by a vampire. Now, he's woken up to one feeding off him.

"It's Sloane!" I say quickly.

His eyes spiral, flicking and frantic. "The mark?"

"Gone," I tell him. "She has to put hers on top."

Sloane adjusts him in her arms. I wonder how much blood she's taking. I know this isn't a normal exchange.

"Doorway," Roanoke croaks. "Gotta close the…" He goes limp.

"Roanoke?" I cry.

Sloane holds her wrist out to me. "Cut," she demands. "Deep."

I cut. She slams the wound against Roanoke's mouth and goes back to feeding on him. He rouses enough to choke on her blood before he latches on. It's two long minutes before she takes her wrist away from his lips and then drains him again. Roanoke wavers in and out of consciousness. I've never seen this done, don't know the process.

Someone knocks on the bathroom door. "You guys okay in there?"

Damien.

Sloane whips upright, the back of one hand pressed against her lips. Her gray eyes are ringed in maroon. Roanoke's blood leaks from the corner of her mouth. "Don't let him in," she whispers.

Her arm curls around her stomach. She eases upright, her face pinched in pain as she climbs off Roanoke and out of the tub. She stands, one trembling arm bent at a strange angle as she holds herself up using the edge of the sink. "He tastes like bleach and ashes. I don't know if it worked. I had to stop." She pauses. "I feel really weird, Willow."

"Are you okay?" I ask.

For a worrisome amount of time, Sloane doesn't answer. "Woozy," she manages. "Can you check on him for me? Make sure he's not having a reaction, too?"

Damien knocks softly. "Guys?"

"One minute!" I call as I move toward Roanoke. His chest rises and falls, so he's alive. But any more than that, I don't know. "What am I looking for?" I ask her.

I hear Sloane say my name, whip around to catch her under the arms as she swoons.

"Hey!" I call. "What's wrong?"

"I'm coming in," Damien says.

Sloane coughs, maroon coating her lips. I've watched her feed. It's never been like this after. "Lotta demon in that boy's blood," she whispers as the knob turns.

Damien takes one look at Sloane slowly sinking to the floor and me struggling to hold her and Roanoke passed out in the tub with his neck covered in barely healing stab wounds and a bite mark.

"You guys never just wanna hang out," he grumbles as he slips beside me and gathers Sloane by the waist. "Never a movie night or cosmic bowling. Those things can be fun, too. Just sayin'." He points to Roanoke. "He good to move?"

"I think so," I say.

"Carter!" he calls over his shoulder, and a second later, Carter's head pops in. "Take Ro," Damien tells him. "Too many people in here, and we've got a vampire down."

Damien hauls Sloane against him and steps aside as Carter wrestles Roanoke's dead weight out of the tub, through the door, and into the hotel room without a word.

I want to follow him. I can't leave Sloane.

Sloane's glance moves from me to Damien. "Second time today I've ended up in your arms," she says weakly. "Gonna start thinking you've got a thing for me."

Damien adjusts her, grinning. "Yeah, well—" he starts and then Sloan's head rests against his cheek. His brow knits with concern. "Hollywood, you're super-hot."

"See? Thing for me," she slurs. Cringing, she tightens the arm she's looping around Damien's shoulders before her pain seems to fade again.

"She's burning up," he says to me. "Feel her."

Reaching out, I squeeze her arm. He's right. Sloane radiates heat. She's usually chilly to the touch. I shake my head, baffled.

"Good news?" Sloane grinds out between clenched teeth. "The mark worked. Bad news? I don't know what this is." She grabs at the collar of her shirt and yanks it away from her skin. "I feel like I'm drowning."

"But you don't breathe," Damien says, confused.

"Christ," I whisper. We know from experience and experiments that Sloane absorbs the blood pretty much as soon as it's down her throat. Having her vomit it up won't help. I wonder if we should try, anyway.

She swallows thickly. "I think the demon infected his blood."

Damien shoots me a worried look over her shoulder. "We might be in some deep shit here, Willow." As if to prove his point, Sloane suddenly droops. He catches the crown of her head in his palm. "Hollywood?"

"Get him out, Wil," she moans. "I don't want him here."

Damien glances up at me as if he's done something wrong, and I feel a little bad for him. I tap my finger against the side of my mouth, the same place on Sloane where Roanoke's blood streaks.

"I'm in a band," he says, surprised, and then he smiles at her. "Half coherent people covered in blood and throwing themselves at me is your basic Tuesday."

"I didn't throw myself at you," she snaps and for the first time, I think maybe she's going to be okay.

"Well, not yet," he says, sounding vaguely offended. "But we both know you can't resist much longer."

Still, she didn't ask me to banish Damien for no reason. "What are we doing, Sloane?" I ask her.

"You've got to get Roanoke's blood out of me," Sloane says, struggling to sit up and free herself from Damien's hold. Her gray eyes are glassy when they meet mine. "But when you do, I'm going to get very hungry and very unsafe."

"She can have some of my blood," Damien offers.

"No," Sloane and I both echo.

"When I feed, you're going to need to be ready with the silver." A moment passes between us as I process what she's really saying. The only silver in the room is the same knife I used on Roanoke. Sloane's trusting me to angle it close to her heart, rendering her helpless but not killing her. All while she's feeding on me.

"Look, I don't think I can—"

Sloane keens. The sound resounds through the tiny room. As it fades, December fills the doorway.

"Sorry, I'm pulling him. Damien, out," she says.

When he opens his mouth to argue, the warning look she shoots him is so caustic I wither beneath it.

"You wanted to help Willow, but we both know what you are is going to become a real problem for everyone once blood gets spilled, isn't it?" She waits for an answer. "Isn't it?" December repeats.

Damien's jaw tightens, his expression furious. "Fuck you, Dec."

"You want me to tell them why?"

He turns to me and I'm ready for him to plead his case, to finally find out what supernatural creature Damien is and why he hides it. Emotion wars over his face as he looks first at me, then Sloane. "I gotta go," he says as he stands. "Sorry."

I watch, stunned, as he leaves the bathroom without another

word.

"What is he?" Sloane asks.

"Not food," December says bitterly as she closes the door behind her. Just before she does, her eyes meet mine. "Ro's waking up."

Everything inside me wants to be beside Roanoke. But I have to do this first. I owe Sloane so much.

It's Sloane and I, and my single silver knife laying where it slid to rest in the room's corner by the tub. I take the two steps toward the blade and scoop it off the ground. "How do you want to do this?" I ask, my voice deadened.

I'm exhausted and scared and if I'm being honest, if this goes wrong, I can't fight off Sloane. She looks deceptively worn through and weak, using the edge of the tub to hold herself upright, but the more desperate she is for blood, the stronger she gets.

"It hurts," she says, her words a whisper.

"Let's get you better then, okay?" I say.

Her eyes fall shut.

"Sloane?" I call and they snap open again.

She lays her head on the porcelain. "Carotid," she says in a shaky voice. "Now."

I don't hesitate. The cut is clean, fast, precise. Sloane whimpers as a spray of red hits the wall, the result of pressure, too much blood in her system. She angles her upper body toward the sidewall of the shower.

"I think you just lost The Raven Shakes their room deposit," I say as one of her hands loses the fight to brace herself. Her palm slides into the tub, skids through the gore, tumbling her forward. Blood oozes from her neck in a strange, glugging rhythm. Sloane's lack of a heartbeat screws up the process.

Two minutes, I think. *No more.* I need her conscious to stop feeding, but drained enough that the blood Sloane takes from me will dilute whatever effect Roanoke's is having on her.

"Willow?" She's gone pallid. "No more."

The words are barely out of her mouth before I'm hauling her up, twisting her over. I'm expecting help, but Sloane's deadweight, her head cracking against the piping under the sink.

"Hey!" I yell.

I scoop my arms under hers, lifting her. Her head lolls on her neck like a rag doll. I grab a handful of her hair, use it to shift her against my neck. She doesn't react. I nick the blade of the knife across my skin, a tiny cut to get the blood flowing. The longer it takes her vampire instincts to kick in, the more dangerous this is.

"Come on, Sloane."

Behind me, I hear the door open.

"Jesus Christ," Carter whispers.

"Get out!" I yell and the door slams again.

Sloane jolts. Her tongue flicks across my skin. I feel a double pinch of pain as her fangs pierce, the pulsing suck. I move the knife subtly, counting up to her seventh rib as she drinks from my neck. One of her hands flutters up innocently, but then Sloane rips me closer, hard and fast. A small sound of surprise squeezes out of me. Her leg wraps around my waist. I'm trapped in her grip. The fangs tear out of me, sink in again as if she's scouting the best place to drain me.

For the first time since Sloane and I met, when I found her huddled over the body of her dead boyfriend, it occurs to me I might have to decide if it's going to be me or her walking out of this bathroom.

Fourteen percent, I think. I can lose fourteen percent of my blood before I have major issues. But how the fuck am I supposed to know when she's taken that much?

I can't tell if my dizziness is adrenaline or something more frightening. Her grip on the back of my neck tightens. Each of her fingers digs. I'm going to have bruises.

"Sloane, stop. Please." The last word is a sob. I don't want to do this. I plant the knifepoint against her shirt, prepare myself to shove.

One, I think. *Two.*

She rips from me, stumbling backward. The wound in her neck has slowed to a trickle as she heals. Her irises are red rimmed. I wonder distantly if the blood on her lips is hers or mine or Roanoke's. She looks half crazed and terrified.

"Better?" I say, my voice barely above a whisper as the room spins.

She nods, and then slumps, shame flooding her features.

"It's okay," I promise. "What made you stop?"

"Him," she says at the same second there's a slam against the door. "He knew I was feeding on you. He's *furious*."

Sloane covers her mouth with one hand to hide the blood, not realizing until she does that it coats her from fingertips to wrists. The knob turns and Roanoke jerks the door open. His eyes find mine and he almost collapses with relief.

His arms come around me, and it's just as well. My legs are like Jell-O. He holds me to him, stronger than he has any right to be after what he's been through tonight. Over his shoulder, I see December, Carter, and Damien in the doorway, watching. I offer them a weak smile. Only Damien returns it.

Roanoke and I cling to each other, swaying slightly. "I'm done," I whisper to him. "I'm about thirty seconds from passing out."

He slips an arm around me and helps me out of the bathroom to one of the double beds. I hear the water turn on—Sloane cleaning herself or the room.

"We all crash together," Carter says. "Whoever that bitch was, she's in town and she's probably super pissed off right about now."

"It was her," Roanoke says. "I thought she was dead."

He can't mean Cassandra. My head hits the pillow and I feel Roanoke slide in behind me. I turn until I'm lost in the warmth of his arms. His lips press against my forehead. I want to ask him more about who took him, but I can't focus.

Everyone's okay, I think, vaguely mystified. *Everyone's safe.*

As I fade into unconsciousness, I wonder how long it can last.

CHAPTER 22

ROANOKE

It feels like a trick. First one week, then the next passing in a series of cities and stages. We settle, all of us, into the routine of being on the road. I don't drink. I don't fuck up.

Not once.

The fever dream of a chance with Willow has become reality and I have hope for my future. I'm absolutely enamored with her, those brown eyes always looking like they're puzzling me out, those soft lips learning my body as mine learn hers, her mind, her wit, the way her mere presence makes me feel like a meteor.

Part of me, though, is waiting for the crash. Because this isn't over. Sometimes, in the middle of the night, I wake in a cold sweat, Cassandra's scream in my head, pounding my temples as Willow stirs in my arms before she settles again.

Nightmares, I promise myself.

Only nightmares. I haven't sleepwalked since Sloane took the mark off me and closed it with her own. I don't have scars.

Instead, two wine-colored birthmarks the size of pencil erasers are on the side of my neck where I'm told Willow cut me and Sloane fed. I don't remember any of it.

It's strangely easy to back off the connection Sloane and I have. The first few mornings, I awoke with the phantom taste of blood on my tongue. In quiet moments, her hunger washes over me, a ravenous hole I can't fill.

Willow snuggles against me as we make the walk from the Winnebago to tonight's hotel. I stall, let the others get their room keys as I lean against the counter with my elbows cocked behind me. Willow kisses me, our smiles contagious. I want nothing more than a hot shower to wash off the sweat of the show and then enough time alone with Willow that I'll need another one.

She shoots me a sly grin. "What's that look for?" she asks.

"Thinkin'," I say, trying to keep my tone this side of innocent. It's a miserable failure.

Pushing off the front desk counter, I nestle against her neck, bury myself in her curls. She smells like ten thousand screaming fans—heat and sex and shampoo—and inside my tattered jeans, my cock stirs to life. "I'll tell you every detail when we get upstairs," I murmur into her ear and she laughs in her throaty chuckle.

Her hands brace against my shoulders. Her mouth meets mine in a series of pecks and presses before the front desk clerk finally breaks us from our revelry.

"Sir?" she says lightly. "Were you ready?"

I have half a mind to tell her no, that I need a minute. I envision sweeping the brochures and jumbo bottle of hand sanitizer off the counter and showing Willow every dirty thought in my head right here and now.

"Sir?" she says again, and I force the thoughts away with a last glance in Willow's direction.

She licks her lips, the motion overly seductive.

Tease, I mouth, and I'm rewarded with another laugh as I scoot over the few yards to stand in front of the check-in computer. "Sorry," I say to the clerk. "What did you need from me?"

Her smile is apologetic. The last thing I want is some sort of issue with the room. My lust slackens.

"Hey," I say, suddenly on edge. "These reservations were made months ago." I point down the hall where the rest of The Raven Shakes are waiting to get on the elevator and go on with their nights trouble free. "You had everything straight for them, so if there's—"

"It's nothing bad!" she says, sounding surprised. "It's just...I love your band. I only had one suite though, so I put in the upgrade for you and Miss Taverson."

"Oh," I say, unable to hide my shock. "Thanks."

"That's so sweet of you!" Willow chimes in.

The girl beams. "It's nothing, really."

"What's your favorite song?" I ask, because I'm thinking I'll doodle her some lyrics, sign it for her, drop it off later.

Her smile wavers as she types into the computer. "Oh gosh, I couldn't pick a favorite."

"Sorry you had to miss the show tonight," Willow says.

The girl looks up, confused. "What?" she asks.

"The concert. You had to work."

"Oh, right, yes, I did." That white teethed smile pops onto her mouth. "But look how lovely it all turned out!" She hands me a folded over envelope with the standard two hotel keys inside. "Enjoy your stay."

I tap it twice against the counter before grabbing Willow's hand. "Cool, have a good night. Thanks again."

When we reach the elevator, Willow presses the button before kissing the rough stubble of shadow on my chin. "It's sexy when people get all star-struck over you."

My gaze strays toward the front desk, but the girl's gone. I've seen fans go a little overboard. She didn't ask for an autograph. A picture. Nothing.

I glance down at the envelope and open it. Shock widens my eyes.

"What?" Willow asks.

"Holy shit." I flip it to show her. "She gave us a presidential suite!"

"Ro, you've gotta bring her something signed. That's so far above and beyond!"

I nod. I know damn well Willow's used to this treatment—I still remember the opulent room she took me to the night we met—but I'm so uncomfortable.

We get in the elevator, the doors closing. I have to put the key into a slot to grant us access to the floor.

Uncertain, I turn to Willow. "Let's give it to Damien," I blurt. "He'll freak."

"Damien?" she repeats. Her head tilts as she studies me. "You don't want to get naked in the hot tub with me?" She lifts her arms to encircle my neck. "Because I want to get naked in the hot tub with you."

Her mouth meets mine, and for a second, I forget myself. Forget these elevators usually have cameras. I twist with Willow, press her up against the mirrored wall as the elevator cycles through floors, climbing. There's the slightest clink of metal against the glass as the silvered knife she's got strapped to her makes contact. My fingers thread through her hair. "Maybe we won't be giving up the room after all."

"Yeah?" she says, her voice low and sultry. "Changed your mind?"

I kiss her hard enough that a moan breaks from her throat and rolls into mine. I want her.

I can have her.

"Willow?" The strange tone of her name must scare her a bit because she stops kissing me to pull back, worried. I lock eyes with her, my thumb stroking her cheek. "I never want this to end. Us."

An almost shy smile blooms across her face as she leans into my touch. "Me either."

It's as close to an out loud I love you as we've dared with each other. The elevator door dings. Willow grabs my hand and leads me to our room. She kisses my jaw, my neck as I blindly slip in the key.

When it clicks, she throws open the door, walking backward into the space. It's dark, stretching, huge.

"Holy shit," I say at the brief glimpse I get over her shoulder before her hands are tugging at the hem of my shirt, lifting it. I strip it up and over my head. Windows line two walls, a view of the city lights beyond.

"Hot tub?" Willow asks, the words smashed between our lips enough that we both laugh.

"Shower sex first?" I counter and she rolls her eyes skyward in feigned ecstasy.

"That sounds glorious."

"I can't wait to—" I freeze. The smile fades from Willow's face as she takes in mine.

"Ro? What is it?" she asks, but my attention locks on the shadowy figure across the dark room, staring out at the city.

"Hi," I say quickly and Willow whips around. I grab her arm and snatch her behind me, protected, as I pick my shirt up off the floor and slip into it.

The shape of the body is female. She doesn't move.

There must have been a mix-up, I think. *The suite was occupied after all and the clerk messed things up.*

"Sorry, we're—"

She turns. The light catches her face, and all the air leaves my lungs.

"Hello, Roanoke," she whispers cautiously, like she's not sure what my reaction will be. Her sad smile rips holes in any façade I ever laid that I was okay, over things, whole again.

"Ro?" Willow says cautiously from behind me. "Who's your friend?"

I try to answer, try to get anything to come out of my mouth, but my head's clustered with all the times the dead girl standing impossibly in front of me told me not to speak and I can't.

I can't.

Her frown digs in and a memory flashes of myself before the incubus, kissing her, wanting her. Out of my head with need. My stomach churns.

"No," I blurt, the sound haunted.

"Ro?" Willow says again.

To my absolute horror, the girl crosses the room, holding out her hand and smiling like we've all bumped into each other at the gas station. "It's so lovely to meet you," she says to Willow.

Lovely. It's the same word the clerk used when she gave me the room upgrade. *Look how lovely it all turned out.* Instantly the clerk's claim of being a fan without being able to name a song, her lack of interest in coming to the show, it all makes sense. She'd been under the vampire's sway. This was all a setup.

Now, Willow moves around me, holding out her hand to shake Cassandra's in a confused welcome.

"No!" I yell as I snap free of my shock. She and Willow turn to me in surprise. "You don't touch her," I snarl at Cassandra. "You don't look at her."

I mean to follow up with a threat. Instead, I take a slow step backward, away.

It's too much. Too much, too much, and I remember her scream in my head as everything in my brain went burned and broken. And before, years before, my bones aching and my insides emptying as she fucked me into the hollow vessel she needed before she turned me into this *thing*.

I get out one shuddered word. "Cassandra."

Beside me, Willow draws a sharp breath.

Demonic amusement dances in Cassandra's eyes, or maybe it's the red glow from the fire exit sign above the door. "Aww, lover!" she says. "You talked about me. That's so sweet!"

"I told her what you did to me," I whisper.

She frowns, as if she's trying to remember what I could be talking about.

"You killed those women, didn't you?"

"I—"

"You're the one that put this demon inside me, the one that made me fuck random people, steal their years. Then you killed them for it?" I ask. Nothing is making sense.

I'm conscious of Willow behind me, her touch on my waist as if to give me strength.

Cassandra's expression fills with disappointment. "Don't blameshift," she says.

I balk. "What?"

"I told you. Every time. All you had to do to stop it was stay with me. I love you so much," she says, and there's such sincerity in it that I cringe. "Almost as much as you loved me once. You just have to remember."

"That wasn't love." I'm shaking. For every step I back Willow and I away, Cassandra follows.

A faint smile drifts across her lips. "Roanoke," she says as if chiding me for being dramatic. "I know you're upset I left you. Do you remember how you begged me not to go? You broke my heart."

Her world-weary sigh tips my fear into fury.

"You used me. Took everything from me!" I swallow hard as the memories claw forward. How I'd choked the demon down my throat, terrified, but more terrified to die.

She looks utterly astonished at my anger. "I could have let you die."

"Am I supposed to be grateful?"

Her smile pinches as if she's fighting against losing her temper. "You were supposed to," she says lightly, as if we're two normal people talking about the weather. "Die."

Her gaze goes calculated and I remember what this means, that she's about to do something terrible to me, my hands, my voice.

To Willow. I keep myself in front of her, the only protection I can offer.

"I wanted to ruin your pretty little life," Cassandra says. Her grin goes victorious at my confusion. "I wanted to rip you off that stage and fuck you to pieces. I wanted your songs to be about me alone and for me alone. And they were. You *existed* for me. Do you remember how much fun we had?" That wretched smile softens. "You remember, right?"

I'm back there, pliable and blinded by her sway in her shitty little apartment where we were king and queen. My memories are twisted, color and black and white, images of what she wanted me to see and my gaunt face, bloodshot eyes from lack of sleep. She made me sing for hours. A soundtrack while she moved about the room putting on her makeup and dressing and I stood there, broken and captivated and caring of nothing but her happiness while my throat went raw and the melodies poured from me.

She can't control me anymore, I tell myself. I want it to help. I want it to give me power. But even in my head, I sound weak and scared.

"Why didn't you kill me then?" I ask. I feel the warmth of Willow beside me, the edge of her shirt brushing my arm. I have to get her out of here.

Cassandra shrugs, leaning against the couch in the sitting area. "It seemed like such a waste," she says evenly. Glancing around me to Willow, she raises an eyebrow. "Do you not tell him how beautiful he is? How talented? He never doubted himself when he was with me."

Willow lifts her chin and stares the other girl down.

Cassandra dismisses her with a wave of her fingers and turns her attention to me again. "I had my exit plan. Being a succubus was boring when I had so much more power available. Friends with gifts to offer me. And I thought, I'll feed my demon your life, and then go find myself a better one."

She pushes off the couch and strides closer as I'm backing Willow and I away, almost to the door. Cassandra doesn't acknowledge Willow exists. She only has eyes for me.

"That was supposed to be the end," she says. "But I couldn't stop thinking about you."

"Don't," I say, the single word a quiet threat. "I don't care and I don't want to know. We're leaving."

I keep Willow tucked close as I start toward the door, my hand on her back, hurrying her forward. I don't bother grabbing our suitcases as I pass.

"This was so much easier before," Cassandra pouts. "You were into me when you snuck out of Willow's room to come meet me. One little nudge and you couldn't get enough. Are you really going to pretend you didn't want me?"

She's lying. That never happened.

Except, it wasn't just her teeth in my neck. I'm remembering her hands on me, her mouth on my mouth. She kissed me. She touched me.

What if there was more? If she's a vampire, she might know I couldn't steal away her life. We might have—

Stunned, I turn to Willow. Tears stand in her brown eyes. And just like that, I know it's over.

"I don't know what I did," I say to Willow, my voice tight with shame. I've lost my life once to Cassandra. Now, I'm losing everything I've clawed and scraped and prayed for. "I'm sorry, I—"

"Don't." Willow's word hits me like a slap. Her mouth opens as her head tilts as if she can't quite believe I'd attempt an apology. Her glare goes cold. "You have nothing to apologize for," she says.

She shifts her rage toward Cassandra. "You never had his consent," she seethes. "Not when you first took him. Not when you made him an incubus. And sure as hell not now."

Cassandra smirks as her arms cross over her chest. "Bold words. You weren't there. You don't know all the beautiful things he tells me. How he sings me to sleep at night. How he worships me. Tell me, Willow," she says, though her eyes never leave me, watching for my reaction. "Did you ever taste me on his lips? Even a bit? That little tang of mystery?"

"You fucking bitch," Willow grates out.

"Why now?" I ask Cassandra. "After three years. Why hunt me down now?"

She doesn't answer.

"Why kill all those innocent girls?" I press. "Were you trying to frame me?"

Her smile wilts. "Why would I do that?" she asks. "I wanted you to remember you didn't need them anymore. You never needed them. Not when you have me."

"Because being a vampire means you can feed my demon without losing life force?" I ask.

Her mouth gapes before she wrestles up a surprised smile. "How did you know that?" she asks as her eyes flick to Willow, reassessing. Between us, the power shifts before Cassandra recovers. "What the hell?" she says. "You ruined my big reveal!"

I ignore her attempt to lighten the mood. "You think I could ever forgive what you did to me, to those poor girls?"

Willow's hand finds mine. Her squeeze gives me the strength I need to end this. Threading our fingers together, I lean forward into Cassandra's face, angry and reckless.

"Fuck you," I say.

It's quiet, but forceful. Cassandra blinks.

"Fuck your little planned villain speech. Fuck whatever happy ending you imagined for yourself."

Some of the bravado fades from her expression. "Roanoke, my happy ending was always you," she says.

My bark of a laugh makes Willow jump. "You are goddamned

delusional."

Cassandra locks eyes with me. The more she speaks, the faster her words come. "When I heard Once and Future three months ago, I knew it was about me. About us. Lovers broken apart by fate and brought back together by time. It was clear you still wanted me. So I did what the song said, and I found you again!"

My brain feels like it's splitting apart. "The song is about King Arthur," I say, mystified.

She examines me as if trying to decide if I'm lying or not.

There's a long moment of silence, and then, I call what she did to me by its right name. "You raped me, Cassandra. For months." My voice breaks with the emotion in it. "You forced me to do things I never would have done. I didn't know where I was half the time, what was happening. And you're showing up again like some sort of fucking nightmare movie monster."

"That's not what happened. Stop lying to save face in front of your..." That indulgent smile returns as she glances at Willow. "What did I call you? Food for his demon? Because that's all you've ever been."

"Shut up, Cassandra," I growl.

"Or what?" she asks. It's a threat.

"You have no power over me anymore." I'm free. I have a future. I have hope. I'm grateful for Sloane and everything she went through to get that damn mark off me, to break the hold Cassandra had on me.

"No. I don't," she says, annunciating each word. "But I have other ways to control you." She turns slowly toward Willow.

Willow tenses. One of her hands slides around to the small

of her back. I remember our ride up on the elevator, when I'd kissed her, pressed her against the mirrored wall, the metal clink as she hit.

"You don't know me," Willow says as the two circle each other slowly. "I'll forgive you for underestimating."

Cassandra belts out a laugh. "Look at us," she says. "Fighting over a boy. Let's not. I'll let you go." She shrugs magnanimously. "You'll live to see another sunrise."

Willow doesn't answer. Instead, she draws a wicked blade from the sheath hidden in the dip at the base of her spine.

Cassandra's smile freezes.

"Willow, don't," I whisper. "She'll kill you." Her confidence is going to get her hurt.

"Willow, don't," Cassandra repeats in a voice cold and hollow. "I'll kill you."

Inside me, something shifts, goes hard. "No."

Before I can say more, a flash of movement whisks past me. Cassandra blurs. I reach for her, but I'm way too slow. By the time I turn to follow the blur, she's on top of Willow, has her on her back. Willow stabs upward, blindly, as Cassandra's fingers claw at her eye sockets.

I jump without thinking. My fists pound Cassandra's shoulders and she's forced to let go of Willow's face to fight me off. It takes one solid fistful of my hair and a yank before I'm airborne.

I slam against the wall hard enough to crack the drywall behind the wallpaper. Pain sears through my ribs. Tumbling to the floor, I struggle to stay conscious.

"Roanoke!" Willow calls.

I get a hand under myself, rushing to sit, move, fight. Stars explode across my vision.

Willow strangles out my name again. She's locked underneath Cassandra. The vampire's fangs are bared, Willow's fingers shoving the other's jaw away from her neck. It's a battle she's losing.

Cassandra gains another inch. Her teeth gnash. Willow brings the knife around, stabs the silver blade into Cassandra's neck.

There's no reaction save a wisp of smoke where the silver enters.

Willow leaves the knife buried in Cassandra's neck and raises her other hand to help fend off the fangs. Her elbow shakes. "Ro, I can't," she gasps before she cuts off. "Help me!"

Willow's brown eyes find mine. I'm not used to seeing her scared. I give my head a hard rattle and the room steadies. This time, I go for the silver handle still plugged into the smoking wound on Cassandra. I rip it loose. Crimson spurts, splashing across Willow's chest.

"Get off her," I growl as I jab the blade into the vampire, hit her neck, the meaty part of her shoulder. The knife glances off a bone and I almost drop it, my grip shifting awkwardly.

"Heart," Willow groans.

Cassandra snarls. She twists and suddenly it's not Willow she's after.

"Shit," I blurt as Cassandra launches herself at me. I swipe, opening a wound even as she strikes and the knife clatters from my hand to the tiles.

Inside me, the demon is quiet, as if I'm not battling for my life.

It knows her, I realize. Slow terror slides through me. It knows her, so it won't fight her. A fear blossoms that I haven't felt in over three years.

I could die here.

It's not me I care about, though.

Cassandra's fangs graze the side of my palm but her teeth slip and she reels from me. "Why can't I feed from you?" she demands.

Sloane's mark. It's protecting me.

Willow gropes madly. Her fingers close around the knife I dropped.

Before she can bury it in Cassandra, the vampire rolls us. One of her hands palms Willow's forehead. A solid thud echoes through the room as Cassandra slams Willow's head against the floor.

"Don't!" I call and it's as if she's suddenly remembering I'm there and that she's hungry. She meets my horrified gaze. Red rims her mouth.

My blood, I think dumbly. It snakes through her teeth as her lips peel in a grimace. But there's more blood, on the floor, a slow trickle spreading from the back of Willow's head. She's not moving.

"Don't fight me, Roanoke," Cassandra spits. Maroon flecks my face. "We'll pass on your demon." She points to Willow's unconscious form. "To her even. As soon as it's gone, I'll be able to make you a vampire like me. We'll be together forever."

The thought of an eternity with her sours my insides. And the demon...I would never do that to Willow. She's still not moving.

Cassandra dives toward my neck and there's the same slam of repulsion as there was when Sloane tried to feed off me before.

"What did you do?" she demands before she comes at me again.

Her hands find my throat. Pressure cuts off my air. I wheeze in half a breath, lucky to get that as Cassandra bares down before Sloane's mark blows her free of me again.

My fingers search wildly until something skitters away. I reach. Snag the knife.

I clasp it tight. As Cassandra leaps toward me, I raise it in a solid arc and bury it in the side of her ribs.

The effect is instant.

With a shrill scream, she withdraws her fangs. Wetness flows as I fight to sit, her blood spilling onto my shoulder from her gaping mouth. Her eyes roll wildly. She reaches for the knife and I still, but it's silver and she can't touch it, can't get it out of her.

"Roanoke." The whisper of my name stands the fine hairs at the base of my skull straight. It's the sound of air over the vocal chords of a corpse. Her chin bobs as she tries in vain to swallow, her eyes hollowing, their color going dull. "What have you done?"

"I ended this." I reach forward, slam the knife deeper, straight into her heart. A pop sounds.

Cassandra slumps toward me even as she shrivels. I don't catch her. Instead, I shove her away, leave her to fall to the cold tiles, dying alone. I crawl toward Willow's still form.

"Wil?" I say, my voice too loud in the sudden silence. I slide a hand to the back of her head, sending up a prayer until I find the skull there firm. My fingers grope through her sticky hair. I lean my cheek next to her parted lips. Her breath is warm, the inhales shallow but steady. She's breathing. She's alive. "Come on, wake up," I beg. "Come on."

For the second time in as many weeks, I've gotten her hurt enough that I'm begging her back from death. I juggle her onto my lap as her eyelids flutter.

I'm worried about a brain bleed. Damage. Until I remember Sloane's blood is still working through her system.

"We're okay," I promise her. "Open your eyes." My own flick to Cassandra where she lies writhing on the floor. I watch as she stills, tempted to stick the knife in deeper, again. But that would mean taking it out and I won't risk her coming back to life. She's already had her movie monster return.

"Ro?" Willow croaks, and my attention snaps to her. She blinks, groggy. "Heart," she groans. "Get her heart."

"I did." I smooth Willow's hair from her face and kiss her forehead, her lips.

"Are you okay?" she asks.

"A bit chewed on, but I'll live. You?" I ask as she struggles herself into a sitting position.

Willow raises a tentative hand to her bump. "Next time, I promise I'll—"

"Nope." I cut her off with a kiss. "No next time. One and done."

She laughs, but it sounds more pained than anything.

"Can you walk?" I ask. She nods and I help her to her feet. Rotating her, I check her head before I help her to the couch and move, finally, to switch on the overhead light. We both squint against the sudden glare.

On the floor is the gray husk of what's left of Cassandra.

"Yeah," Willow says with a surprised sigh. "You definitely got her in the heart."

"Come here," I say as I run my fingers over Willow's skull. The bump is still swelling, but the bleeding seems to have mostly stopped.

She swallows hard against me, her face buried in my shoulder. "If anything had happened to you…"

Inside me, the demon stretches. My heart beats in time with Willow's. For the first time since this weird purgatory of a life started, I'm clear headed and sober and free from looking over my shoulder. I'm ready for whatever's coming. Fame, fortune, or fangs.

"I love you," I tell her. I'll remind her a thousand times, every day, for the rest of my life. I don't know why I ever thought I should hold off. "I've loved you since the second I laid eyes on you, and I'll love you until my last breath."

"I love you, too." She leans back to meet my mouth, her kiss needy in a way I echo.

Willow's phone rings in her pocket. "Sloane," she says.

I nod. I'm surprised it took her this long. I hold out my palm to Willow, show her the shallow puncture marks Cassandra had managed. "The mark kept her off me," I say.

Willow drags the phone from her pocket and answers it, sounding slightly bedraggled as she explains the events of the last five minutes to Sloane.

"I can't believe I got my ass kicked by a vampire," Willow says when she hangs up. "I must be out of practice."

"Can we talk about you retiring from anything that involves silver knives through the heart and getting your skull cracked?" I say, threading my fingers gingerly through her hair.

"Done," she says, sounding more relieved than I dared hope for. Her eyes meet mine, the worry in them making me uncertain. "Doesn't mean I can stop practicing, though. Those wolves are still hanging around my house."

"Sloane told you?" I ask, and Willow smirks.

"Well, no," she says. "You just did. But I'm well aware they're not about to back off that easily. We'll have to be ready for them."

"We will be," I promise. "Together."

"Together," she repeats.

• • • ● • ● ● • • •

A Note from Rekelle:

Hi! I just wanted to thank you real quick for reading! I hope you loved reading Roanoke and Willow's story and the supernatural found family of The Raven Shakes as much as I loved writing it. If you have a second, please consider dropping a review or mention online—it makes a huge difference for me in finding readers. The next book, Sirens and Snares (December's story!), will be out soon! Head to my website to get updates on releases, read bonus chapters, and more!

Made in the USA
Las Vegas, NV
05 February 2025